THE LAUGHTER

THE LAUGHTER

A Novel

SONORA JHA

HARPERVIA

An Imprint of HarperCollins*Publishers*

This is a work of fiction. Names, characters, places, and incidents are products of the author's imagination or are used fictitiously and are not to be construed as real. Any resemblance to actual events, locales, organizations, or persons, living or dead, is entirely coincidental.

HarperCollins books may be purchased for educational, business, or sales promotional use. For information, please email the Special Markets Department at SPsales@harpercollins.com.

FIRST HARPERVIA EDITION PUBLISHED IN 2023

Designed by Terry McGrath

Library of Congress Cataloging-in-Publication Data

Names: Jha, Sonora, author.
Title: The laughter : a novel / Sonora Jha.
Description: First HarperVia edition. | New York, NY : HarperVia, an imprint of HarperCollinsPublishers, 2023.
Identifiers: LCCN 2022037628 (print) | LCCN 2022037629 (ebook) | ISBN 9780063240254 (hardcover) | ISBN 9780063240285 (ebook)
Subjects: LCGFT: Thrillers (Fiction). | Novels.
Classification: LCC PS3610.H33 L38 2023 (print) | LCC PS3610.H33 (ebook) | DDC 813/.6--dc23/eng/20220815
LC record available at https://lccn.loc.gov/2022037628
LC ebook record available at https://lccn.loc.gov/2022037629

---

23 24 25 26 27 LBC 5 4 3 2 1

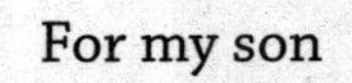
For my son

Let the new gods of the earth try as they can,
They cannot hear the sob of her ecstasy.

FAHMIDA RIAZ, "The Laughter of a Woman" (in *We Sinful Women*)

Since the beginning of the world all men have hunted me like a wolf—kings and sages, and poets and lawgivers, all the churches, and all the philosophies. But I have never been caught yet, and the skies will fall in the time I turn to bay. I have given them a good run for their money, and I will now.

G. K. CHESTERTON, *The Man Who Was Thursday*

Contents

CHAPTER ONE

It Began as Lust

It began as lust, that much I will admit. The events and emotions that came after were harder to reconcile. I, Oliver Edward Harding, am not one to trifle with the truth. The thing about truth, though, is that it sometimes reveals itself in the recounting, not in the living. So, while it is still fresh in my mind, I must revisit the events of these past weeks, in particular, the matter of the boy.

The straight and sure lines within these pale margins of my mind leave no other trail but those of my design. Only here might one find a true "safe space," as it were, to borrow a phrase from the luminaries of our time. Do I take a risk, then, by spilling my thoughts in ink? Do I dare reveal the workings of my heart in some clumsy assembly of words? Oh, but it is such comfort to hear the scratch and whisper of pen on paper, to write by hand the way I once did as a boy with a journal. Here I am, then, on a page, in a fresh notebook, committing my story to sight. My story and theirs.

Before I dwell on the story of the boy and his aunt, I must state that something has been taken from me, something precious and tender, and the loss of it is so great that it may smother my account with searing emotion at times, of the kind no associate of mine would generally ascribe to my personality. I will attempt to sluice out such emotion, lance this open wound of the ghosts within, although I will not delude myself that a complete exorcism is possible. I must remember that the police prefer a clean retelling of incidents. Unblemished. The gendarmerie, the boy would call them. They are leaning on me to make sense of all that happened. I must organize my thoughts here so they can have the spotless narrative they so desperately need. I won't, of course, share my written accounts with them, for I hardly imagine them avid readers, but I will deliver to them as lissome a truth as they deserve. Were it not for their urgent and unannounced visitations multiple times a day, I would have more time to discern the most pressing matter at hand, the matter of the letter.

What is to be done with this letter that is in my possession? This question has kept me sleepless until this hour of 3:45 a.m. I must choose one of two alternatives. This letter was given to me by the boy, less than a week ago. He asked that I mail it to someone in time for a birthday, someone in France. I am familiar with the contents of this letter. I did not read it in a furtive lapse of ethical judgment but, indeed, at the urging of the boy himself. Adil Alam, the boy, came to imagine me as some sort of mentor to him in the matters of the heart. Be that as it was, I did not advise him to change a single word in the letter. I found it rather charming, his declaration of love, driven by a clumsiness endemic to those forced into solitude in adolescence. The letter was all the more endearing, I thought, for being crafted by hand, despite the poor penmanship that has resulted from the millennials' practice of texting, which has rendered all correspondence among them to be, quite literally, all thumbs.

The contents of this letter are remarkable not merely for their sophistication but also because they will have a significant impact on the investigations of the police. And this is where my dilemma cuts deep—the boy extracted from me the sincerest promise that I will not share its contents, not even in part, not even orally, not even in concept, with anyone. The letter was meant to leave my address and arrive at the address of one Ms. Camille Harroch in Toulouse, France, as close to her birthday on December 1, 2016, as was calculable by ordinary post. Today is November 3.

Of course, all of this is rendered with greater poignancy because the author of the letter, the boy, now lies fighting for his life. If he dies, will this letter live beyond him? If he lives, whom will this letter serve? My journey of discernment must lead me to now deploy the letter in the service of love, or in the service of the law.

If one must speak of love, one must begin this story at that point. Although, as I noted earlier, it began for me as lust. That impulse, too, caught me off guard, because Ruhaba Khan was not the kind of woman to have inspired lust in me in all my years.

It helps to return to it. In these sleepless hours here, at my desk at home, I must return to that man I was at my other desk just about a month ago, in my office, a man far less bereft than I am today. It helps to play back those early images of Ruhaba in my head, before she knocked on my office door. In fact, those nascent fantasies I'd had of her did feature her knocking on that door. In the scenes of my imagination, she would knock, she would walk in, and she would stand over my desk. I would rise to shut the door behind her, "to keep the noise of the Department of English out," I would tell her. Then, as she spoke of something—it was different each time in my fantasy—as she spoke of committee work and how it ought to be divided on the basis of disciplinary expertise of the faculty, I would come up to her, put a finger on her lips, and shush her.

I wouldn't startle her, but I would no doubt see surprise in her eyes. And then, as she realized that goodness, yes, she had been expecting this, she would smile against my finger. My free hand would brush up against her buttocks and smooth the fabric on the ample mounds of flesh there. Things would go so quickly from here, and I would be assailed by the colors and scents of her flesh. She would be speaking of her workload on committees, negotiating with me for a reduction as I'd lay her down on my desk. I would enter her. She would fall quiet except for the tiniest sighs and moans. I would cover her mouth to protect her interests. Department walls have ears, especially those of the Department of English.

So you will understand when I tell you that I felt flustered and somewhat exposed the first time she actually knocked on my office door. I hurriedly put away my knitting and turned the key on the lock of my desk drawer. When I heard her voice outside say, "Dr. Harding? It's Dr. Khan," I had a moment in which

I thought I must hide something else, some physical evidence of her that she would spy on the desk or on the rug on the floor. But there was none, just a lot of books and papers from my years of work on a literary biography of Chesterton.

Ruhaba wasn't looking around my office. I wondered if she could smell the wool and yarn of my knitting, or the heat of my desire, but she seemed to have very little curiosity about my little world in that room. She walked in with a sense of purpose and said, "Dr. Harding, I have a favor to ask of you."

"Oliver. Please," I mumbled, as I stood up and motioned to her to take the seat before me.

She gave a half-smile and a nod and sat down. "I'll get straight to the point," she said. "I must ask to be relieved of my responsibilities on the Building and Space Committee."

This was so close to my fantasy, I squirmed a little as I sat back down.

"Any particular reason?" I said.

"I have some personal commitments coming up and I anticipate having less time to devote to committee work. I know we are in the middle of a huge push to demand more space for Liberal Arts after that STEM building was approved, and I just think you'd be better off with someone who can devote more energy."

Dear God, she was pregnant. I had entertained so many requests of this sort over the years from female faculty heading into maternity leave. Family Leave, they call it now. Of course, I heartily support it, even though colleagues like David Meyer make awful jokes about what I see as strides for more gender equity. What was it he said recently? "Personal commitments" was code for "I have been recently fucked harder than ever and now you must all bow before my biology and divide up my work while I go get fat and distracted." Men like Meyer are increasingly a relic in academia, thank the heavens.

I reminded myself that Ruhaba wasn't married and then reminded myself that this was not a thing that mattered these days. As if reading my thoughts, she said, tentatively, "Although I am not required to say what my personal commitments are, I feel it might be collegial of me to share them with you. A nephew of mine whom I have never met before is coming to stay with me. He arrives in two days and I have no idea what to expect."

"Nephew?" I said, trying not to sound too relieved.

"Yes."

She felt compelled to fill the silence that followed, although she frowned as she spoke, as if irritated with herself for not living into her political beliefs about women's rights to privacy at the workplace. "He's a teenager and he . . . needs a change of scene . . . I am told. That's all I know. He's my sister's son and she's asked for help."

"Ah, I understand," I said. "Well, I will have to grant your request, of course. Although I do think your voice is so useful on that committee." What I meant was that her voice and her skin and hair were the only reasons I was chair of that committee. Discussing the blueprints of buildings and their layouts as reflective of the mission, vision, and values of a university was the dullest work to which I had consented in years. Let me be candid and state that one of the reasons that women of color are asked to do disproportionately high service on committees on the American campus is that men of pallor like me are no longer asked. We have proved to be obtrusive and resistant to change and have thereby earned ourselves more time sitting back in our offices or getting out to play golf. I, especially, had a system that worked well to make me the least desirable man for committee service: I would passionately argue every position and kick a committee's decision-making in its bluest balls. The only committee I now served on with any enthusiasm was this Space one and the one on Rank and Tenure. I was coming up on my final two years of my third term as chair of the Rank and Tenure Committee. I will be the first to admit that the reason I did this work was to weed out the riff-raff to whom universities were awarding tenure these days. I was fair, and I was tough as nails.

Ruhaba said, "That's very kind of you, but you and I both know that the Building and Space Committee is a joke. We're just little pawns in the hands of the administration. They already have a blueprint for their own little campus universe."

I was so stunned by her candor, I let out a roaring laugh that I instantly realized seemed quite disproportionate to her words. She startled and then smiled. Oh, would that it were so simple to put my finger on those lips now.

I cleared my throat. "True," I said.

"Please don't take that as rudeness on my part," she said.

"Oh, no, I won't. Trust me."

"Well," she said, pushing herself away from my desk with both hands.

I recognize that my thoughts then were entirely inappropriate, but, although they were mere thoughts, I want to keep my writing here honest, close to the bone. So, I will admit I wanted to reach out and hold those hands and place them firmly back, pin them down to the edge of the desk, but instead, I stood up to shake one of them.

"If there is any way I may help with the nephew situation . . ." I said, knowing I might be implying more familiarity than we had between us. We only met on committees and at the occasional work event. We weren't even in the same school at our university—she taught law and I, English.

"Oh, thank you, but it may end up being less trouble than I am anticipating," she said. Then, she hesitated. "It's just that his parents and I have been estranged and I . . ." Her eyes started to wander around my desk now and it took me a moment to realize that she was looking for signs that I may have had a family.

I quickly jumped in. "Oh, I understand about being estranged from loved ones. My . . . my ex-wife and Kathryn—my daughter . . . well, they keep to themselves more than I'd like."

"Oh. I'm so sorry."

"It is what it is," I said. It was what it was.

I wanted to talk about her, not me. "But perhaps the arrival of the nephew means that things are on the mend? The easiest way back into a family's heart is through the children and all that."

"Yes, I suppose so," she said, sounding unconvinced.

She started to take steps backward toward my door.

"They're sending him to *you*, which implies trust."

She stopped and looked at me. "Trust?"

I stared at her. Her eyes were inky-black and frank. Some sort of evolutionary thing in her genes, perhaps, to render themselves penetratingly human behind a burka. Even though her traditional dress had been minimized to a headscarf, old manners die hard. I had encountered this strange thing about her before, this taking of things literally and seriously. It's as if her part of the world did not have the same rules of small talk and niceties as ours. I found it so beguiling.

"Certainly," I said.

I was ready to play by the rules of her part of the world. I added, "Your sister must respect you and your life here or she wouldn't . . ."

"Oh, I doubt that," she said waving a hand dismissively and taking those black pin-points of her eyes off me. "My sister and her husband don't approve of my ways. You study all the way to a Ph.D. and your family tells you it makes you less marriageable. Then they ask why you live by yourself in your late thirties. Why you move around like this in the Western world. They didn't like that I once had a lover. That was the last straw for them. Oh, wait. Not that. The last straw was that he wasn't a practitioner of Islam."

I stood there in silence. She drew a sharp breath in, widened her eyes, and looked at me as if she had forgotten for the last few moments that I was even there. Her hands flew up to her face and she looked away and smiled with embarrassment. "Goodness, Dr. Harding. I can't believe I am prattling on and on like this about such . . . such personal things. You will have to excuse me. I am clearly out of my depth with this oncoming . . ."

"Oliver," I said, faintly.

"What?"

"Please call me Oliver."

She smiled and gave me an odd look. She was peering at me, as if noticing for the first time that I am a handsome man. Some twenty years her senior, but blessed with the distinguished look of handsome men who age well.

She looked away then, as if it were all suddenly too intense. She nodded, thanked me for listening, and walked out my door.

I sat back in my chair, weak. She hadn't quite ruined my fantasies with the untidy reality of her circumstances. The images of my own mind had stayed for a while, and indeed, she had now gifted me the whiff of a scent from her hair to work with. She had given me a better sense of a voice in a lower octave, more inquiring in personal space than the declarative voice she held in meetings. She had offered a fuller sense of her chin and neck.

An academician's office is a dismal place. Semesters go by in the predictability of students' papers arriving on one's desk and coffee mugs drained and forgotten during glassy-eyed grading. Office hours are a puddle in which minutes drip and drip and drip with no students in sight, as if they indeed had no debate with Chesterton's arguments against modern relativism. Janitorial staff came in at night to dust around the bookcases, but they were trained to never touch the piles of journals—even those from as far back as 1998—nor the shattered spines of books left open to a page since 2002 on the academician's desk. So, they'd miss the drying peels of mandarin oranges and leave the academician to find them blackened or moldy every time he had the spark of an idea and shuffled into paper in search of a reference.

This month of October bore down especially hard on the academician's office in our town of Seattle. Take my office windows, for instance. I had the best office in the Department of English, better than that of even the current department chair, a fine Nigerian woman who taught postcolonial studies. My office had a row of three windows, and hers, one. But what I hadn't considered when I made a power play for the office with the three windows was that I would have three times the swath of gray sky for the nine months beginning in October. Three times the view of the row of full moon maples as they lost their leaves and turned to twigs. Three times the damp seeping in through the glass. Three times the view of students shuffling around through the quad below, dressed in their black Uniqlo puffer jackets. Three times the dread of the penetrative advance of the gray as it dealt the great seasonal sadness we would all either feed or deny, we faculty and students. The latter, at least, would seek treatment, and then we would be awash in Adderall-driven attention or Zoloft-muffled anxieties.

So, it would be cruel to question the warm ripple of lust in the wake of Ruhaba's visit to the academician's office in October. In the fantasies that followed, I was able to have her face me as she lay back on my desk. I was able to remove her headscarf because I now knew where to untie it. I could fill in the length of her hair with my imagination and have it tumble in endless curls over the breadth of a desk hurriedly swept clear of years of debris.

Reliving these images in my head and writing of them at this feverish pace feels macabre given the terrible nature of things that happened in that very office on November 1st. Goodness, was that just two days ago? No one is allowed in that office now, and the whole floor of the Department of English has yellow police tape around it. I do not want to ever go back in there, not even to retrieve my Chesterton book notes and my knitting.

What could I possibly find there in the middle of all that loss? I feel like a dirty old man, and my fantasies that once soothed me now feel tawdry. Predatory.

Reality, you see, had rewarded with me with so much more—moments in flesh and blood, with voices and shouts and laughter and fights and letters and promises—oh so many promises. The dreams I began to build in the quiet moments between reality will have to see me through the months to come.

As for the police and federal agents, they could knock themselves out in that office of mine, looking for Truth. If they had read their Chesterton, they would know that a bullet is quite as round as the world, but it is not the world.

They have their questions. But, truth be told, the question that is beyond their ken, the question that overwhelms me, even more than the matter of the boy and his letter to Camille, is one of love. How much and how quickly I came to care for these people. I am haunted now by this—did they ever come to care for me at all?

CHAPTER TWO

Welcome Back to Fall 2016

To: Sugar High Bakery
From: Khan, Ruhaba

Dear favorite baker,
I'm craving a good cake. Do you have any options for a delicious cake for a feminist living a delectable life alone?
xoxo
Ruhaba.

The sun has risen, or rather has cast a feeble yellow wash on the skyless clouds. Still, I sit here and write, moved afresh into a frenzy so my mind can grasp and clutch at memories. I find myself parsing through the moments, sorting, cataloging, then shaking my head helplessly as they all flutter away like a hundred starlings on the wing, pulsing and wheeling as one. And what is that one singular sense I seek to make of such a flight? I seek, in particular, any hint of missteps or errors of word or judgment on my part in all the things that came to pass.

The first time I saw the boy, I knew he could be no one but a relative of Ruhaba's. This wasn't because he looked like her. In fact, they seemed to bear little resemblance. I noticed immediately that he was paler in skin, almost like an olive-toned white boy, Spanish or Italian. His hair, even in the indoor lighting of the party we were attending, was more of a dark and impenetrable brown, as if a thick cloud of Eastern dust had settled forever on a black-haired boy's head. He was dressed formally—in a long-sleeved shirt, buttoned at the cuffs and collar, tucked into khakis instead of hanging over jeans. And brown leather shoes. He was dressed in the manner of a boy whose parents held great store by impressions and had worn their child down long ago. The care and cultivation of a unique personal aesthetic was what signaled to me his ties to Ruhaba.

The "thing" we were at was the first in the limitless string of parties that our university's Provost threw in his waterfront home all year round, in an effort to be liked. This one's evite was titled "Welcome Back to Fall Quarter 2016!," which someone should have pointed out to him was an impossibility, since this was the beginning of the fall of 2016 and we had been nowhere before this but in the summer of 2016.

The Provost lived a short drive from Seattle over Lake Washington, on the upscale enclave of Mercer Island. Upscale, because that's what one did on Mercer Island, where one's neighbors were Bill Gates and Howard Schultz. Enclave, because his wife was an attorney who worked for Amazon. The Provost did not need to be Provost but everyone knew he stayed Provost so he would have a job to go to from nine to five instead of thrashing about in a seven-bedroom, five-bathroom micro-mansion.

In the years he had been Provost and I had been faculty, I had come to this party and only twice seen his wife, and briefly, at that. People wanted too much to talk about Amazon, and her job was predicated on not talking about Amazon. Rumor had it she was lead attorney on a case that had the city abuzz—an Amazon employee had jumped off its twelve-story headquarters building after sending out an email threatening to kill himself if he wasn't given the transfer he wanted. The Provost's wife was drafting a pledge for every employee to sign, swearing they wouldn't kill themselves on company premises.

No matter how many times you went to the Provost's home, the sharply uniformed help would hand guests an ivory-colored brochure with a map to the many pieces of art in that house. In the past few years, I had started to collect these and anonymously mail them out to the local media, especially the journalists who covered the rise of socialism in this town. That we never saw a story on the ostentatiousness of this home was a tribute to how good the Provost's wife was at her job.

The Provost had no swimming pool, though, and he talked a lot about not having a swimming pool, about not wanting one because it was just pure vanity in Seattle, even a heated pool, because the temperatures even in the summer lent themselves to barely eight or nine days a year of actual, organic swimming pool pleasures of "cool water against warm skin." As much as he talked about not having a swimming pool, the Provost talked about having African hardwood floors and limestone on the living room fireplace.

This annual event of his couldn't have inspired much of a spirit of revelry in anyone except the fresh new assistant professor recruits, and even in them, it might only have provoked anxiety. Few sights are as heart-rending as university faculty dressed in their best. Few events are as shorn of mirth as those in which well-dressed faculty attempt to party. Every time I stepped into such things, I was once again convinced that the academy was where intellectuals came to hide from their chance at greatness.

But one had to admit that anxiety pervaded the nation at the time, as it still does, just five days away from the election. The second presidential debate was on that same night as the Provost's party. The Provost's administrative assistant had sent out an email to faculty to apologize for what she said was entirely an oversight on her part in scheduling the party on that evening. Those who wanted to watch the debates would not be disappointed, she promised, because all the Provost's flat-screen LED smart televisions would be turned to that channel and perhaps the faculty in political science would provide an analysis afterward? (Ah, but we all knew the faculty in political science would be shit-faced by the time the debate ended, which was just as well, given that their expertise in most matters relevant to today's politics became irrelevant more than a decade ago when a Black man started to dream of the White House.)

The Provost had almost canceled the party and only a few of us faculty whom he trusted knew of this. He had set up a conference call with me and a couple of other, trusted, senior faculty to ask whether he should go ahead with it despite "the possibility of awkward and inappropriate conversations likely to come up at the party." The university's legal counsel (and, I suspect, the Provost's wife) had recommended caution, he said. People were atwitter about a videotape released by *The Wash-*

ington Post. Women were coming out of the woodwork to accuse Mr. Donald Trump of sexual assault. "We don't want people using words like 'pussy' at my party. The female faculty could file lawsuits all over the place," the Provost said, perhaps forgetting the fact that a female faculty member was on the conference line, or perhaps not caring that she was. I'd assured the Provost that I'd keep an ear out at the party, make the rounds, break up conversations as needed. The others on the call offered to do the same.

So, I'd mingled a bit at the party, moving from the large expanses of split-level living room to the waterfront patio to the dazzling kitchen and back to the living room area. Donald Trump and pussies and women's outrage were all that anyone was talking about, so I abandoned any attempt at intervention. From the looks of it, we were headed for four years of a strong female leader. I was all for it, but let these poor people have their fun while they still could.

Besides, I was riveted by Ruhaba's young visitor. The foreign boy had an inscrutable expression on his face. He was holding an orange plate (the color of fall) and staring at a platter of gourmet nachos, layered with beans and salsas and cheeses and guacamole and whatnot. He picked up a large spoon that he spied next to the platter, matching the muck on the tip of the spoon with the colors and textures of the food on the platter, and he started to poke at the nachos. I almost stepped forward to help.

I stepped back. A young Black girl came up to the boy, laughing. Why did they allow students at these parties? Ah, yes, free labor. Despite the upscale residence, the party itself was scaled to the stature of the attendees. Minimally catered and no catering staff. For the students, the barter was free food or free booze. The Black girl dramatically held her hand out to take the spoon from the Pakistani boy's hand. The hooded look in the boy's eyes dropped away. He looked flustered. He handed the spoon to her. I wondered if his discomfort was at her Blackness—understandable, since he could not have encountered too many Blacks, if any, in Pakistan. Or was it at some perception of his own lack of etiquette? That was understandable, too, if the boy was unaccustomed to ladling things onto his own plate. I imagined they had servants and mothers do that sort of thing in Pakistan.

"I know, our food looks a little crazy, right?" the girl said. Her voice sounded familiar. I guessed she might have been in a class of mine and I took note of her as having a unique name—Conscience or Essence or something.

Today, of course, I know this person's name is Essence. More about that one later.

"I'm guessing you guys don't have nachos en Français?" the girl tried again.

The boy smiled, ignoring the girl's ridiculous error in language and avoiding her eyes.

That was when I learned he was from France. I hadn't known Ruhaba had family in France. I certainly had never detected a French inflection in her voice or manner. Even if she had attempted to conceal such a connection, it would not have escaped me. I spoke some myself, and I do love the French accent.

Another girl joined them. I recognized her as a student in one of my classes, one of the less attractive students, Lindsay or Libby or something. She was trying hard to seem casual and friendly. No doubt she was one of those students who *adored* the lovely Dr. Khan, and wouldn't mind the boy putting in a word for her. The Black girl had put a heap of the nachos on the boy's plate, even though he had tried to put up a protest by waving his free hand. Now he was just standing there while the two girls chatted with him. He fixed his gaze over the Black girl's shoulder and nodded vigorously at everything. He didn't have a fork and he didn't seem to be using that as an excuse to get away from their company.

I watched him fidget uncomfortably. I wondered about his life in France. Did he live in Paris? Elsewhere? Hadn't Ruhaba said something about his parents being worried for him or wanting to give him a change of scene? A brooding Muslim teenaged boy in France—I was never one to leap to conclusions, but recent events urge us to consider that everyone should be worried about such boys. Be especially worried about the ones who dress well, I thought, and immediately felt some shame. Come on, Harding, don't let the madness of these times get to you. Or such was my thinking on that day.

"That's the Pakistani gal's nephew," a voice said next to me, too close to my ear and probably too loud for politeness. Before I turned to see who it was, although I sensed the identity of the speaker, I glanced at the boy. He had heard. He was staring right at me. He looked quickly away now, to save me the embarrassment or to save himself the awkwardness.

I turned to the voice—Betsy MacDowell, who, if she'd been capable of a fraction of that foreign boy's shame, would have stayed home. Over the summer, someone had scrawled the word "Fugly" over her office door in the Department of English. But there seemed to be no shaming women like her these days. Everything was fine, they were "embracing it all," all their imperfections, turning the scorn back on the scornful, *shaming the shamers* as they called it, making up new nouns as they went along, spotlighting the "fat-shamers," the "slut-shamers," the "skinny-bitch-shamers."

But I did feel a little sorry for Betsy. She and I were somewhat of the outsiders in the Department of English, along with my dear friend Meyer. She, for all her . . . well. And I, for having been the "freak hire," the Chesterton scholar in the midst of the postmodernists and postcolonial theorists (although I did, for a while there, coauthor a paper or two on post-structuralism, enough to be the well-rounded golden boy on the job market in 1991). I earned tenure and full professorship, and all through it they kept wondering whose side I was really on. I study them now, closely, these desperate seekers, these self-declared progressives who will be-the-change-they-want-to-see until they are maimed from the brutality of change and blind from seeing. Intellectual discourse, debate, disagreement, and certainly academic freedom, were dying swiftly in this terrible fire, this pretense of progressivism.

The closeness of my study had been alerting me these past few years to something new in the air. Something electric, a self-righteousness in the student body, a bracing-for-impact in the faculty. Our curricula were under scrutiny, the pigment of our skin stretched thin under microscopes, our every lecture frozen for a moment on our lips, reconsidered, for its potential to stir the shit-storm of the politics of identity.

"Look at you, Ollie, looking as handsome as the day you were hired!" Betsy leaned in to air-kiss me and I held my breath as I tilted my head lightly toward her, nodding at her husband Rob or Jim or something. The man would come to each of these parties dressed in the single taupe suit he owned and he would speak to no one at all until the end of the party, when he would effusively thank the host for the great time he'd had. This man Rob or Jim will murder us all one day. And they won't find a splatter of blood on that taupe suit.

Murder your wife, I mouthed to the man silently as Betsy went on about something. Her hand was leaning so heavily on my forearm that if I shifted my weight in the slightest, she would probably fall down, and in falling, clutch my sleeve so hard that she'd bring me along to the floor with her. After giving her approximately forty-five seconds of audience, I set my glass of whiskey on the knuckles of her clutching hand and bounced it up and down there, playfully but hard enough for her to remove her hand with a look of confusion. If I held my thin smile a second too long, she would take it in her head that I was flirting, somehow, so I frowned suddenly and looked past her.

"I must go watch the downfall of Mr. Trump, my dear," I said to her, splashing some of the liquid on her shoes as I turned to walk away, hoping she would be distracted as she attended to the little accident. She yelped exaggeratedly, in a manner that would imply not clumsiness or rudeness on my part but, agonizingly, again, flirtation. She started to wave at a napkin on the table, as if expecting me to fetch it . . . and, what, stoop down at her crotch and play at wiping her shoe? I brushed rig' past all this and walked away.

Before I realized it, I had walked up to the foreign boy. I know it wasn't intentional. In any case, the boy was now surrounded by other students of Lindsay's or Libby's kind. The Black girl had left and all of these kids were white, shabbily dressed. Some of them were drinking and others were probably holding back until they could binge-drink in their dorm rooms or wherever else and show up hung over to my class the next day.

"And how do you say, 'Girl, I already swiped left on you, so stop hitting on me IRL,'" one of the gay boys said, and the whole group laughed.

The foreign boy's face was flushed, probably from wanting to bolt or from struggling to translate that gibberish into French. He spoke softly and stumbled just a little on his words in English, which made his audience titter even more. They offered reassurance, of course, with their "awws" and their "oooh-la-las," to comfort him that they weren't laughing *at* him but *with* him.

I inched closer to the food table and surveyed it with a frown. I realized I wanted to eavesdrop, to get a better sense of the foreign boy and thereby his aunt. This irritated me. Couldn't Harding be content with fantasizing? Reality is always a downer, a boner-crusher. And what reality was I trying to draw close to, anyway? For all I knew, things didn't quite add up with the aunt and nephew scenario. I didn't quite subscribe to the hate-mongering of Mr. Trump and his men who said that it had begun, the infiltration of these radicalized Muslim youth from France into America, but one did have to wonder how the boy so easily got a visa. Perhaps because he was still a child? Although, they would argue that at fifteen, a Muslim male was hardly a kid, at least not one who came from Pakistan, "originally," or otherwise.

And where was the aunt now? I turned to look over the split levels and past the try-hard, well-dressed intellectuals, out onto the patio. I spotted her there, wearing a yellow and orange headscarf (tasteful, but fall colors nonetheless), nodding her head to something the Provost was saying to her. From this distance, I could bring myself to imagine her not as a dark-skinned woman from the Far East but as Mediterranean—Greek, perhaps. And her headscarf, if I imagined it a little looser, could easily bear the elegance of a foulard draped around Tippi Hedren's head in *The Birds*.

I watched her for a while, making sure to look away often enough and down at the food table to load my plate with nuts and cheese and a couple of meatballs. I could hear her clear little laugh every now and then, like the chink of a knife against a champagne flute, making an announcement to me of the tumult to come in my life. I could see I wasn't the only one to be stirred by that sound from her throat. The Provost beamed every time she made it. Men who stood within hearing, in this clutch or that clique, were compelled to turn their heads in her direction. Each glance lingered for a bit. Roamed.

Did she ever notice that she provoked this response in men? If she did, she didn't show it. She wasn't one of those women whose eyes darted around at a party even as they rested their cold fingers on the speaker in front of them. But still, I felt an odd sense of relief when I saw Ruhaba throw quick looks in the direction of her nephew every now and then. Good. She hadn't just thrown this boy in here and forgotten about him.

I recall feeling some surprise in that moment that I gave a shit. I wondered if something about the boy had tapped into a sense of solicitude that I hadn't felt for some time now.

I looked over at him again. The crowds around him had thinned. It was down to the gay boy and Lindsay-or-Libby. Their faces were less animated now and they seemed to be nodding at the boy's words with flagging interest. He turned around for a moment, to scoop another helping of nachos onto his plate. He was still talking, smiling now, as if leading up to some sort of punch line. Before he turned around, the gay boy and the girl were distracted by someone calling out to them and now they stepped away and toward another group of people, so that when the foreign boy turned completely around, still speaking, he looked into blank space. Even though his face was only partially visible to me, I could see that it fell. His smile vanished as he spotted them, their backs to him, walking away. He looked quickly down at his plate and then glanced around the room to see if anyone had noticed this terrible moment.

I averted my gaze just in time. Dear God, the awkwardness of youth. The foreign boy ought to learn a thing for two from Fugly.

I made a good show of looking around the room as if I, too, were in need of a friendly face in this horrid crowd. "Hello, there," I heard myself say, stepping up to him. "You must be Dr. Khan's nephew."

He nodded and smiled politely. Then he looked away.

"Bienvenue!" I said before I could stop myself.

The boy turned his smile from polite to a faux-perky. He could be an academic someday.

"What brings you to the P-N-W?"

He frowned. He cocked his head to the side. "Je ne comp . . . I don't understand?"

"Oh, the PNW? Seattle is in the Pacific Northwest."

"Ah, okay." he said. "I have heard that before. I forget. I forgot."

"Learning English rapidly, I see," I said. If my intention had been to make the boy feel a little easier, this was not cutting it.

"I speak English only okay," he said flatly. "My parents speak English to us." He didn't sound churlish or offended. He sounded like he was providing factual information and had spoken those very sentences several times before.

"Are you going to be with us a while?" I asked. "I'm sure your aunt would like that."

"Maybe. Not sure," he said, moving his weight from one foot to the other and looking at my neck.

"Well, perhaps we'll see you on campus. Have you been yet?"

"No," said the boy.

"Oh? Why not? Let's go find your aunt and tell her you must . . ."

"No, no, please. It is okay. I will come sometime. That will be super."

"You're lying, aren't you?"

"Pardon?" He looked right at me then, and his eyes seemed fierce. His jaw seemed to come into some definition, pushing out against the childish plump of his cheeks. Come to think of it, I was startled, too, by what I'd said. Had I meant to simply impose a jocular familiarity, or was it that the boy had already stirred in me a need to be confrontational? But, at the time, I was more interested in his response than in my trigger. Was he accustomed to being called a liar? Was his indignation a signal of a life of respect or one of ignominy?

"You're lying about it being a nice idea," I said quickly. "You don't want to come to campus. All those young adults, I suppose? Or does it just not seem cool? Being that it is your aunt's place of work and all? Filled with us old farts." I hadn't worked so hard in years.

The boy looked from my neck to his own shoes and back.

"I don't like the American university. I mean American campus," he said.

"You don't *like* it? *Any* American campus?"

The boy shrugged.

"Why not?" I asked. Was this a Muslim thing? A disdain for the American way of life, of educating the Lindsay-or-Libbys alongside the gay boys and straight boys? Or was it a French disdain, for the high cost of college or something?

"I don't like the . . . the shooters."

The shooters. Had I heard right?

"The shooters?" I said stupidly.

"The university shooters. Campus shooters? I know, I know, not every day. Not every campus. But we don't know when, yes? Any day could be the shooting, n'est-ce pas?"

I blinked at him, incredulous. That's when I realized what seemed so familiar about this stranger, what made it clear that he was from Ruhaba's world. It was a sensation one had, a pull toward a different axis, where unexpected things would be said. You'd sense a certain crackling energy of intelligent discontent, and if one allowed oneself to be propelled into this gravity, one would look right into planet-size eyes asking questions as odd as the universe.

"Surely you are joking, young man," I said. The boy was fifteen. I reminded myself firmly that the boy was fifteen.

He said nothing.

"So, you are afraid of a campus shooting? How do you go about your day in France? Aren't you afraid of a terrorist shooting? Or are you . . ."

I let my voice trail away. I wanted to say, "Or are you in the know when terror attacks happen?" I was surprised at the fact that I bristled at the boy's words, his presence here, on this soil, and there, on French soil. Pull yourself together, Harding.

He was peering at me, waiting for more words. When nothing else came, he said, "I am not afraid. I don't like to go to places where I will have to run."

I let the outlandishness of those words settle in my head for a bit. Just moments ago, the boy had been animatedly talking to kids just a few years older than him about god knows what, flustered and seeking their approval. And now, he was talking to a fifty-six-year-old academic, eye to eye, mind to mind, serious and unfathomable as the Koran.

"Allahu Akbar!" the boy said. I startled and spilled my drink, on accident this time. I took a stumbling step back, away from him, disoriented at the brightening of his face. Then I noticed he was looking over my shoulder, past me.

"I see you have met a professor," Ruhaba said to him, coming up behind me.

"Yes, Khala Ruhaba," the boy said. "But I don't know monsieur's name now, I am sorry." His manner had changed. He projected an enthusiasm toward his aunt that suggested a politeness toward me that certainly hadn't been there a moment ago.

"Khala means Aunt in Urdu," Ruhaba said to me.

Ah. So, that's what the boy had said. Khala Ruhaba. Not Allahu Akbar. He pronounced his *r* the way the French did. The languages and pronunciations of people roaming the world collided and colluded to fuck with everyone's heads. I tried to ignore the fact that my pulse had quickened, either from what I had misheard the boy say or from the presence of Ruhaba so close, so exclusively with me and her closest kin here.

"This is Dr. Harding. Professor Oliver Harding, a senior colleague of mine," Ruhaba said to the boy. I shook his hand.

"You teach law, sir?"

"Oh no, I teach English literature," I said. I watched Ruhaba look from me to the boy and back with a pleased smile on her face. Was she pleased at this scene before her or was her pleasure residual from her conversation with the Provost? Had she been offered something by him? Would that thing put her closer within my reach or farther from it?

Betsy MacDowell found her way to us. She clutched Ruhaba's hand in her own and tried to pull it to her lips to kiss it or something, but Ruhaba managed, quite deftly, I thought, to retrieve it.

"How do we pronounce that woman's name?" Betsy said, gesturing to the television. Someone had turned up the volume on the presidential debate.

Ruhaba frowned at Betsy, unsure of her question or where she was to direct her attention. Betsy gestured more expansively and pulled Ruhaba by her arm, a step closer to the television. "There. That *beautiful* creature."

A woman in the presidential debate audience was asking a question. "There are 3.3 million Muslims in the US. And I'm one of them," the woman in the television debate audience said.

Ruhaba didn't bother pronouncing the name as Betsy had requested. Instead, she skipped past the woman's name on the screen and read aloud what it said next: "Uncommitted Missouri Voter. There you go."

Betsy smiled, looking convinced Ruhaba was an idiot. Then, she frowned, reconsidering her conviction.

I looked back at the screen. I must say, I didn't think the woman was a particularly "beautiful creature." In fact, she decidedly was not. But one didn't point at women from other cultures and colors around here without using the word "beautiful." It's just what we all did now. Even women who were themselves decidedly fugly. Such pandering, such patronizing . . . did poor Ruhaba have to endure this sort of thing all the time?

I missed the Muslim woman's question, something about people like her needing protection from America's Islamophobia, but I saw Ruhaba lean in closer to the television. Her nephew leaned against a wall and showed less than a mild interest. I stepped back so I could watch him and his aunt. On television, Trump said something about Muslims having to report the problems when they see them.

The room fell silent when Hillary spoke. She said something about her vision for America where everyone had a place if they worked hard and did their part and played nice.

The boy started to look around the room, back toward where the students had been chatting with him.

"We need American Muslims to be part of our eyes and ears on our frontlines," Hillary said.

I recall that line clearly because something about it made Ruhaba cross her arms over her chest. I saw her face harden. I saw it shrink from the quick, sideways glances a few people in the room threw her way. She was a live, exposed wire in a roomful of toddlers.

Hillary was saying, "I've worked with a lot of Muslim groups around America . . ."

Ruhaba, as if responding to her covert audience, forced a smile on her face. I could see it took work. I must have been staring hard, for she looked my way, right into me.

Even today, I am struck by my swiftness in that moment, my sense of presence, the alacrity with which I seized upon the right thing to do.

I rolled my eyes.

Her face lit up.

". . . part of our homeland security, and that's what I want to see," Hillary said.

"I need to refresh my drink," I said loudly to the room. "Call homeland security."

The joke got what it deserved—weak laughter. But it allowed those of us who wanted to step away to step away.

I am grateful for this, among other talents with which I have been blessed—I know how to modulate my quips and deploy my wit for just the kind of laughter occasioned by any given circumstance. At this, I never fail.

"We should be leaving," Ruhaba said, looking at her watch. "Adil, fetch your coat."

I clutched at something to say to hold them back for just a minute. It had to be something neutral, nothing about the pronunciation of names or about whether this woman and this boy had reported on their friendly neighborhood Muslims today.

"What was the Provost talking to you about?" I said. It sounded intrusive and I kicked myself for that.

Ruhaba didn't give any sign of finding my question odd. She said, "Oh, about a wine cellar he is planning to add to the house," she said, grinning.

I took that as a sign to get chummier. "Do you have school tomorrow?" I asked Ruhaba. "Do *you*?" I asked the boy.

"*I* do, but not him," Ruhaba said, stepping closer. "He's here on a tourist visa, so he can't enroll in anything just yet. I will have to get some paperwork done, to, you know, show him as my dependent, so he can go to school soon."

"But I may go home before that is needed," said the boy, looking at neither of us. Then, with a quick nod at me as a way to say goodbye, he turned and walked away from us. It was only then that I noticed that he walked with a limp, not very deep, but visible especially because he was the kind of person one would be likely to watch, approaching or leaving.

"Did he hurt himself?" I asked Ruhaba. Maybe I could still draw her into a conversation.

"No, he has polio."

I blinked. That explained the boy's remark about not wanting to be in a situation in which he might be called upon to run. "Polio? Hasn't that been . . ."

"Well, no, it hasn't been stamped out in Pakistan. Adil's polio is one of the biggest misfortunes of our family. He was born in France but contracted the virus when his mother took him as an infant on a trip to Pakistan. Now he's a Generation-Z Frenchman with polio. I suppose the boy's been teased a good deal growing up, even in France. Do you think so?"

"Do I think what?"

"Do you think he would have been teased by children in France? Taunted?"

I frowned. Another odd question, of the same quality as the boy's a few minutes ago. Their faces would look so earnest, with a sense of immediacy in seeking a response, an open inquiry, as if I were right now the only person in the universe, and I held the wisdom that would free generations from misery.

"Well, children the world over can be quite cruel, can't they? But, no, I don't suppose he was teased, not very much, I'd think. That sounds quite medieval," I said.

She nodded slowly, searching my face, but looked unconvinced.

I had failed generations by using too many qualifiers instead of a plain, declarative sentence.

"Perhaps we should ask the boy," I said, as he came toward us then, wearing a dapper, well-fitted tweed coat. This item of clothing set him even farther apart from the other young people at this party.

"No," Ruhaba said quickly in a low voice. "Why ask him such a thing? I don't want to make him uncomfortable in any way." She put her hand on my arm, pressed down on it, as if to impress her point upon me. Her grip was firm even through it was fleeting. Oh, how different it was from the fumbling grip of Betsy. Oh, how I wanted more of this. A grip of a hand, a grip within her arms.

As Ruhaba and the boy started to walk away, I felt an almost gravitational push, as if I were plummeting away from something. I saw her pull out her phone and punch her finger on some app. I seized my opportunity.

"How are you getting home?" I asked.

"Uber," she said. "It was too rainy to drive here tonight."

"Ah, forget Uber," I said, in as casual a manner as I could muster. "I'll drop you off on my way."

"Oh, no, please don't bother," Ruhaba said. "We probably aren't even on your way home."

"Where do you live?" I asked, as if I didn't already know. I had done some casual Googling once. She lived in Columbia City.

"Columbia City," she said.

"It's on my way," I lied.

On the way to her home in my Jeep Cherokee, I allowed myself a moment of pure pleasure. It had been a while since a woman had sat in my passenger seat and a child in the back. I was so overwhelmed by these locations of human bodies in my shapeless, scentless spaces, I let myself yearn for more. As I tried to concentrate on the blind hairpin turns and their sharp dropoffs on this island of multimillion-dollar waterfront homes, Ruhaba lowered her window a bit and turned her face to the wind.

"Adil, lower your window and smell the fall," she said. "Not too much or you'll let in the rain."

I glanced in the rearview mirror and saw the boy lower his window for a polite three seconds, nod, and shut it again. I looked over at Ruhaba and shook my head. She smiled.

We drove in silence for a bit longer as I went over I-90 and the glimmering cityscape came into view. Beneath us, Lake Washington grew icy-cold. If it had been the daytime, Mount Rainier might have loomed up on our left, and I could have pointed it out to Ruhaba and the boy, told them about the time I hiked up to its summit. I considered telling them anyway but stopped. It would have been a ridiculous thing to bring up out of nowhere in the darkness of the night.

And then Ruhaba spoke of work. She spoke about the Space Committee. About whether the university would seriously entertain the proposal to move from the quarter to the semester system. About the new hire in Enrollments and the ridiculously high salary he was to be paid, a sign of the growing allegiance to investing in administration rather than academic excellence. Administrative bloat, they call it. She asked me what I thought of the new curriculum students were demanding.

She looked at me with a sideways glance at this last thing. Ah, I realize now that she had, indeed, tried to warn me of my own impending annihilation. Her glance had been a signal to me, of the hostilities afoot that would render the likes of me irrelevant in the ivory tower. But on that night, all I could see was that her lips seemed redder in the shadows within my car.

"What new curriculum?" I said, not even trying to sound interested.

She hesitated. "Never mind," she said.

I was relieved. Discussions of enrollments and curricula were a surefire way for a man to land in "colleague zone," a purgatory whose temporal punishments were impossible to endure with any grace on one's way into the plenary indulgences offered by a woman.

Traffic was unusually and annoyingly light that night, no

doubt because the residents of this city were taking the presidential debates too seriously, huddled indoors with their popcorn and their pumped-up fears. The parts of the city I knew well started to fall behind me as I drove into South Seattle and its poorly lit streets.

I braked hard for an old Black man crossing the street with a walker. The light changed but he seemed to care as little as anyone else in his world probably cared for him in his senility, clear from the way he was shouting at a clutch of lowlifes who stood by a cannabis store. The city had painted a mural dedicated to these people and it came into view as I drove slowly, afraid that someone may run out in front of my car. The mural was called *The Rainbow of Diversity*, for these neighborhoods in the south of the city claimed to have the most diverse zip code in the country. The mural bore a mawkish earnestness in the depictions of women in headscarves or gypsy earrings, men in a mariachi band beside a man in an Osama turban. They'd thrown in a busty blond woman on the mural. Had I seen a single one of those walking around here yet? Nope. Someone should have scaled back the heavy-handedness of all this. The greater irony was that this mural was painted on a street-facing wall of the Darigold Creamery, a bona fide American institution, a cooperative of Northwest farmers whose milk and superior dairy products we Whites had enjoyed for years. The people who lived here deserved fresher spaces. They deserved better than irony.

"Why did you choose this neighborhood?" I asked Ruhaba once the car was moving again. I failed at making that sound casual.

She looked at me and chuckled. “I have a view of the Cascade Mountains from my bedroom window.” I took my eyes off the treacherous road and glanced at her for signs of seduction. Women don’t mention their bedrooms without intent.

She had turned away by then and was looking straight ahead. “Make a left here,” she said, and I know I heard that smile still in her voice.

“I’m looking for a dog walker,” I said. Then, speaking in broken French, I said to the boy, “Someone to walk my dog for me, twice a day. Would you be interested in walking Edgar, young man?” I looked at him in my rearview mirror while keeping Ruhaba in my peripheral vision.

The boy shook his head firmly. “No, thank you,” he said, staring out the window into the rainy night.

Bastard.

Ruhaba shrugged at me with a somewhat apologetic look. “I will ask him to reconsider,” she said. “It would be nice for him to be able to speak to someone in French. And perhaps you could encourage his English.”

Yes, this was good. I felt almost euphoric at the mild interest she had shown toward the possibility of a continued alliance of some sort. “Of course. *And*, if you walk him twice a day, I’ll pay $30 a day,” I said. “With our city heading for $15 minimum wage and all,” I chuckled.

But that remark seemed to have caught Ruhaba’s attention.

“Well,” she said. “I don’t want him to make a small fortune to get up to trouble with,” she said, quickly turning around to wink at her nephew as his head shot up.

He looked at her with a deep frown and a question on his

face. She shook her head at him as if in clarification. I could have sworn she looked a little flustered, nervous. I had to focus hard on my driving.

She strained to reach out and tap him on his arm. "I mean, I don't want you to, you know, have extra cash to buy up a whole lot of pot or something." She gave a short laugh.

The boy nodded. He waited for her to speak again.

"If you'd like to do the dog-walking, I'm fine with it," she said. "I would actually be happy if you did. Better than playing video games at home all day."

"No, thank you," the boy said, pulling his earbuds out of his pocket and tucking them into his ears, drifting away from us, taking his sweet aunt with him, out of my desperate reach even as she sat close enough to touch.

CHAPTER THREE

"Do You Hate America?"

To: Khan, Ruhaba
From: Khan, Ruhaba

Pick with care the kind of fools you will suffer.

The secret you bear this time isn't one to let slip even to the village idiot. It will be your undoing, and what an undoing that will be, babygirl.

Do not imagine that a single person you know will understand. The one who may support the part of you that is woman will not stomach this kind of woman. The one who may support the part of you that is Muslim will not support the kind of eruption you devise. The one that loves you as the radical will abhor the part that summons the exquisite. Men, mothers, lovers, professors, friends, students, grocers . . . the world will say you are evil from head to

When Ruhaba and the boy alighted from my car, I willed myself not to dwell on whether I would ever find her at such closeness again. Already, she and her ward were fading into blurred shapes within the wet onslaught of the October night.

I stepped out and lingered, as politeness would allow me, the gentleman who waits until a lady has at least entered her front door. She lived in an odd house, not one of the many brand-new swanky ones that had sprouted up in this part of the city like bright candles on a moldy cake, but a somewhat older, somewhat beaten-up one. There was no order to the other homes on the street and there were no sidewalks. To the right of her was what looked like a crack-house, complete with a chain-link fence and an old white Cadillac with a shattered windshield. In a house across the street, a dog on a chain in the front yard barked without a sense of purpose. The townhouse to her left sat dark and immutable, with not even a porch light but with a neon sign in its window that read I Heart My Muslim Neighbor.

Jesus.

Just as I was about to get back into the comforting familiarity of my car, I saw the shape of two men rise from Ruhaba's porch. Ruhaba halted in her tracks and grabbed the boy's arm. The two of them took a few steps back. I froze. I had no instinct to step up and throw myself to their defense, but my eyes were riveted and my hands gripped the door handle. My brain scrambled for a response. Honk the horn? Call 9-1-1?

The men flashed something at Ruhaba, an ID of some sort, that made her drop her hand from the boy's arm and step toward them. I could not hear a thing, but after exchanging some words, the group started to walk toward Ruhaba's front door. I was awash in relief that I wasn't to be witness to . . . an assault.

I was spared the prospect of being the coward skulking in the shadows, a half-a-hero, making a call and waiting for the authorities to arrive. And then, I became alert to a new possibility—I was within reasonable minutes and distance for a solicitous inquiry of some sort. A three-quarter hero.

I jumped out of my car and, keeping my finger hovering over the green button after punching 9-1-1 on my phone, I called out, "Ruhaba? Is everything okay?" just as her front door was about to swing shut. I kept a safe distance.

Ruhaba stepped out toward me and beckoned. "Oh good," she said. "I am so glad you're still here!" Her voice sounded thin, higher pitched than I'd known it to be, almost intimate in its request.

I hesitated. I took two slow, deliberate steps forward. "Is something wrong?" I asked, trying to determine the ethnicity and intent of the two shadowy men behind her.

"These people are from the FBI," she said.

I felt a rush of relief at this information. Oh, good. Just the FBI.

"They say they have a few routine questions for Adil," she said.

Her face looked strained, even in the night. Then, as if suddenly aware of how she looked to me—vulnerable—she turned her face into a mask of detached, professional certainty of the kind I knew from our meetings on campus. She cleared her throat and spoke steadily into the night.

"Ollie, I'd like to ask you for a favor." Looking over her shoulder at the men in her door, standing with the boy, she said, loud enough for them to hear, "These FBI agents are fully within their rights to question a minor, with no warrant or warning. They tell me they do not suspect him of any wrongdoing. He will cooperate with them. I am now presenting myself in the role of his lawyer. And I'd like to invite you in, Dr. Harding, Ollie, as a family friend, which you are, to simply bear witness to our cooperation."

I swallowed. What the fuck was this. Somewhere in this city, an Uber driver should right now be thanking me. But she had referred to me as Ollie and my heart had skipped a beat. Women. They have their ways.

"And to help if Adil has trouble expressing himself between French and English," Ruhaba said.

I felt foolish standing there with my jaw open, trying to form words. None came—not in French, not in English.

Ruhaba took a deep breath and said, "That is, if you are not afraid. I urge you, Ollie, to be unafraid."

One of the agents behind her had reached into her house and switched on the porch light. I looked at the men. Regular, American men. One of them waved at me.

I snapped my jaw shut. I looked at the boy's face and then at Ruhaba's. The two of them looked afraid, even Ruhaba, through her mask of detachment. But something told me at that time that it was a fear of their situation, not of their story. And yet, they were asking for *my* fearlessness.

I cleared my throat and said, "I'm not afraid. Please, lead me in."

I was very afraid. But, within the fear was wrapped an assurance of my own safety. I was a tenured, full professor of English literature, and the FBI agents looked almost relieved to have me there, a figure of harmless familiarity albeit a bit of nuisance, like a housecat. No, I gathered from their marked lack of interest in me, they didn't think of me as someone having an involvement any deeper than a polite offer of a ride home, an act of kindness—American, Christian, gallant. I found myself feeling surer of my role by the minute. I feel chagrined as I think about it now, but I must be honest about what I felt then.

I glanced around Ruhaba's home. I feared for her. I hoped to God we would not see Islamic prayer mats or wall hangings or some other such overt expression of her religion. I would have loved to encounter those things at any other time, all the accoutrements that made her the alluring woman she was, but in the intrusion of these FBI men, I was relieved to spy no such thing. Indeed, the interior of her home seemed normal, if a bit sparse.

I settled into an overstuffed chair to which she ushered me, leaving the FBI agents to sit uncomfortably together in a loveseat while Adil and Ruhaba pulled up straight-backed dining chairs. Ruhaba switched on every single light in the room, even the lamps on the end tables by the loveseat. She didn't turn on the heating. She had no intention of letting these agents linger long enough to warm their bones.

The first FBI agent introduced himself as Agent Ray Waters Jr. The second, the one who had waved at me, who I noticed now was a stocky, square-faced woman, not a man, introduced herself as Agent Sarah Kupersmith. That was the only thing she spoke that whole night. She took notes while Ray Waters Jr. asked questions.

They had been asked by French authorities to do a drop-in and inquire into Mr. Alam's well-being, he said.

Ruhaba thanked him and said Adil was doing fine and to thank the French authorities for their concern.

Ray Waters Jr. looked at the boy, who was staring at the floor, gloomy and silent.

"We have heard from the French authorities about your misguided activities in Toulouse. For our assurance at our end, we would like you to recount to us the matters that brought you here. Are you able to do that, Mr. Alam?"

"Please refer to the child as Adil," Ruhaba said, making it sound like the meekest yet firmest of requests. "Just a reminder that he is a minor."

"Adil," Ray Waters Jr. said, pronouncing it very differently from the way Ruhaba had. A manner of showing distance, perhaps even disrespect, I thought. I would have to make the effort to pronounce it correctly. That is, if the events of this evening left me with any desire to continue my association. I looked at Ruhaba and the elegant curve of one thigh crossed over the other. An expanse of skin between knee and mid-calf was visible under fishnet stockings. Yes, I hoped for a continued association.

I looked over at Ray Waters Jr. to see whether he had noticed the fishnets. He had to have noticed. He was a man in his forties. Wedding ring on his finger.

"What made you want to come to America?" Ray Waters Jr. asked the boy.

The boy looked at him with a frown. "Nothing," he said. "I do not wish to come to America."

"Ah," the agent said. "And why is that? Do you hate America?"

"No. "Just I love *my* country."

"And which country is that?"

The boy frowned. "What do you mean? You said that the gendarmerie phone you? My country—France."

And then, the dams opened.

What was it that I felt when the boy told them that he loved his life in Toulouse? As I sit here now, in the comfort of my own home, setting my pen down to crack my knuckles and think back to that night, think of my uncertainties about my place in the world and theirs, can I summon up the empathy I felt then? Can I feel now the same lurch in my heart as I did when the boy said he missed home and ached for it every day since he'd been here in America? He said he missed his mother and his little sister. He missed his friends. He couldn't bear to think that their lives were going on without him, that they were planning movies and playing football and video games without him. He missed Jean and Ali and Gabriel and Sam and Armand and Camille.

What was it that I looked for that night as I glanced around from the corner of my eye, past Ruhaba's living room into a section of her bedroom visible from where I sat? The light reached in there and revealed to me part of an unmade bed on which a richly embroidered red silk comforter lay disheveled and slipping almost to the floor. Beyond the bed, red silk curtains. Beyond that, I supposed, way beyond, the Cascade Mountains. Hadn't I felt a deeper sense of belonging with those cold mountains in the distance than with the warmth of silks and the breath on these voices so much closer within my reach?

Had I leaned in when the boy said he had been angry? Had I flinched when he'd said he still was? Had he felt my glare as strong as those of the agents when he spoke of tender things like his birthday a few weeks before that day, a birthday he'd spent at a park with his friends? They had planned a barbecue, he'd said. His mother had insisted on bringing a cake. The boy hadn't wanted the cake, said he was too old to be sharing one with his friends. French teens did not do such things, he'd told her. But do it for the sake of your mother from Lahore, she said.

"Your mother is from Lahore, Pakistan," Ray Waters Jr. said.

"Yes," the boy said. "But she is now French citizen. She lived in France from when she married my papa, very young, like twenty-one."

"Eighteen," Ruhaba said.

Ray Waters Jr. nodded. Sarah Kupersmith noted.

The boy continued his story. When she arrived at the park, his mother texted him to say she was looking for him. He looked around for her and he saw two of the many policemen at the park that day step toward his mother and say something to her. He saw, even from the distance, that they had startled his mother.

"I wanted to go to her, but I can feel like the embarrassment. She wears . . . she was wearing the abaya."

"Do you mean the hijab?" Ray Waters Jr. said.

The boy looked at Ruhaba. She said: "They call it abaya in Pakistan. For your purposes, it's the same thing."

Ray Waters Jr. frowned and seemed about to say something, perhaps about the FBI's purposes being far more nuanced than she was implying. But he let it go. Sarah Kupersmith noted.

All this had made my skin crawl. I didn't know who I was, who I was meant to be in that moment. These people who had only moments ago made my heart soar with possibilities of intimacy were being rendered distant, foreign, by people meant to protect me. *Let me out*, I'd wanted to shout. *Let them in*.

Yes, yes, I do recall feeling that way, thinking those thoughts.

The boy said he saw the policemen at the park gesturing to his mother to take off her scarf. They were pointing to the sign seen at all parks, forbidding dogs, drunks, and symbols of religion.

"My mother's scarf was not even like this . . . traditional . . . not even like tied like Khala Ruhaba ties," the boy said to the federal agents. He didn't look at his aunt when he said this, which implied that he had noted the manner of her headscarf before, had thought about these things. Looking at Ruhaba's face, I imagined I saw the same thought as mine there, even though her eyes were lowered, looking at her hands in her lap as she sat erect in her chair. She didn't take the trouble to explain any more to the agents or to the boy than she already had.

He said he regretted even today that he hadn't walked over to his mother that afternoon at the park. He had been a coward.

"You are not a coward," Ruhaba said. All of us in the room were startled a bit by the sharpness in her tone, more so than by her interruption.

"I *was*," the boy said softly. He said he didn't want his friends to see his mother being humiliated by the police. He didn't want them to think that such things happened to their friend Adil's family and that he was different from them.

"I did not want Camille to feel bad for me," he said almost to himself.

He said Camille had spotted his mother, too. He said she had followed his gaze and grabbed his elbow when she saw his mother put the cake down on the ground at the park and quickly take off her headscarf. He said his mother kept looking at her phone as she did this, expecting her son to text her back to say where he was. The park was filled with teenagers, so she couldn't see him. She stuffed the scarf in her purse and the policemen walked away. Before leaving, one of them picked up the box of cake from the ground and handed it to her. He wanted to seem polite.

"That policeman's face . . . is in my head for many days. Even today," the boy said. "He was a gros . . . fat man with a moustache. He is grinning at Ammi as if nothing happened. As if he was welcoming someone to his country for their first time. I wish I could . . ."

"Adil, what happened after that?" Ruhaba interjected, less sharply this time.

He swallowed and then returned to his narration. "Camille was also waiting, for a moment, same like me. And then we walked to my Ammi. We wave at her to come over." By the time his mother got to his group, he said, she had composed a smile. She had searched his face to learn if he had witnessed what had happened. He had pretended to be distracted, tossing a Frisbee up and down in the air, cheerily greeting his mother. She looked convinced.

She'd said a quick Hello to his friends and then left hastily. They asked him to cut the cake right away and he had.

"What kind of cake?" Ray Waters Jr. asked.

"A birthday cake," Adil said, his voice distant, his face fighting back emotion.

"What flavor?"

The boy closed his eyes for a moment. He opened them and said, "I don't know. Chocolate?"

"A chocolate cake," Ray Waters Jr. said. Sarah Kupersmith noted.

"I think so. It said 'Happy 15th Birthday, Adil!' on the top of it."

When the agents were silent, the boy continued. He said all he could think of as he cut his cake was how disheveled his mother's hair looked after having to unexpectedly expose it to the world. She usually was so smartly dressed and wore good makeup.

For the next few days, he'd had nightmares. Always, he had woken up in a sweat and then fallen back to sleep and been able to intercept his dream and change the outcome with the police. Sometimes his mother wasn't wearing a headscarf. Sometimes there were no police and she would walk right up to him and his friends, stay for the cutting of the cake, tell them stories of how her father would take them to get ice cream on Mall Road in Lahore after the city cooled down following fourteen hours of scorching heat.

The boy paused. He stared at the federal agents. He asked his aunt for water. I wanted some, too, but I did not ask. Yet she brought water for everyone, in clean, tall, glass tumblers laid on a wooden tray stained with a rough gold polish.

The boy continued. He had begun looking things up online after that. He had started reading news reports of other women being asked to remove their headscarves. He read about other humiliations on French Muslims—Arabs, Pakistanis,

Iranians—and he read an essay from a member of a youth coalition that wanted to stand up for their families. He commented online on the essay and got a response the next day thanking him and saying he should feel free to attend a youth meeting that Friday, where a group of French Muslims and their friends would discuss coping strategies.

"I went to that youth meeting and I feel very welcome," he said. "But also I notice that it is all French Muslims and really no friends or something." But the young men told him they had all seen their women—mothers, sisters, cousins, girlfriends—humiliated the way Adil's mother had been. In some towns, they said, mothers wearing headscarves had been forbidden from picking up their children from school. Big and small stores were routinely searching veiled customers.

I remember thinking back then, to my visits to Paris for conferences, to Aix-en-Provence with my young family, to those panoramic views from the cable cars in Chamonix. I recalled the French disdain for the American tourist, but also the nonchalance and perhaps even some cheery self-absorption . . . all these things the boy was speaking of seemed like ugly untruths, exaggerations at best. But he had my ear, that child, as he spoke of his own strange little world in a France unrecognizable to me.

Some women had even been violently attacked, he said. One of the young men, barely eighteen, said that his cousin, who was pregnant and wore a headscarf, had to be hospitalized after being beaten on the street by a young man who called her a "dirty Muslim."

Adil said he went back for two more meetings. At the last one, they talked about taking an action. He grew nervous and went home and wrote them an email that night to say he was grateful but wasn't going to join them anymore because he didn't feel he fit in well with direct action. He didn't get a response.

The police had arrived at his doorstep. It had all been very confusing, but what they said was that his email sent to the server of the youth group had been intercepted because of some phrases he had used. They had arrested a few young men and wanted Adil to identify them. Adil's family had been terrified for him. His little sister had cried and cried, thinking her brother was going to jail. His father had called up a policeman who ate regularly at his restaurant and he took Adil to meet the man. They had talked for hours. There had been so many questions.

In the end, Adil still had to identify those men by their photographs. He did that and then his father said he should take the year off from school and go live in Pakistan with his family in Karachi.

"Not Lahore?" Ray Waters Jr. said.

"No," the boy said. "Only my mother is from Lahore. My father's parents live in Karachi."

His mother had said that would be like going from the frying pan into the fire. Pakistan was not a good place for an angry Muslim boy. His parents had fought. His sister had cried all those days, even more than she had cried once to get a dog. Adil was not allowed to call any friends, not even the ones from school. He prayed he wouldn't be sent to Pakistan.

"What is your sister's name?"

The boy had hesitated. His aunt nodded at him, so he said, "Naomi."

"Spell that, please," Ray Waters Jr. said to the boy, looking at Sarah Kupersmith's notebook.

"N-a-e-e-m-a," the boy said, slowly. Had he deliberately mispronounced it the first time, or was it my ear that had heard it wrong, heard it in ways familiar to me?

The French police had told him not to open his email and to disable all his social media accounts. They had taken his laptop into their custody for any other clues to militant radical Islamist groups. "Then, my parents they come to me and tell me I have an auntie in United States," Adil said. He looked over at Ruhaba and hesitated. "They never tell me and Naeema about you. They say they disapprove of your Western ways."

She looked blankly at him and then smiled a brief smile.

"I am sorry, Khala Ruhaba," the boy said. "I am telling all of the things I told to the French policemen before they give the visa."

"It is okay," she said, leaning over to squeeze his hand.

"They told me my auntie was my mother's sister and if my mother will beg her for pardon for being harsh and quiet for all so many years, Khala Ruhaba would take me to live with her for one year."

He was given no choice in the matter, he said. He had begged and screamed and sworn to never communicate with bad elements again. But they had pleaded with him. His father said his business was beginning to suffer already as word was getting around about their possible involvement with terrorists.

"My father said, 'We are not like the other Muslims here, early-on Muslims—the Algerians, the Tunisians and Moroccans. The French have old hatred for those people. We Pakistanis were not in the same leaky boat as them,' my father said."

His parents said they would have him come back as soon as they felt it was safe. Until then, he and the family might be in danger. It was all too much. Think of Naeema, they said.

So, the policeman contact had helped expedite Adil's tourist visa to visit his aunt, and here he was.

We all sat in silence for a while. Then, clearing his throat, Ray Waters Jr. stood up.

"Well," he said. "We will be checking some of these details with our French friends. Meanwhile, young man, please stay out of trouble."

"He will," Ruhaba said, brightly. She stood up and, straightening her skirt, ushered us toward the door.

Ray Waters Jr. looked at her ushering hand and rooted his feet down, stood his ground.

"What activities does he plan while he is here?" he asked Ruhaba.

"Normal activities of teenagers," she said quickly. "Video games. Music. I have bought him a bicycle. Netflix. Halloween. Thanksgiving with family friends. Christmas."

"And he will walk my dog twice a day," I said.

The agents—and the boy—spun around to look at me. It was as if they had forgotten that I had been there this whole time, in my chair in the corner, like a child placed in time-out.

"Yes," Ruhaba said. "He will walk Ollie's dog."

"What is the dog's name?" Ray Waters Jr. asked.

"Edgar," said the boy.

Ruhaba and I stared at him.

When the federal agents were gone, Ruhaba turned from the door, threw her arms around the boy, and held him for a long time. He did not struggle.

When she let him go, he spoke again, in a low voice. He told us he felt friendless, a stranger to his aunt and her world, a ghost to his old friends and their world.

He said he had wanted to say this to the federal agents but had held back. Sometimes in his nightmares of that incident with his mother in the park, she would trip and the cake would fall from her hands and his friends would groan but scramble up and eat the clean bits of cake anyway, laughing. Sometimes his mother couldn't see him even when he walked right up to her, waving. Sometimes, Camille would take the cake from his mother's hands and walk away with it, away from him, from their friends. Sometimes, little Naeema would bring the cake but when she came close, it was a dead dog she held in her arms. Sometimes, someone came and shot the policemen in the back of their heads. The last one was his favorite, he said.

Ruhaba shuddered. We were all still standing by the door. I offered to fetch her a blanket and then leave. She shook her head and asked me to please sit back down. She offered me coffee and I said yes, decaf, please. She rose to walk to her kitchen and then stopped.

Turning to the boy, she said, "Didn't you tell your Ammi that you saw what happened with her at the park that day?"

The boy slowly shook his head.

"Dear God, why not?" Ruhaba said.

He replied, "I see that day at the park that she wants to hide that thing from me. The . . . shame. I think she even hid it from Abbu. I did not want to bring that thing in our home."

Ruhaba sighed. She rubbed her eyes with the back of her hands. Dark smudges of eye makeup appeared like smoke trying to snuff out a fire.

She looked at him and shook her head, as if to dislodge some of the language that floated there. "I have been nervous," she said. "And to be honest, a part of me was perhaps resentful and judgmental toward your Ammi, for so many years. Do you understand?"

The boy nodded.

"And you should know that your Ammi only told me the last part of that story. That you had somehow become mixed up with bad elements but were completely innocent. They begged me so much to take a leap of faith. You know what I mean? They asked me to believe. I asked your Ammi how she knew you were innocent. I asked her why you would get involved with those young men from the mosque, and she said she didn't know the answer to both those things. But I understand it all now. My poor Adil."

"Khala Ruhaba, you have to give to me a promise. You can never say it. Only Camille and I know about that thing that happen that day. She with me also never talked about that thing. It makes me want to have a vomit even now when I think of it."

Ruhaba sighed again and nodded her head. "I will promise to leave it alone for now. And I promise never to tell her without asking you first."

Then, she added, "And you have to make me a promise in return."

The boy listened intently. "If those agents ever come back, do not speak to them outside my presence."

She asked him to repeat that three times.

I will not speak to the police outside your presence. I will not speak to the police outside your presence. I will not speak to the police outside your presence.

I couldn't sleep that night. It wasn't from coffee, which Ruhaba had forgotten to make in the end. My thoughts raced and, as I often do to calm myself, I pulled out my knitting. I was working on the collar of a charcoal-gray Irish-collared men's pullover. In my office drawer was another project with which I was halfway through—a recto verso sweater in a deep forest-green. This past year, the knitting at my office had moved at a better clip than the one at home.

I thought of red silks. The click and clack of the knitting needles brought focus to the event I had witnessed at Ruhaba's home. I could make better sense, as I knitted, of why I had lingered, why I had conceded to stay back where a saner citizen would have demurred.

This old fool Harding was stirred by the accident of being part of a story that wasn't his.

I had found myself yearning for their story, no matter what dangers in it had brought the FBI to their doorstep. Stories are the things that you miss when you have strayed away from people. You think at first that you will miss telling someone your stories, but soon your solitude lays bare this truth that it is *their* stories you will miss, their stories with the steeper arcs of desire and ambition—even the tacky ones that young couples tell, of how they met for the first time, or stories of the present minute, of tinier shafts of pleasure and pain, of birthday presents received or of embarrassing office emails on which somebody accidentally hit "reply all."

What stories had I expected from the Muslim woman and boy as I followed them into their home? Stories certainly very different from what the FBI sought. I wasn't seeking to know more about the ways in which their worlds were different from mine. I am not the typical, precious Seattle Liberal. No, I wanted the stories that felt like they could have risen not from their living room but from mine, stories that made us the same somehow, of failure, of misunderstanding, of repressed rage, of withheld beauty pressed in like strands of saffron in a glass bottle, or even the stories of their own tiny darting eels of fear.

Every cell in my being had strained toward the story, and thereafter, it was all I could do not to stumble like an earnest fool, over and over, into the thrall of Scheherazade, who bid me to sit by her on a rug.

CHAPTER FOUR

The One Great Love

To Whom It May Concern:
I was lying in the grass in a clearing in the woods and I saw a bird flying sideways. I laughed and called out: Is that a THING? I don't recall exactly what he said, because he was flying so high there, but it may have been: Sure. If lying in the grass like that is a thing.
—Ruhaba

My eyes are dry and aching and my hand almost numb from writing, writing, writing all this down, but my memory of that night whirls insistent within my head, a carnival in which I am at once on a carousel and also aiming darts to pierce the hearts of red balloons. I imagine I have left my desk a few times in these hours, yes, as morning turned to noon to dusk. I know I have let the dog out once or twice. I see I lit a fire that must have roared and is now extinguished. I see crumbs of a meal of ham and canned butternut squash soup I must not have bothered to warm up. But my mind hums only with these people's story, which demands to be told. For me to succumb to any rest for my body would be a betrayal to storytellers of all time. Indeed, any reprieve now, before all of it is said and done, would feel like no reprieve at all but like an intrusion. A drink of water, perhaps, and then I write again.

I recall I awoke the morning after that night at Ruhaba's, grateful I didn't have to teach that day. I had managed but an hour or so of drugged sleep, and Edgar was whimpering in urgency to be let out. I wished I had asked the boy to begin the dog-walking that very morning, but I'd needed a day to get my things in order, pick up a thing here and there, draw signs of my sodden lifestyle inward, push them under a rug or stuff them into a closet. Pity that I had frittered, over the years, the pride with which I could once throw open the doors even to unannounced visitors. Any clutter back in the day would be overwhelmed by the stunning views from my living room window, of Puget Sound, Pier 91, and the spectacular Olympic Peninsula.

My mind went to the promise of the view from Ruhaba's bedroom window. Indeed, we lived in this city with a hierarchy of views, we provosts, we senior faculty, we recent immigrant faculty. Wraparound, sweeping, waterfront, immediate, unobstructed, partial, distant, none.

Not upscale, not enclaved, but the Harding house still was a trophy that had come my way from happening upon Seattle in the early 1990s, the rightest of times to build a life in this town. Emily had fallen instantly in love with this 1909 craftsman on the western bluff of Queen Anne Hill. By the time she'd left me, she'd wanted to have nothing to do with it. So, I was one of those rare men who didn't lose his home in the divorce.

I dealt with the dog and with my headache. I put away my knitting in the back of my closet and looked at my cellphone. I had two text messages and a phone call. The first text message was from Meyer. "Call me when you . . ." My eyes skipped to the next one because, although I didn't recognize the number, the first word almost made me drop my phone: "Dad, can we get lunch?"

Dad. I hadn't had a message with that word in it for years. I looked with fumbling fingers to see if the voice message, too, was from Kathryn. But it was from another number I didn't recognize. It still could have been from Kathryn, perhaps from a different phone of hers or from the phone of her fiancé.

It was from Ruhaba. She sounded bright, rested. She wanted to meet for coffee. "Please forgive me for being such a terrible host last night. I forgot about your coffee! Please let me buy you a cup. Any time you're free."

I rushed to my desktop computer and pulled up Facebook. Kathryn had never accepted my friend request, but she often posted updates that were set to "public." That's how I had learned of her recent engagement. Emily should have called to tell me that news. A father should not have to learn of his daughter's betrothal by stumbling upon a post shouting "I SAID 'YES!'" and a fuzzy picture of her with a young man on bended knee silhouetted against a sunset. Kathryn was only twenty-three! She was too young to marry. And, despite some of my discreet inquiries, no one had filled me in on the young man who had persuaded her otherwise. How had Emily let this happen?

Maybe Kathryn had come to her senses and broken off the

engagement. Perhaps she was reaching out to her father for solace or sound advice. I texted her instantly: "Little One, yes, we can get lunch. Come over at noon?"

I waited. I peered at her pictures online and waited some more. I started to clean the house. What a tremendous project that would be. Perhaps if I cleaned only the living room and kitchen? I considered rushing to the store to pick up a pack of macaroni so I could cook her favorite mac-and-cheese. I put a couple of beers to chill. She probably drank beer? I put a bottle of white wine to chill as well. I'd have to go out and get the tiramisu cheesecake from Trader Joe's. She loved that, I remembered. No, that would take a long time to thaw and would not be ready on time even for a late lunch. And if I left for the store now, I might miss her call. There were patches on Queen Anne Hill that were poor zones for Sprint . . .

My phone sounded a text alert. It was Kathryn. "I was thinking more like next weekend, but if you're free now, can you come meet me at Portage Bay Cafe? I'm having a fitting near there so I could be up for a quick bite after."

A fitting. So, she hadn't called off the wedding. And what was "*now*"? And what did these millennials mean by "*I could be up for—*"? How many avenues for bailing could they possibly set up in half a sentence? I sat there staring at my phone. Should I wait until next weekend? It would be nice to have her here in my home. The last time she had been here, she was fourteen. Edgar was a puppy then.

My text alert buzzed again: "?"

That last message was not a good sign. It was the sign of a question mark, yes, which one may say is inherently always a bad sign, but what I mean is that it wasn't a good sign for any promise of sustained interest or possibility of a long-term plan actually coming to pass. A lot can happen between a question mark and next Saturday. I foresaw canceled dates and a total exit from blinking dots in text boxes to a blanket of white.

"I'll be there in a half hour," I texted back.

As I dressed, I scanned the breadth of sweaters in my closet. I owed each of these to little Kathryn. I should tell her that at lunch, should tell her the story of her father's knitting. Would she remember? Was she still friends with little Olivia? When Kathryn was twelve, she wanted so badly to be friends with Olivia. Find out what Olivia likes and see if you can like it too, I told her. Olivia was learning to knit. She wanted to start a knitting club with other girls from their grade. I rushed Kathryn out to buy needles and yarn. She was terrible at knitting, had no patience for it, and had poor small-motor skills. I bought another set of needles and I learned to knit. Emily had been too busy at work in those days, and we were growing apart. I sensed an impending divorce. I needed to build something with little Kathryn, a ritual to which we could return. As I got better at knitting, Kathryn got better, too. She came home one day to say Olivia had invited her over for a knitting playdate.

When Emily left and took Kathryn with her, I planned knitting playdates with my girl. When she would come over to visit, we'd bring out our knitting. We would knit headbands and scarves. I asked Kathryn to invite Olivia over for knitting playdates. The next time Kathryn came over, she said Olivia's parents had said No. All the adults around Kathryn said they didn't want their girls going to playdates in a home where no mom was present. By the time Kathryn and I graduated to knitting mittens, her own visits had dwindled. More and more, she would return only to repeat stories she had heard about me from Emily. Bad stories, untrue stories. And then one day, mid-mitten, Kathryn said she wanted to spend all weekends at her mom's, because her friends would be able to do sleepovers there.

I kept up the knitting. Naturally, I had to hide it from the prying eyes of excitable idiots who would consider me "a sweet man." The word "hipster" was just around the corner back then, but I had already aged out of that one.

I started to restrict myself to knitting men's sweaters. For the past eight years, I have knit two sweaters a year. For myself. I began to get compliments for my sweaters. Once, the ridiculous Betsy MacDowell even tugged at the back of my sweater's collar to look for a label so she could get one for her husband for Christmas. So, I ordered custom-made labels from Amazon and sewed them onto the neck of every sweater I knit:

The Frances Gilbert Sweater Company
London, United Kingdom

Too exclusive, too elusive, I told people. Available only through orders I placed through old friends in London. Thanks to the multiculturalists teeming amongst us and the fall of the literary canon, few would recognize the combination of the first names of G. K. Chesterton and his legendary sweet wife.

Few would imagine, either, that I—perhaps the only faculty member on my campus and one of the too-few residents of this town who champion the Second Amendment, shoot guns at the range, and own a fine selection of pistols—would also turn loving attention to needle and wool. Execrable, the way we pigeonhole our fellow humans.

Would we, as the human race, embrace imagination over reason (or, increasingly, indignation), we would see the joys of paradox. Indeed, a preoccupation with paradox is what led me to G. K. Chesterton, which in turn yielded my most profound learnings, my richest teaching, the most eloquent of my lectures, and the best of what I have had to offer to the world as a thinker and human being.

Chesterton, described as "the prince of paradox," believed man to be the highest of creatures and the greatest of sinners. He advised every one of us to think of ourselves with sober judgment, and yet, his best writing was steeped in humor. In fact, one of my favorite lectures, which students of our Honors Program invited me to deliver as a "Last Lecture" (the lecture one would give if one were on one's deathbed), was titled "Love, Sex, Humor, and the Other Places Chesterton Would Somberly Go." Of course, the "sex" part was a bit of a stretch, especially if students bothered to look up a picture of the unforgivably heavy-set saint (and yes, I would join in any call to confer upon Chesterton a sainthood, although I do not personally care much for religion—how is that for a paradox?).

Chesterton described sex as an instinct that led to an institution. His measure of the success and the very purpose of sex lay on whether it produced a family, and I have always found this somewhat touching. "The moment sex ceases to be a servant, it becomes a tyrant," he said. My students have had a lot to say about that over the years, and oh, haven't I suffered the tyranny of sex when she turned me into her servant? I have often wondered about how Chesterton tamed this servant in his marriage to Frances.

But then, she was a woman of another time. An educated woman herself, Frances wrote poetry and songs but dedicated herself to her husband's career as his amanuensis, typing up all that her prolific genius of a husband dictated to her, managing his expansive writing life, perhaps, one hopes, even sparring with him, nudging his notions of paradox. In fact, it is well known that it was sweet Frances who brought Chesterton to the cross.

Chesterton examined the better parts of Christianity. He spoke of charity as a paradox, as meaning that we pardon unpardonable acts and love unlovable people. He urged us to live within the tension, the topsy-turviness of things. Indeed, he described paradox to be "truth standing on her head to get attention." One literary critic, Hugh Kenner, has said that Chesterton "makes truth cut her throat to attract attention."

Perhaps that is what I am doing here as I write, cutting open truth's throat, laying bare all paradox in the bloody mess of things.

As I drove to my lunch with Kathryn, I imagined she would be delighted with the story of my knitting. And, if she were to have a wedding and I were soon to have a son-in-law, perhaps I could draw them into my secret and knit a sweater for the young man. Thinking of the wedding made me think of what matter had urged Kathryn to break her silence with me and call. The phone started to ring right then.

It was Ruhaba. I imagined her still lying in bed, wrapped in silks. I decided to take the call.

"I'm calling to ask again about coffee!" she sang into the phone.

"Yes, yes, I'd love that," I said. My cheer sounded genuine. It startled me a little.

"This afternoon?" she said.

"I . . . I'm having lunch with my daughter and it might go on for a while. How about tomorrow morning?"

"Oh, how lovely. Lunch with your daughter. Is this a regular thing?"

"I wish it were," I said. I felt reckless, open, giving. "I haven't seen Kathryn in some years. But now she's engaged to be married. Too young, of course," I said quickly. "She's a baby."

Ruhaba laughed. "Perhaps Kathryn wants her father at her wedding, then. To walk her down the aisle? Such a wonderful thing for you."

"Perhaps," I said. I wondered if that's what Kathryn wanted. Yes, that would be a wonderful thing. A vision leapt to my mind then, of an unfinished mitten from years ago, shoved to the back of my desk drawer in my university office. I didn't dare hope for too many good tidings. How did that Steve Taylor Christian rock song from my youth go?

Life unwinds like a cheap sweater,
but since I gave up hope, I feel a lot better.

But I had Ruhaba on the other end of the phone line with me, and I remembered the terrible tidings that had landed on her doorstep the night before. “Is everything okay with you and your nephew today? Any more visitations?”

“All is well,” she said. “At least, all is quiet. No more visitations.”

“Speaking of which,” she continued. “Adil is still quite willing to come walk your dog starting tomorrow. Nothing changed overnight. Would you still like that?”

“Oh yes,” I said. Giving—yes, that’s what I was. “Yes, that would be terrific. I’ll text you my address.”

We said goodbye and hung up. I thought of her smiling, which took me to the view of her thighs from last night. I shook my head to dislodge the image from my mind. I was going to lunch with my daughter.

I’d found a lovely spot for us at the restaurant, close to the fresh fruit bar. I got worried when Kathryn was fifteen minutes late, and I texted her. She replied, “I’ve been here a while now. Where are you?”

I was at the wrong branch of Portage Bay Cafe.

I drove from Roosevelt Avenue to South Lake Union in fewer than ten minutes. When I arrived, Kathryn was texting someone on her phone. I stopped to take a look at her from a distance. She was beautiful, radiant, and too grown-up. She was a woman.

She stayed seated and held out a hand to squeeze mine. When I leaned over, she offered me her cheek and then quickly gestured to me to sit down. She had already ordered her brunch, a salad, that she was already halfway through.

“Not sure you know this, Dad, but I’m getting married,” she said.

I said I knew, through some mutual friends. She frowned and seemed to decide to let it go.

"Congratulations, Little One," I said. "When can I meet him? Who is he?"

"Oh, Phillip? He's a Ph.D. candidate at UW. Robotics."

"Ah," I said. I concealed my surprise as best as I could. I had expected Kathryn to be drawn to people from Emily's world—artists—but my girl had been drawn to people from mine—academics. Even from within academia, she had chosen responsibly. The humanities were all very well and enriching as a discipline of study until it came to your little girl and the starting salary of her suitor.

The waiter came by. I ordered coffee and pancakes. Kathryn glanced at her watch. I asked her if I could buy her a decent meal instead of just the salad. She shook her head. The waiter left.

"It's two weeks to the wedding," she said. "I'm sticking to salads."

"Two weeks?" I said, hoping my face hadn't darkened.

"Yes. Didn't our mutual friends tell you?" she said. She poked her fork into a piece of grapefruit in her salad. Even now, she had the same tell—looking away and poking at the food on her plate.

"Aren't you hurrying this a little?" I said. "As it is, you're too young to be getting married. You just graduated college last year." There. I'd said it. Someone had to say it. The world was too full of people who were not saying things that needed saying the way they needed to be said.

Kathryn drew a breath. "I considered that with good care," she said. I saw the twelve-year-old serious child who once had examined my manuscripts for spelling errors. "Phillip and I have attended premarital counseling. We went on a retreat with the Gottman Institute, which predicts whether or not your marriage will last."

I contracted a hundred muscles around my eyes to keep them from rolling. "And?" I asked, with gentle interest.

"And ours will," she said, raising her chin and poking her fork into the air in front of me, as if pinning me against a wall in a duel. "We have what is called an intimate friendship."

My eyes broke away from the contract. They rolled.

She drew back into her chair. "Go ahead, hold my age against me. But children of divorce mature quickly. And twenty-three is not that young, so stop infantilizing me. Besides, the one great love of our lives arrives when it does. There's no timing it, is there?"

I thought carefully about what to say next. I wanted more conversations with my girl, even if they were to be as troubling as this one. In fact, I might come to find such sparring with my daughter to be invigorating. Perhaps, if we met several times in the next two weeks, I'd even have enough time to talk her out of the marriage or talk myself into her new world.

"The one great love," I said. "Surely you don't believe in that stuff?" I was aiming for "light-hearted."

"I do," she said. "Perhaps you, even, could stumble upon it still."

I was taken aback. A tragic thing, when your child is so grown as to realize that her parents' love wasn't the one great one. And, I wondered, was she mocking me or being tender, with what she'd just said? I had a desperate urge to tell her about Ruhaba, tell her something random, even reckless. I didn't.

"But," she added, "the way to love anything is to realize that it might be lost."

Her eyes twinkled for just a moment. I smiled. She was quoting Chesterton. I would find myself in my daughter's life yet.

Then, the moment was gone.

"I can't stay for your pancakes to arrive, Dad. I just wanted to talk to you in person to let you know, to be up front. I thought it was the decent thing to do."

"Let me know what?"

"Let you know that although I'd have liked my dad to come to the wedding, I'm just sorry I can't invite you. I want my special day to be worry-free. I'll have you meet Phillip later, if you still . . ."

"Worry-free? You're eating a salad with no dressing. Looks pretty worried to me."

In the old days, this could have gone down as a joke. But we live in humorless times.

My child fixed me with a cold stare.

"You have nothing to worry about with me, Little One," I said.

My eyes flickered. Hers were steadfast in their glare. I felt a cold lurch in my stomach. How much had Emily told our girl? She had promised never to speak of the one time I went too far, the one time I sort of lost control, sort of crossed a boundary. The one time I was rough with Emily in our lovemaking. She had promised to never speak of it, to protect me, of course, but I wagered also to protect her own esteem, given that women judge other women for staying too long in a marriage in which they have felt violated. I'd promised her it would never happen again and it hadn't. Surely, Emily hadn't decided, after all these years, to pollute our child's innocence with . . .

"Really? You ruined my birthday parties by flirting with other moms or students you'd invite. You picked loud fights with my mother."

I waited for more. Nothing came. I was awash in relief. My stomach righted itself.

"Are *these* the memories you are left with? Or are these the ones kept alive from the telling and retelling by Emily? Think about all our good times!"

"Too few, Dad," she said.

"Remember the knitting?"

She frowned at me, impatient, her face blank, distracted, bereft of memory.

"I'm your father, Kathryn. Don't you want me to walk you down the aisle?" I wondered whether I sounded plaintive. Or maybe I sounded like I was alerting her to something that hadn't occurred to her yet.

It had. "I don't need you to do that. I've asked Gerome."

"Gerome!" I said with a laugh. "Your mother's lover!"

"Also known as my mother's husband. Also known as my stepfather of eight years."

The waiter arrived with the plate of pancakes. He set it down with a flourish and started to name the three syrups and sauces that accompanied the pancakes. I swatted him away at rhubarb-strawberry. Kathryn was fishing inside her purse for money.

"Gerome," I said. "So here we abandon feminism. Didn't you major in Women and Gender Studies? And you still must have a man *give you away*?"

Kathryn set down a twenty-dollar bill, half-tucked under

her half-eaten salad. "Yes, Dad. I'm a miserable excuse for a feminist. So, shoot me." She stood up and walked away.

I had to stanch the swell of rage in me then (or was it merely anguish?), so I willed myself to picture her as a little girl toddling away. My little girl. Not a woman asking to be shot but her daddy's golden, wayward, lost princess.

"Fare thee well, Child of Divorce," I called after her. "And remember, a great man once said—marriage is a duel to the death." I left out the rest of Chesterton's quote: ". . . which no man of honor should decline." I was in no mood for paradoxes.

I texted Ruhaba my address as I'd said. Then my finger hovered over her number. I wanted to call, ask her out to a drink instead of coffee, take her back to my place and do things to her for which the FBI wouldn't have the words to put in their notebook.

I didn't call. Years of therapy had taught me not to take the cruelty of one woman—and yes, Kathryn was now a woman—to an encounter with another. No good ever came from it.

I called Meyer. He was always up for a drink. But his in-laws were in town, he said, and they were hosting a dinner, so he couldn't get out. I was about to hang up, when he asked, "Did you get my text?"

I remembered his text message from that morning. I hadn't finished reading it. I scrolled to it. It said: "Call me when you get this. Something to tell you about the woman you left the party with last night."

His choice of words gave me a thrill. *The woman you left the party with last night*. In his imagination, at least, there were still women and nights and *leavings with* in my life.

"I thought that's why you were calling me," Meyer was saying. "I have to go run some errands now, but just so you know . . . not much I can tell you about this . . . but that woman, Khan, is under investigation."

"Under investigation?" I wondered how Meyer knew more than I did about Ruhaba and the boy and the FBI.

"That's right. Best keep a distance, Ollie."

"You'll have to tell me more. This dinner for your in-laws . . . I'm coming, too."

"No!" Meyer almost shouted into the phone. "Sorry, that was rude of me. But you know Pat. She doesn't like surprises."

"Who's investigating Ruhaba?" I said.

"Ah. I see you are on a first-name basis. I hope it hasn't gone any further. As I said, I don't know very much. I hear there's a small committee. It's all pretty hush-hush. But it was . . ."

"A committee? At the university? This isn't the FBI?"

"The FBI? Jesus, Ollie. What kind of racist track . . . wait . . . is the FBI involved? With the university committee?"

I grunted in exasperation. "No. I just made a big ol' leap there about the FBI. Just find out more, would you? Then call me."

"Why? You aren't . . . are you trying to get in . . . are you up to your old tricks here, Ollie?"

I hung up.

Knitting didn't help me that night. I poured myself a whiskey and then another. I sat staring out at the night, my glorious view shrouded in the leaden, starless sky, and I wondered whether I had been played. Had Ruhaba singled me out from the start as a lonely man, not young enough to pose a serious threat to her as an obvious suitor but also not old enough to be devoid of lust? Could she and the boy have been plotting something that I didn't know then?

That is when I should have walked away.

It is now midnight and I am sleepless, the same as I was on that other night, but I know so much more than I did then. Each of the questions I had that night has been answered. Be careful the questions over which you agonize for answers.

I will attempt to sleep soon. I had to halt my writing and attend to two rounds of visitors earlier this evening. The first wasn't so much a visitor as just a knock on the door, around 7 p.m. It sent Edgar into a frenzy. Upon opening my door, I found a basket outside, filled with food. A neat little card was tucked on the basket's corner. It said, "Glad you are safe! XO, Janet." I looked around, and there, down the street, was Janet, my neighbor from six houses away, peering at me, ready with a wave.

The card would have been enough. It would have left an air of sophisticated compassion. The lingering to wave seemed a bit excessive. But that is precisely why we hadn't kept up our "Friends with Benefits" relationship, wasn't it? It had been so convenient for both of us, our lovemaking on some afternoons when her husband was at work and I was home grading papers. We kept it up for four years, give or take, until around six months ago. She wanted more of a friendship than I had in me to provide. No, let me not conceal that it was more than that. Now, how do I put this? It felt, to me, like a bigger breach of faith to her husband that Janet wanted an emotional intimacy with me. Physical intimacies in a marriage wax and wane, fizzle out and smolder, wander and often return. But, if you'd rather talk to your neighbor, six houses down, about why you love pets more than people, or your plans to "go fiercely gray" at menopause, or your fears of breast cancer because of a family history, you need to look your husband square in the face and deliver the cold, hard truth about your marriage. I just couldn't sneak that banal beauty of a shared life from under another man's hearth. Emily and Gerome had done that to me, and I could not pass that kind of thing on.

I waved back at Janet and shut my door. In the basket was a menu card, written in Janet's careful hand: Cottage Pie. Olive-oil Roasted Delicata Squash. Endive Salad with a Hazelnut Vinaigrette. Raspberry Lemon Pound Cake. I fell upon the meal with a hunger so fierce, it surprised me. I missed Janet's kindness, her smile, and I hoped we could one day reconnect in some other way.

My thoughts—and indeed my meal—were interrupted by another knock on the door. It was Ray Waters Jr. and Sarah Kupersmith. They have been to my home twice before in the past two days since the incident. Unlike that first night when we met in Ruhaba's home, they now hang on to every word I say. Tonight, I offered to pour them a whiskey. They politely refused.

Ray Waters Jr. asks me things, and in his tone and his words I detect that he imagines me a fool, a sitting duck for a conspiracy between aunt and nephew to enchant me with their alluring foreignness and their false vulnerability. I ask him how he has the time for all this when his boss Comey has blown the whistle on Hillary's emails, and shouldn't every agent of the FBI be investigating that matter instead? He snorts, so I fall silent. I could nod dully as he asks me his barbed questions and then goes back to plowing through the detritus of the event in my office on November 1st, sifting through computer records and text messages and on-site interviews, leaving no stone or sentiment unturned. I could ask him to inquire into how much Ruhaba already knew about me and my almost solitary life. Did she know how estranged I was from my ex-wife and daughter, my hours and words like barnacles too rough for most, but tender enough to either be fed or be sloughed off with the right application of attention, leaving me exposed, porous?

But instead, I ask after the condition of the boy. They fear he could fall into a coma. Some medical staff disagree. They say he is a fighter.

A fighter, I say out loud. Ah yes, remember his aunt said he was no coward. Something fuels him from within to fight, doesn't it, I say under my breath, but I think Ray Waters Jr. hears it, because he nods, and he says they will be right there waiting if the boy fights his way to recovery. We must ask so many questions even though we may know the answers, he says.

They have just left after their questions, or rather, Ray Waters Jr.'s questions and Kupersmith's notes and recordings. They wished me a night of good rest. I must be shaken, they said. It might hit me later, they responded when I shook my head. Get some rest.

Perhaps I must attempt to shut my eyes, shut down my brain down, tend to the frailties of my physical self. When I return to the page, I will once again fold deep inward. I will restrict my narrative to the way I recall it unfolding in the moment, for, although, as I suggested earlier, an account may be enriched by the recounting, it may also be atrophied in truth or fattened in untruths by unseemly dwelling.

When I write again in the morning, we will encounter here the footfall of a flutist.

CHAPTER FIVE

The Flutist

Today is Friday, November 4th. I have indeed slept a dreamless sleep of exhaustion for six hours. It is just as well that the university has given me time off to recover from the horrors that befell our campus. The department chair has taken over my class, although how she thinks she might be able to teach my signature course—Paradoxes of Ideals in 19th-Century Literature—I have no idea, even with access to my syllabus and lesson plans. I imagine students dropping the class in the coming days. She will be mortified, and I truly feel for her.

But this is no time to dwell on such quotidian things. I must return to my account of the boy. He arrived at my doorstep at 8:30 a.m. the day after I met with Kathryn, the day after Meyer told me to steer clear of Ruhaba. I had to scramble to find the leash to hand to the boy. This irritated me, but one could hardly hold such punctuality against him, at least not until the university committee and the FBI had more for me. I decided to be cordial.

"Young man, meet Edgar," I said, ushering the boy in at the front door. He looked bright, friendlier than the other night. One could hardly imagine him a fugitive from a terror cell in Toulouse.

Edgar was wagging his tail and sniffing at the boy's shoes. He let Edgar smell his fingers and then crouched down to scratch him behind the ear.

"Named after Degas?" the boy said.

My eyebrows shot up. "No, but guess again," I said.

"Ah. After Poe."

"Yes," I said, squinting at the child. I couldn't have expected my students, those who had walked my dog before, to have heard of Degas—and the boy had an advantage, having been raised in France—but none of them had even made the connection with Poe. Or, if they had, they hadn't cared to state it, perhaps for fear of sparking a literary conversation.

"How do you know of Poe?" I had to ask.

"My mother. She loves poetry from all over the world. Urdu poetry, French poetry, English . . . we have so many books in our house."

The boy was watching my face, and I quickly wiped from it my expression of incredulity.

"Do you have a dog back home?" I said. "I mean in France, not . . ." I stopped just in time. I had been about to say Pakistan, for what reason, I do not know. That probably would have been what the French call a faux pas.

But the boy had caught on. "You mean *not Pakistan*," he said, still not looking up from the dog, who was now sitting there, enjoying his belly rub.

Without waiting for me to respond, he said, "No. My parents—they say they are too busy to get us the dog. Me and my sister—we always want one. She even cried once. Four days. No stopping. But they will not agree. Just no. I think they grew up with a fright of dogs, in their childhood. In Pakistan. Dogs are impure. So we just play with the dogs of our friends in Toulouse."

He stood up and reached for the leash I was holding. "What is the best way?" he asked.

"The best way for what?"

"The best, how do you say, route? For walking the dog. Where does he like to go?"

The boy had taken care to pronounce the word "route" the American way, but still with a hard *h* sound in place of the *r*. I fought off a smile.

"Oh, I usually just take him six blocks to the west—to the park. You can go where you want, I think he'll like just about anything." I was about to add something about how little exercise the dog got with the lazy regular dog-walker Juanita in the mornings and me alone in the evenings, but I decided against it. It wouldn't help my cause any to speak of myself as a creaking old man to Ruhaba's nephew.

He nodded, smiled, and took the leash from my hand.

I watched him go down the four steps at the front of my house, one at a time, proceeding with his good leg first and letting his bad leg catch up.

"Oh, and don't worry, he doesn't pull at the leash. He'll walk at your pace," I called out after the boy, but he didn't acknowledge anything, just took some swift steps down the front lawn. I would have to be careful not to embarrass him like that. I stood there ready with a wave, but the boy didn't turn around, his back stiff, as if aware of being watched. He seemed to want to keep his gait as erect as possible. I felt a twinge of something, an awkwardness for myself, for not knowing the best thing to do—I believed I ought to act just like I would with anyone else, but I couldn't summon up what that would be—watching and waving, or just going back inside and averting my gaze. It wasn't as if the boy's limp was that bad. The poor child shouldn't have had to think about it at all.

I found myself distracted over the next hour, found myself waiting for the boy's return. I went to my desktop computer to log on to Facebook, to Kathryn's profile page. I couldn't bear to look anymore, but I did.

Yesterday, she had "checked in" from Portage Bay Cafe.

Ah. As she waited for her father to arrive so she could tell him he wasn't invited to her wedding, let alone requested to take his rightful place by her side to walk her down the aisle, my daughter had idly posted a picture of her little salad. I toyed with the idea of disabling my account, withdrawing from all social media, leaving the world to its devices.

I quickly switched to my own page, with its profile picture of the Olympic Peninsula. I wasn't terribly active on these media, except to post pictures from my hikes and an occasional political commentary from *The Economist*. Lately, I'd been finding some interesting commentary on Reddit, some subreddit groups that enjoyed healthy debate from all angles. On Facebook, though, I found myself drawn in by posts from people I knew, in support of Donald Trump's presidency, and I'd egg the fools on with a "like" that I'd later go back and remove, to fuck with their heads.

Now, my own head felt fucked with.

I looked at the front door, wondered now about the boy. But it did little to ease me back into an even breath. I wanted to reach for my knitting, but it would only remind me of Kathryn again. I forced myself to return to thoughts about the boy. I'd spent more than twenty-five years of my life around students, kids just a little bit older than he was, yet I'd rarely felt so tongue tied as I did around him. I'd have to overcome this sort of thing, and quickly. The boy had an unsettling quality to him, a watchfulness even when he wasn't looking, or perhaps especially when he wasn't looking. One got the feeling, too, that he was listening for more than you were telling him. And saying too little, far too little. Did his fiercely protective aunt know enough about him?

I had to shake off such thoughts. She was safe and I was safe. America was taking care of this problem in a mostly moderate way. Candidate Trump had proposed an all-out ban on Muslims entering the country. Over-the-top, of course. Totally unnecessary. Reactionary. And just the kind of thing that would keep him a good many votes shy of being elected. But one had to have a grudging admiration for the man for putting a thing or two on the national agenda. Hillary was already a hawk, sure, but perhaps the good men at the Pentagon would have their Madam President do a deeper examination of these matters.

I must confess to being somewhat nettled that I should feel this sense of . . . what was it . . . displacement, in my own homeland. The world was interconnected, yes, and wasn't that a beautiful thing, but to pretend that the movement of people across borders did not occasion scrutiny, or that citizens' minds did not need the time to adjust to this borderless age that had come suddenly upon us, such political self-righteousness served neither the rooted nor the wanderer, did it? Was I being an idiot, leaping recklessly about in my lust? How perilous was this journey to Ruhaba's bed? Wouldn't the FBI have tipped me off after that night, nudged me, as an upstanding citizen, to not get mixed up in all this? Or, were they now going to watch my every move, imagine me as an ally? Or, worse, had they forgotten that I was even sitting there, this citizen, on his own soil?

Really, what was I doing inviting the boy in and letting him walk my dog, *paying* him to do it? The last thing I needed, especially if I wanted to one day have Kathryn call me again, was to fumble around in a pall of terror activities. Was I that hard up for sex? It had been a few months since Janet, and there had been nothing since. What had Meyer called it—old tricks? I had worked hard at the pursuit before, taken some profound pleasure in it, but this thing with Ruhaba was a bit of a woebegone grope.

I wondered if the boy picked up on it, this suspicion that had started to bear down on me, about him. That night with the FBI, had he wondered also about me? Had Ruhaba? Perhaps they were accustomed to it, to suspicion. Was that why Ruhaba was calling me out for coffee, to see how far my suspicion had educated me?

Perhaps the boy was especially accustomed to suspicion in France. I wondered about his life there. It was, after all, a wrinkle in my picture of the world Ruhaba came from. Even though she hadn't lived in France herself, her ties there made her . . . either closer within my reach or perhaps farther away from it.

I entered the boy's name into the Facebook search window—Adil Alam, the FBI had called him. I found a page that belonged to an Indonesian girl by the same name and another that belonged to a fat man in Cairo, and then another that was a closed group, not owned by anyone. I tried again. This time, I found a profile page with the boy's face, smiling, with a couple of white-looking French boys in the frame with him, all three of them making some sort of ironic expression. I clicked on the page. It led to a message saying the profile was disabled. I tried it again and got the same result.

I sat up straighter in my chair. The boy had mentioned the other night that he was forbidden to be on social media. But I wanted to follow every trace. I picked up my iPhone and looked for signs of him in the oceans of human data on Twitter, Instagram, Reddit, and Tumblr. Nothing.

A Google search led me down a dungeon of foreignness from which I wanted to quickly retrieve myself. The world was bigger and farther beyond my ken the more the years went by. It used to be different—the older you got, the more you traveled, the closer and smaller the world seemed. I loved the world that arrived in this country and legally stayed, enriching us all. I would fight for their right to be my neighbor. But the internet has a way of showing you the worst of difference.

Just as I was about to close my Google search, I saw a line that caught my eye. It was the middle of a sentence and it said, "mon ami, le doux Adil Alam, qui ferait pas mal a une mouche . . ." I clicked on the link. It was the blog of a girl named Camille Harroch, on Tumblr.

I squinted my eyes past details that jumped out at me. Camille, I learned, lived in Toulouse, France. I made it past several soft-focus pictures—girls eating ice cream, bicycles with baskets, sketches of Japanese-style comics, museum paintings, music album recommendations, pictures of girls in shorts that wrinkled up almost to the crotch . . . things that might have delighted Humbert Humbert but simply cluttered up my electronic path, until I found the blog post from which that truncated sentence had been drawn into my Google search. It was all in French.

I stood up and walked to the one window in the room, my home office, to look down the street. It had been forty minutes and the boy was still out with the dog. How long did he think . . . oh, he probably thought he'd have to walk the dog for an hour in order to earn an hour's minimum wage, given the way I had worded my offer that other night. I walked to my front door and locked it from the inside. Then, returning to my desk, I read the post, which was a few weeks old, dated September 26, 2016. My French reading wasn't as good as it used to be, but it's remarkable how that language rushes back.

Our hearts should be broken. My friend, the gentle Adil Alam, who would not hurt a fly, is being questioned by police. He was pulled out of his mosque along with some older boys whom I don't know and whom I don't think Adil has known for very long. Anyway, he was pulled out and held by the police overnight. The other boys, who are old enough to be men, have been kept in custody but Adil has been let out with a warning, maybe because some police guys knew his dad from the restaurant. We think they are still watching his home and his family. They were at our school, questioning us. We all said good things about Adil because fuck, there are only good things to say. They asked me if his mother wore a headscarf and I said I didn't know. Maybe she used to wear it. I don't know if I should be writing this. Why do we have to be so scared? Can't we all just love? I trust Adil and I always will.

I slumped in my chair. So, the boy's story held up, I thought. I clicked on other blog posts by the girl and found little else but journals from a trip to Paris, musings on the nature of love, excerpts of poetry from her favorite writers, and lyrics from songs. I remember thinking so many things, but also one practical thing about copyright violations.

I clicked on the photographs. I was looking for information, anything at all, that would tell me more about the boy. I found what I was looking for. A couple of photographs of Adil. One of these was the same photo I had seen on Adil's deactivated Facebook profile. Another was of him blowing out candles on a birthday cake. The picture had an uneven mood to it. Around him, his friends were either laughing or making more of those ironic faces and gestures, like hip hop artists or gangsters or ducks with fat bills. But Adil himself didn't look very happy in the photograph, was in fact looking away from the camera and deep into the cake, as if he either wanted to never have to look up from it or expected it to blow up.

The cake wasn't chocolate. It was white. Why had the boy told the FBI it was chocolate? Why had he lied about the cake?

I rubbed my eyes. I was being ludicrous. The boy had been distraught, after all. Allow him the forgetfulness of Chantilly over chocolate.

But, then, why had the French gendarmerie let him off so easily? How had they been so sure he hadn't been more deeply involved with those young men at the mosque? What were their ways of determining that these boys hadn't been plotting to kill tourists at the Louvre?

A thick emotion lumbered up on me, something I had no name for, something I couldn't attribute to an exact party. It wasn't an anger for Kathryn now, was it? The anxiety we feel from scrolling rapidly through lives online, stumbling from one human's account to the other, hardly allows us to have singular emotions, but rather, sends us stumbling through portals of disenchantment and desire for things we do not want to believe we seek.

My anger—if it was anger—was probably intended for the boy, or Ruhaba, or Emily and Kathryn, too, for leaving me so bereft, so open to the flotsam that drifted in from other worlds. I clenched my jaw and chided myself for my hateful thoughts. I was determined to find something affirming about the boy, or at least his kind. I entered more searches into Google, now with general terms, seeking news. What I found could have swallowed me whole for days. I let my browser and my eyes settle on this or that at random.

> According to a confidential French intelligence document leaked to Le Figaro, a form of Muslim ghettoization is gaining ground within the French school system. The report says that the Muslim students are effectively establishing an Islamic parallel society completely cut off from non-Muslim students . . .

On January 6, 2014, two 15-year-old boys from Toulouse ran away from home to become the youngest ever European jihadists to join the fighting in Syria. Toulouse is also the hometown of Mohammed Merah, the Islamist who murdered seven people in and around the city in March 2012 . . .

On February 25, 2014, a 14-year-old girl from the southeastern French city of Grenoble was intercepted at the airport in Lyon. She had a one-way ticket to Istanbul and was about to board the plane. Police were alerted when the girl sent her mother a text message saying she was running away from home because she had been selected to "join the jihad" in Syria . . .

Some 60% of the prison population in France is culturally or originally Muslim . . .

More than 1000 French supermarkets, including national chains like Carrefour, have been selling Islamic books that openly call for jihad and the killing of non-Muslims . . .

I cleaned up my browser history, stood up on watery limbs, and wobbled to the kitchen to put on some coffee. Then, even before it had brewed, I reached for my coat, shoved my feet into my slippers, and headed off toward the park, unsure of what I had in mind, but sure that if the boy had any ugliness to unleash upon this soil, I would spot it if I just watched him for a moment from afar.

I walked into a stunning morning. I distinctly recall it, for it seemed to me like the elements were scurrying about, either beating me back or luring me deeper toward something. Of course, I could put it down simply to the fact that I had dashed out in nothing but my slippers and the October wind nipped quickly at the thinning skin of my feet. I could either turn around like an aging coward or rush about and urge blood to pump warmth upward in my veins.

A fog had rolled in through Puget Sound. I walked into its dense quiet, hoping the boy had followed my instructions and headed toward the park. Beneath my feet, the narrow street had turned into a giant slimy eel of red, yellow, pink, and burgundy as the fallen leaves of a bad year turned to mulch. As if I weren't already forced to watch my step, I was also compelled to slow down, by the idiot citizenry of the city, who drove like startled mice with every turn of weather. I could see their headlights as they approached, but I couldn't tell if they could see me, because no one told these folk that the fog lights in their cars were meant for precisely a day such as this. No, it wouldn't be *rude* to turn those lights on.

At Rodgers Park, the fog had already started to burn off in patches. This caused the eerie effect of some things falling into shadow and others rising up in sharp relief. I spotted the boy easily, sitting on a park bench, his bad leg tucked under him. I ducked from his view and stood behind a tree and only then noticed a spectral form looming up beside him on the park bench.

A beast?

Pull yourself together, Harding.

It was a man. Something turned cold in my throat at this. An accomplice? But upon blinking my eyes a bit against the thin curl of moisture on my lashes, I saw that the man sitting huddled by him on the bench was rocking back and forth, bundled up in oversize fleeces and threadbare blankets. A homeless bum. The boy sat facing just a little bit away from him. Smoking a cigar.

No. Wait. That wasn't a cigar. He was holding something up to his lips that wasn't a cigar. A bugle?

I looked for Edgar. Where was Edgar?

The dog was rolling in the grass not too far from the boy's feet. Rolling and rolling. I hadn't seen Edgar do that in years.

More movement. Like zombies, a jogger or a cyclist or a clutch of ladies on their group walk took shape against the fog, bathed now in the light of a weak dawn. I thought at first that I was imagining it, that there was something odd and sluggish about their presence, like they were all trapped in some warp of the blanket of vapor that now held us and could only twitch on occasion a leg or arm or expression of face. I rubbed the wool sleeve of my coat against my eyes and wrapped my gloveless palms around my damp head.

They were halted, these people. They were halted and were staring at the boy. I looked back at him and at the thing he held to his mouth.

I saw now it was a flute. He was blowing upon it but no sound emerged. I looked back at the people, wondering if this peculiar little detail had slowed them down. Why would something so trivial catch their attention?

But it seemed that they could hear some sound. From the way they looked at the boy and, every now and then, at each other, it became clear that they could hear more than some sound. They heard music. They heard music they liked.

They stood noiselessly, unobtrusively. The boy's eyes were closed. His fingers, bare like mine, moved swiftly along the instrument. He seemed to be warmer than me in that cold, held in the embrace of some chord of melody rising from deep within him. I tried to strain against the wall of soundlessness that had me in its grip. I shifted quietly from one tree to another, still hiding. At one spot, I thought for a moment that I did, in fact, hear a note of sound rise, but it slipped into the thin burn of the fog before I could catch it. It was as if an implacable force were pressing against my ears, turning them into flattened graves.

I fought against panic and sought to make sense of it all: my ear canals had clearly numbed and shuttered in the cold. My brain was dimmed from a deprivation of its usual flood of caffeine. The fools who stood swaying before me in the throes of the boy's little concert in the park wore the classic expression of the martyred and the meek. The homeless man on the bench was rocking back and forth from a methamphetamine-addled brain, not a sophisticated appreciation of the sound emerging from a wind instrument. As for Edgar, the rotten bastard, anyone who knew anything about dogs would know that their rolling in the muck was not a display of glee but a primal instinct to camouflage their scent in the presence of a predator.

I retreated from the sight before me. I don't know what I had expected to find on that stupid sojourn, but the confounding little scene, as it had played out, was not to turn me less alert. I walked with purpose back to my home. The air was turning warm and a terrible dread rose up in me, but it was soon quieted by a trusty draught of chill that came curling down the street and sighed upon my chest.

At home, I waited for the boy to return. When I heard the

knock on my door, I took a deep breath and readied myself to politely tell the boy that I had changed my mind, that I thought it would be rude to fire poor Juanita, that his services were no longer needed.

Upon opening the door, though, I had a little more to deal with.

Along with the boy and Edgar was Ruhaba. I was taken aback and stumbled a little as Edgar knocked into my legs and ran through the door toward his bowl of water.

"Goodness, sorry to startle you, Ollie," Ruhaba said. She was beaming.

She spoke again. "Good morning! I thought I'd come by and make sure my young nephew here was doing a good job on his first day at this new opportunity. Also, I was worried, with the fog and all. He left home early and insisted on taking the bus so he could enjoy looking out at the city. I saw him tossing a Frisbee to your dog in the park down the street. I had to tell him about the leash laws. He'd better not go breaking leash laws and bringing the FBI to our doorstep again," she laughed.

I stared at her in silence. I looked at the boy. His cheeks were flushed, his hair was damp from the fog, and he was grinning. They both looked like they believed they were just like anyone else from the street I lived on. They expected to be invited in.

I offered a half-smile and stepped to the side of the doorway to let them in. I felt a measure of annoyance with myself for my embarrassment over the clutter of things in my living room, the unclean floors, the dust everywhere, my own body—rheumy in the eye and bedraggled in my pajamas. I bore down upon my twitches of doubt and told myself that I ought not to feel any sense of apology on their account.

I tried to think of something to say but nothing came. I couldn't possibly say anything about the boy and his flute. There was no way to explain how and why I'd been a stealthy witness to that. And I couldn't say anything about my misgivings after what Meyer had told me, about the university inquiry into something to do with Ruhaba Khan.

They seemed to pick up on my hesitation.

"Is everything okay?" Ruhaba asked, looking around my living room and back at me. "I don't mean to intrude. How silly of me . . . unannounced, so early in the morning. Our plans for coffee were tentative, after all."

I still couldn't think of something to say. "Sorry. We should go," Ruhaba said.

She patted the boy on the shoulder. He nodded.

"Was I gone for too much long?" he asked me. "I am not sure for how long he likes to play. Edgar looked like he had so much fun. He made a good shit."

His aunt chuckled. "That's disgusting," she said. "T-M-I. But it's cute how you say it."

Then, turning to me, she said, "We won't keep you from your Sunday. And I got here straight from the gym . . . I should go home and shower."

Her mention of the shower . . . I couldn't help the image that vaulted into my mind . . . of a naked Ruhaba in a glass cubicle, trapped in steam, her dark brown nipples pressed against the glass, her mouth contorted in a shriek of pleasure . . .

My eyes fell to her body standing there in my living room. How had I not noticed that she was dressed in gym clothes—

tight yoga pants in turquoise blue and a sweat-soaked black thing on top that I could tell was no more than a sports bra even though it was under a rain jacket fastened halfway up her torso. And there, on her head, the scarf.

The boy shuffled his feet and looked at me and then at his aunt. She put her hand on his elbow and turned back toward the door. Had she noticed my brooding stare? Had my eyes slithered over her too long, hooded from suspicion, coiled in desire? Had the *boy* noticed?

Why was he here?

I couldn't leave her to his design. Yes, he was just a boy, but in their part of the world, with its old mores and its rising might, he could be imbued with an untimely dominion over her, or, worse, in pursuit of a brutal supremacy over us all.

And this unsuspecting woman before me—did she even pause to wonder about what she had let in? She was floating about, from cafes to gyms in this liberal bubble of Seattle, as if the FBI had been a pesky old cousin showing up for an uninvited visit on her doorstep. Perhaps the university inquiry, too, was a peril that the boy had somehow ushered in for her. I felt something stir in me, a protectiveness. I didn't want to regret one day that I could not find it in me to be the one she could turn to should she need a rescue from a predatory male relative sent to restore the family honor.

"Ruhaba," I said, my voice thick with desire and a rising dread. "If you give me a few minutes to get dressed, I'll take you up on that offer of coffee."

CHAPTER SIX

Look for the Shame

Dear Mr. Paulson,

I just wanted to follow up on my previous email to you in response to your kind invitation to me to write an Op-Ed for your newspaper. I was wondering if you'd given some thought to my alternative offer—of writing on why we must oppose the new youth jail in Seattle.

I hope you weren't offended by my refusal to write about whether Muslim women support Hillary Clinton in the upcoming presidential election. As I explained, that is nowhere near my area of expertise. I am not a professor of political science or religion or sociology. I am a law professor and I study the incarceration of Black women in the United States. The proposed new youth jail (which is being euphemistically named "The Children and Family Justice Center") is an abhorrent effort by the state to jail more juveniles, a disproportionate number of whom are Black children. I have the expertise and the credentials to write such an Op-Ed and would be happy to work on such a submission for the *Seattle Times*.

I hope to hear back from you at your earliest convenience.

Sincerely,

Ruhaba Khan, Ph.D., J.D.

I interrupted my writing this afternoon to call Ray Waters Jr. He asked if it was something we could discuss over the phone, but I asked him to come over. I wanted to show him the searches I'd done on my computer that morning a few weeks ago (which he would have found anyway, the thorough investigator that he is). He arrived with his usual companion, and I wondered whether he just didn't like taking notes. I also began to get the sense that they liked to meet with me on their own terms, in their own time. They looked churlish at my summons.

We stood huddled over my computer, and I showed them my browser history and clicked on each link in almost the exact sequence. Ray Waters Jr. asked me why I had done the searches and I told him his visit to Ruhaba's had rattled me. Just like the FBI, I needed at the time to make sense of the boy's arrival here, I said, and I had merely the tools that any ordinary citizen had at his disposal in the face of such things—an internet search. If you see something, say something, yes? I hadn't gotten around to saying something, but I did search something.

And how is the boy doing now, I asked them.

He is likely to survive, the man said, his eyes on me, unblinking. Sarah Kupersmith nodded and noted something.

These agents may find other searches of mine from those days, frequent searches, for translations from Urdu to English and from French to English. So many words swirled up around me in those few days. My brain would capture each one from

Ruhaba's tongue, file it away until I could be alone, in search. The agent may find searches on Sufi poets, YouTube videos of the streets of Lahore, and the stumbling, rapid queries of this or that foreign reference misspelled over and over until my inquiry and the computer's intuition colluded toward the right revelations. I will answer the federal agents' questions on these if and when they are posed to me. I couldn't be faulted, surely, for having a love for foreign languages and cultures?

Someone has suggested I hire a lawyer. I am just the kind of person they like to go after these days, some well-wishers say. Nonsense. I have greater faith in the law and its fair process.

Perhaps, though, I should tell them of this sensation I had this morning as I took Edgar for a walk, a sensation of being stalked. But if I tell them that I suspect someone has started to follow me, perhaps it could result in an annoyance to me, in case they give me some sort of companion or guard out of solicitude for my safety. Besides, all I have to offer them by way of elaboration is a mere sense of a shadow, something dark and furtive behind me as I turned a street corner here or sat on a park bench there for a bit.

I understand that the nature of their investigation must be exhaustive and they must be as invasive as cancer, here in my city and in the boy's hometown, perhaps even in his parents' homeland. They have decided not to allow the boy's parents to fly to be by his side. They have delayed granting the parents their visa. I, for my part, have tried, at every attempt, to reassure them of the innocence I witnessed in the child. His voice holds conviction, I tell them, and his eyes lack the shift of the devil.

I told them about the many attempts in which I tried to catch the boy off-guard, do my due diligence. For instance, the time once when, as I handed him a Starbucks caramel latte, I said, "Here you go, young takfiri." I had taken great pains to pronounce the word as close to the way he may have heard it in his world, and I watched his face closely. Where I had been looking for a flinch or even a slight quivering of his lashes at being referred to as a soldier of ISIS, I saw nothing but deep concentration of his brow in taking the cup out of my hands without scalding his fingers if they landed outside the cardboard Starbucks sleeve.

"What does that word mean?" the boy had asked me once the delicate handover was complete.

"I don't know," I said. "I thought you might know."

"Say it again? Is it Urdu? We could ask Khala . . ."

"Oh, never mind," I said hurriedly. "I must have it all wrong. I think I was trying to say 'poet.' What is Urdu for poet?"

What do these people of the law see when they look at me? What does Ray Waters Jr. imagine led me to continue to associate with Ruhaba and the boy, draw them into my heart and let them roam my home, rifle through my drawers, mingle my hours with theirs? I can tell in the timing of his glances at his associate that they think of me as a lonely man, cast out by his own family, indeed, rejected by his own kind, compelled to buttress his self-esteem through making himself indispensable to brown-skinned immigrants, hoping for the attentions of an exotic woman to whom he strived—with one last lurch of his fading youth—to appear more amorous than avuncular. This is how they think, these trained xenophobes. I can tell they are biding their time before they ask what I knew of her, for I have reason to believe that she had revealed to me more of her heart and her ways than to anyone else in this town, but they think making me hold out as they inquire on campus, in her department, among the women who fawned over her, will send me to the point of bursting.

We are four days away from the presidential election on November 8th. I can almost smell their despair. Oh, how they would want their Klan clown to win, but instead we are headed for a female commander-in-chief, and the only thing that keeps me from feeling sick over the paucity of our alternatives is watching them feel sick over a qualified albeit aging woman in a white pantsuit.

I see how they look around my home, turning their training with laser focus to divine signs that would classify me as either dangerously savvy or incautiously stupid. In their bloated sense of purpose over battling ISIS while they fight back flatulence from a lunch at IHOP, they seem to conclude that I was neither of those things—I was merely stuffy, the pompous English professor who was probably too full of himself to notice the nuanced moves of a jihadist.

Well, fuck them. I will tell them the least they need to know. As I said before, the best part of this narrative is to come to a decision about that letter to Camille. These agents have given me little reason yet to hand it over to them. I hold it in my hand now, for that sweet child far away.

To say what I have to write next would take the breath out of me. I will recount some memories of my first real encounter with Ruhaba, as a meeting of a man and a woman. I feel as unprepared to write about it as I felt unprepared to go through it then. When I think about it now, I can see that I was not the one in control. Ruhaba was.

She'd let the boy take the bus home that morning after he'd walked Edgar. She said she'd wait for me at a coffee shop not far from my home. I would like to think of it as a date, but that would be as much a lie now as it would have been a lie then. It had all the trappings of a date, a perfect Seattle kind I perfectly loathed: a coffee date. She even chose a cafe I didn't care for—it called itself El Diablo, because it was Cuban-inspired, the way you could choose to be inspired by any place on the globe and create a taste and aesthetic that belonged really nowhere in the world.

I arrived at the cafe and spotted Ruhaba through the glass windows while I was still outside. I slowed my step and watched her sitting there in the faux fireside glow of the cafe as I stood in the whispers of the disappearing fog. She seemed to have freshened up a little, and her lips were now painted a deep red. For me? I felt my pulse quicken.

She was peering deep into the foam of her coffee, circling an index finger on the rim of her cup. She blew on the foam and lowered her skin toward the steam that rose up. I was revisited by my earlier vision of her in the shower. She dipped a fingertip into the hot coffee and licked it.

I looked at the people around her. Seattle has found a way to throw quick glances and never quite stare. But a young man with headphones and a laptop, wearing a T-shirt that declared "Gender Is Over," seated at a table across from hers, was breaking these rules of disengagement. He—if he *was* a he—seemed to me to be in a high state of arousal—an across-the-gender-sexuality-spectrum arousal—from Ruhaba's odd little attentions to her coffee.

A feeling twitched dully inside me. A flicker of an eye, perhaps, a corner of Ruhaba's eye, arched toward the aroused young man. Was that the briefest exchange of a suggestive glance, or was it an arthritic tug of my imagination?

A deep sense of ownership coursed through my veins. A feeling from years ago arrived, pushing me through the doors of the cafe with a misplaced but beloved thrill of walking toward someone awaiting me, who was mine. I shook an imaginary rain off my jacket and, as I'd expected, the movement caught Ruhaba's attention, causing her to look up. As I walked to her, she greeted me with the warmest smile I had seen turned toward me in a long time.

I sat down and my sense of ownership receded quickly. The feeling that replaced it was that she was somehow in charge. This wasn't always a good thing, as I had learned. I'd have to work a little to ensure that my desire for her was front and center, so I wasn't sidelined to be a bystander, a friendly, asexual senior faculty member with a dog to be walked. I summoned up the charms of my not-so-distant past and said, "You look ravishing."

Her face registered surprise, though not an unpleasant one. Still, I felt the need to qualify my words, given the times we lived in, where the feeblest compliment could be accused of an intention to plunder. "Especially given that you're coming from the gym," I said.

"Oh, thank you, Oliver," she laughed.

My heart skipped a beat. My name sounded strange on her lips, the *r* not entirely audible, in the manner of speech of the men who had colonized her ancestors, and the *l* spoken deep as an Indus Valley, prolonging my presence on her tongue by one beautiful microsecond.

We were interrupted by a barista who gaily laid a large cup of coffee before me. "Sixteen-ounce Mexican Chocolate Mocha," she sang as if at an opera.

"I took the liberty of ordering this for you," Ruhaba said, smiling into my eyes, her octave pitched as pure sophistication after the barista's.

"We're known for our coffee art," the barista said, lingering. "Happy almost-Halloween!" She gestured at the face of a screaming ghost crafted within the foam of my coffee and the word "Boo" scrawled above. I smiled thinly at her and thanked Ruhaba. She thanked the barista and sent her along her way.

"About the other night," she said, leaning across the table toward me. "The visit of those . . . agents. You must have been thinking, '*What have I got myself into?!*'"

Yes, that's precisely what I had been thinking. Nailed it, as the kids say. But I waved my hand as if shocked that anyone could have such a thought, and I joined in her laughter. "It's just the world we live in now, isn't it? And mostly, it was just family drama. Your transnational family drama is safe with me," I said, holding her gaze. She did not look away.

"Thank you. I am still reeling from it all myself. Dear God, how easily our boys can go astray. I am so glad Adil's association with those people in Toulouse ended when it did. I feel for my sister. Goodness, how do people raise children?"

"Don't ask me. I seem to have failed at that."

She shook her head. "I forgot to ask. How was your lunch with Kathryn? How old is she, by the way?"

I was pleased she remembered Kathryn's name. I jumped to her second question. "She's twenty," I lied. Twenty-three put Kathryn closer to Ruhaba's own profile of independent adulthood. Ruhaba wanted to talk about the raising of children. So, Kathryn would be a child.

"Oh. Definitely too young to get married. Did she ask you to walk her down the aisle?"

"Yes, she did. But I said 'No.'"

"Oh, you did? Why?"

"I don't like that she is marrying at twenty. And I discourage the idea of a young woman being given away by her father into the custody of another man."

She raised her eyebrows. Admiration? Disapproval?

"You will go to the wedding, though?" Ruhaba said.

I grunted noncommittedly. I distracted her by reaching over to circle my hands around her coffee cup, as if to warm my fingers. An old move of mine, to herald intimacy.

She put her hands over mine and wriggled the coffee cup from me. She held my gaze and, raising the cup to her lips, drained it as I watched. Behind her, on a wall of the cafe was painted a voluptuous red female devil seated on a bar stool, her legs crossed at the knees, one hip thrust outward. The devil was topless. Her perky red breasts had no nipples, but the way she held her espresso cup and saucer at a tilt, she seemed to offer up one breast as a delicacy, her eyes imploring, almost pining for a connoisseur. I was struck by the thought that perhaps Ruhaba had chosen this cafe on purpose, sat silhouetted against the bare-breasted devil on purpose, that everything she owned was bold in color and everything she did was pigmented with promise.

We sat for a moment, Ruhaba and I, watching each other. With any other woman, this would have been where I would reach out and hold her hand, pull her close, tell her we should go back to my place. With Ruhaba, I needed at least one more cue.

"I worry about Adil," she said.

I should not have waited. I should have reached for her hand.

She spoke again. "What do your instincts tell you? About Adil."

I was beginning to learn not to be taken aback. And I could see she wanted a straight answer.

"I am inclined to believe him. At least most of what he says. There is one thing I believe he is hiding from us, though."

Her face darkened.

I said quickly, "His feelings for this . . . Camille. She's the only girl he mentioned."

She broke into that smile again. We chuckled together. I could perhaps steer us back yet into the realm of desire. Laughter, as we know, is an aphrodisiac, and I had a certain flair with which to stir it up.

"His parents are worried and phone me every day," she said.

Nope. We were to linger in the realm of terror. The world has marched us all into a War on Desire.

"My poor sister calls from their friend's phone, to avoid disclosing to anyone where Adil is, in case some of those bad elements are . . . it all sounds so . . . menacing. I don't know whom to trust."

Me, I wanted to say. Trust *me*.

"We live in a world where people are rapidly growing alienated," I said. "The alienation of young men, in particular, is striking." I kicked myself for talking of young men like an old man. An old man called in to pontificate on a primetime news program.

"Yes," she said. "All this pressure to conform to a toxic masculinity . . ."

Now that was going too far, I thought. But I had learned, over the years, not to respond with "boys will be boys."

"You have friends you can talk to, though?" I said, with as much nonchalance as I could muster.

"Yes, yes," she said quickly, pushing herself up by her elbows to sit straight up in her chair. "A friend here and there and such. But . . . this might sound odd . . . I feel like they . . . their political beliefs, their liberal little souls, will want to intervene, to *do* something for Adil and me. And I don't want to draw that kind of attention."

Ah. So, this was where I fit in. My lack of an activist political drive would be the thing that could get me laid. Who would have thought.

"I know what you mean," I said. "Well, my lips are sealed and I promise to do nothing for you."

She laughed again, lightly. She turned her body and, gripping the edge of her chair, twisted into a stretch. She closed her eyes. This allowed me to watch her torso openly. Slender, limber, aching under her sports bra, to be kneaded out of whatever knot she was feeling. I almost didn't hear what she said next.

"Well, I do know you are . . . I have noticed that you . . . lean center?" She said this with her eyes still closed and then sprung them open at me at the last word.

I made a dramatic gesture of being shocked, offended.

We laughed again, together. "No, my dear," I said. "But I suspect your allegiance to the Left is probably as complex as mine is to liberty."

"Fair enough," she said, holding my gaze.

"And no, I will not call the FBI on young Abdoool."

Her laughter was genuine now, louder, verdant. We were getting along.

I wanted to order a slice of red velvet cake and share it with her, fork to fork, and then lift the dribbled frosting off the plate with our fingertips and vanish it on one another's tongues, leaving everything sticky. But the scrawl on the chalk board behind the cafe counter listed nothing more promising than a dry pumpkin bread.

Ruhaba caught me looking at her neck. She appeared a little flustered for a moment, I thought, and then, almost as if admonishing herself internally, she looked back at me and told me about all the things she wanted from her life.

Ruhaba. My Ruhaba, seated in the same space as me, eyes flashing with eyeliner smudged at their outer ends, her skin lit up from within in an olive-gold glow that I would never see on a white woman. Her voice dipped and swam and halted in that strange accent, and all these things were exquisite. I ached to move with her in her rhythm.

It was her thoughts that terrified me. Perhaps that isn't the right word. For I don't think it was terror I felt, as much as an unsteadying. She pushed me away with the nature of her obsessions even as she pulled me into my obsession with her.

These were not the dreams of an ordinary woman. In fact, as I found out, Ruhaba Khan was a dangerous woman.

Which parts of these stories that she told me should I share with Federal Agent Ray Walters Jr.?

Ruhaba Khan wanted, with all her will, to focus only on the innocent young being that had arrived into her solitary life. But, for a few weeks before he came, she had been consumed with the death of a stranger. Trying to find her way out of that preoccupation was beginning to feel, she said, like she was an ant trying to climb out of the crevice of a jigsaw puzzle. The puzzle was large and tightly packed, offering clarity, even beauty, to some world above, yet so impossible for the ant to know. All Ruhaba knew was the crevice and the promise it offered in its airless darkness.

Ruhaba said she lived these days in the head of Sandra Bland, a woman who had driven from Chicago to Waller County, Texas, and was found hanging from a dustbin liner in a jail cell three days later. Sandra Bland had been arrested after a state trooper pulled her over for failing to signal when she changed lanes.

Ruhaba Khan was waiting to find out whether she would get a grant to go to Texas over the summer to discover what exactly happened to Sandra Bland during those three days. More precisely, Ruhaba's first waking thought each morning for more than a year had been—*Was Bland required to extinguish her cigarette when Texas state trooper Brian Encinia told her to do so?*

I never told her how little I knew of all this. She didn't pause to consider how little I cared about the things that caught in her breath as she talked and how much I cared about putting my lips on her beautiful throat. Still, fueled as I was by the rush of chemicals within me, every word she spoke landed deep in my imagination. I was even able to ask her questions, relevant questions, every now and then.

"*Was* she?" I asked then.

Ruhaba said, "No, she wasn't. She wasn't required to extinguish her cigarette. The whole thing was a rotten arrest." Ruhaba said she knew this perhaps better than anyone else in this country. She had presented papers at conferences on precisely such questions.

She told me her days were punctuated with flashes of words and images and sounds from the dashcam video of the state trooper asking the Black woman to exit her car. These broader questions were thick with semicolons and legal phrasing, but Ruhaba had thinned them out, she said, whittled them down to imbue them with the urgency and focus they deserved. Urgency and focus, not obtuseness, was the imperative of the national Race and Criminal Justice Grant that she was waiting to hear about. For all the words that she had written into the seven-page grant application, for all the years of work on her dissertation and on her research agenda as a law professor and scholar of race and police science, for all the murky intersectionality of race and gender and citizenship and policing and justice and profiling and masculinity, and the toxicity of masculinity, especially in policing, Ruhaba was a woman in rage.

She spoke to me of male rage, but her own rage sat so thick and rancid in her chest, her sensuality began to recede past my fingertips, far away into the counties of Texas and the gullies of Lahore. The lines on her face hardened and her voice turned dry.

As if seeing something in my face, she smiled, a half-smile. "It's nice to be able to talk to you," she said, softly, now. "I have to measure my words all day."

She had to imagine her sentences in her head, she said, before campus meetings. She had to take a breath before any response to a student question, no matter how quotidian. She had to grant coffee shop baristas a whole ten minutes of delay in her head as she waited for her coffee, so that when the delay was only three or four minutes, Ruhaba wouldn't lose her mind, because she'd factored in all those extra minutes of almost meditative calm. She had begun to avoid social situations where she would not be able to predict conversation or, worse, banter. She would allow herself attendance at only one talk on racial justice a week—and yes, there were so many in these past weeks in Seattle—and even for those, she would scrutinize with a compulsive attention the leanings and allegiances of each speaker.

She could not attend, for instance, anything that advertised itself as a "collaborative" panel discussion on racial profiling and police safety. She had almost lost it when she was in fact invited to speak on one such panel. "When Black and Blue Lives Matter," the panel was called, and the title alone had made Ruhaba stand up, shut her office door, return to her desk, and rip a random, already-graded student paper to shreds.

I remember laughing out loud over this. I also remember how Ruhaba tried so hard to join me in mirth, feigning a chuckle. But it stuck in her beautiful throat.

She must have imagined that my laughter also demanded an

explanation from her, because she went on to explain a method to her madness, with some sort of odd deference to my senior faculty status, perhaps. She could always ask the student to submit another copy of his paper, she said, although such a demand would cost her a point or two on "instructor effectiveness" on the teaching evaluation and/or earn her a "disorganized" on the qualitative comments, which university administrators had begun to weigh with as much gravity as the quantitative these days, out of kindness. Ah, but to rip an already-graded student paper afforded an absorption both sweet and exact of the rage, she said, because it carried the recklessness of destruction and the ruefulness of punishment to the self. Self-flagellation.

"There you go," I said. "Self-flagellation goes down well in your community."

"My Muslim community?" she asked, frowning.

"No," I responded quickly. "Your Untenured Faculty community."

We both laughed together then. I was grateful.

"Ollie?" she said, searching my face.

My heart stopped.

"I just wanted to . . . give you a heads-up. A storm is coming."

"A storm?" I blinked. Oh, God, let her be talking about a storm of sexual desire rather than a literal winter storm.

"Students . . . well, I am not allowed to say much, and I think I mentioned it to you the other day, but . . . students want a new curriculum."

Fucking hell. What was it with her and the students and their silly curriculum? I had no desire to derail our little-engine-that-could of chemistry with the meaningless red flags she would raise from time to time.

"Change is good, change is good," I said.

She searched my face again, more closely this time, and, finding nothing but my steady gaze there, she nodded.

"Tell me more about the things that trouble you, Ruhaba," I said. I had found that it was sometimes just a hop and a skip from speaking of trouble to whispering of passion.

She told me then about an email folder that she found a useful tool to keep her rage in check. She would write three-paragraph emails to herself about things that enraged her during the day or in response to emails that drove her to the brink of madness. To the one inviting her to speak on the panel, Ruhaba wrote an email addressing the nature of sustenance such a panel provided to white fragility and, indeed, the nourishment it promised to the bastards in blue.

The folder she had titled "Save for 24 Hours Before Sending" was meant for precisely such an email. She rarely returned to this folder of draft emails twenty-four hours after transferring something to it, which was why she had made it far enough now to the tenure line that she could "almost smell the epic, hot dump" she would take when she crossed to the other end.

Needless to say, I didn't find Ruhaba in my bed that night.

I just phoned Ray Waters Jr. and told him to look for that folder on Ruhaba's computer, to scour it for anything she may have written in the days leading up to November 1st. They were probably already aware of the university committee that had been inquiring into her, but they should also look for references to anger, to longing, to maybe something that happened to her back in Pakistan, perhaps in her girlhood, and her dalliances here. It will be a matter of a sensitive and shameful nature, I said to him. He asked me how I knew. I told him she had said something about it to me in my office on November 1st, very obliquely.

The truth is, it is *I* who wants to know. So many parts of Ruhaba were hidden from me, so many parts were withheld from my gaze, so many stories made unavailable to my imagination. I could hardly bear it. I deserve to know.

I have told the federal agents they could bring back to me anything they find of her writing and I can perhaps be of some help in connecting the dots, piecing together the puzzle.

I know I took a risk in leading them toward that hidden folder of hers. I risked Ruhaba, my love, and all that we had between us. So little and so much.

You will find rage in her writings, I told the federal agents. But look past the rage. Look for the shame, I implored.

I suppose they would have eventually found her folder on their own, no matter how well she had concealed it. They would uncover her rage and it would lead them to conclusions about Ruhaba that are so different from mine.

All I have now are my conclusions.

Her rage. Her blinding rage.

Even her laughter was tinged with her rage.

CHAPTER SEVEN

As Dead as the Dead White Men

DRAFT:

To: Sharma, Shivani

From: Khan, Ruhaba

Dear Shivani,

Thank you for your lovely invitation to your annual Diwali bash. So rare to get a real physical invitation card in the mail these days!

I know how much you want Muslims, even Pakistanis, at your party, even though I don't hear from you at any other time of year. And I know you like to call it a South Asian Diwali, be more inclusive and all, but frankly, darling, I get so bored at these things. The same old matar paneer and chana masala in the potluck. The same old husbands and the brush of their fingers during hello-ji-hugs. The same singing of Bollywood songs with ironic mimes and little appreciation of those gorgeous Urdu lyrics. I go to your parties in the hope of connection and I come away lonelier than ever.

Perhaps next year?

SENT:

Dear Shivani,

Thank you for your lovely invitation to your annual Diwali bash. So rare to get a real physical invitation card in the mail these days! My misfortune that I made another commitment that evening that I can't get out of. Bummer, as the Americans say.

Let's get coffee one of these days?

Wishing you and yours a happy Diwali!

DRAFT:

To: Harding, Oliver

From: Khan, Ruhaba

Dear Ollie,

Thank you for the lovely conversation over coffee. I'd love to have you over for dinner sometime. This matter with the students is taking up a lot of my time, but perhaps we . . .

It hadn't occurred to me to be offended that Ruhaba had said so much about herself to me over that coffee meeting but had, apart from the brief reference to Kathryn, inquired so little into my life. In fact, I was relieved at this. People didn't draw closer to me upon hearing my stories. My only hope was they would tell me theirs. And what exactly would I have told Ruhaba from my past that would have her lean in? Especially in the light of the tumult that was soon to be upon us, I was grateful for the quiet hour we spent over coffee.

I recall telling her that I hoped she would make tenure and that I was *sure* she would. I do think she could sense the sincerity in my words. Truly, to reassure an untenured woman of tenure is the closest one can come to a tender whisper in her ear.

Much has been said about academics laboring toward tenure, but I recall that journey as the one time in my life when I felt vital, alive, in a perfect toil of mind and madness, my heartbeats set to the rhythms of peer review, revisions, resubmissions, acceptances, rejections, and publication. To publish or perish—ah, it held the dread of shame and promise of glory that tinted each day with urgency. Each semester of those six years of labor—at a liberal arts university in Pennsylvania—called upon me to show up day after day with my best self. Teach with a passion. Have your students hang on to every word. Have them crowd into your office hours, have them whisper in the hallways about your high expectations for them and how they want to rise to them. Present papers at conferences where your peers stand up to challenge you in exactly the ways you predicted.

On campus, be outspoken enough to be noticed and deferential enough to be mistaken as collegial. Tenure was a sword nestled in its scabbard of leather and blue velvet. It would reveal itself to you in one of two ways. It could be a gleaming blade of honor meant to knight you into an ivory tower of fools. Or it could be a blunt weapon of rust and resentment, tipping you with the tiniest shove into a sea of humans with ordinary wisdom. Which one would it be for me? Oh, the delicious agony.

I ate breakfast back in those days. Emily and I sipped orange juice and nibbled on toast at the breakfast table. I loved poached eggs on the weekends. We had a dog, Sylvia. Emily believed I had suggested that name as a nod to Plath. In truth, it was my wink to A. R. Gurney's play by that name. He'd earned some unfair critique for his story about a man more in love with his female dog than his wife, leading to the wife wanting to shoot the dog right between her eyes. I never let Emily in on the joke.

Emily worked at an art gallery, as a cross between a saleswoman and curator. She was close to her family sprinkled about the East Coast, visited them often, and this worked well for me, for the solitude I often craved.

And then, word came down that I wasn't going to make tenure.

The tenure committee mumbled something about a female student's complaint that they couldn't ignore even though they were certain it had sprung from jealousy over another female student who'd performed better in my classes. But I knew the true reason—they needed to make room on the faculty for multiculturalists, for cultural relativism and its daughters. Usher in the postcolonialists. Begin the great march of mediocrity.

I was a traditionalist, the canon wars were upon us, and my career was deemed to be as dead as the dead white men on my curriculum. My syllabi were a tribute to fossils, some said. Whatever happened to academic freedom? We had made room for everyone, and now they sought to topple us over the edge. Such intolerance was hardly what we'd fought for. My scholarly agenda stood little chance before the marauding bigots who turned education into a battle cry in place of what should be its real motive—the search for a good life.

My own search for any life at all for Emily and me turned desperate. I sent out feelers far and wide. My old friend Walter Cummings came to my rescue—he was an associate dean at a university in Seattle, and he didn't like what was going on with the assault on the canon and its good men.

Absurdist, he said.

Reductionist, I agreed.

A blow to the pursuit of beauty and truth, he said.

Tribalistic, I offered.

He made a case for my hire at his university as one who retained the traditional ethics of rigorous pedagogy and noble self-examination. I imagine he pulled in some favors and lost some political capital. Emily and I arrived in Seattle, I took up my new position, and we bought this perfect house with its breathtaking view. Emily started to grow a garden.

She got a job at the Seattle Art Museum. We set about the task of finding friends. We threw parties. We invited the assistant and associate professors and the dean. We mixed them in with artists and with senior library staff or the director of the Writing Center or, if we were planning to throw caution to the winds, even faculty from computer science or physics.

When I was awarded tenure the following year, the newly promoted Dean Walter Cummings threw a party for the three of us newly tenured—Betsy MacDowell, David Meyer, and me. My department chair threw another party, at which I got drunk. It didn't matter, everyone laughed. I had earned tenure, and with it I had earned the right to be soused.

Emily threw a surprise party. Amongst others, she invited some of my favorite students. When I walked young Susan Martin out to her car, she kissed me. I kissed her back. I had earned the right.

The following year, Kathryn was born. Beautiful, blue-eyed, laughing Kathryn, bathed in springtime light and my post-tenure bliss. I had just started my sabbatical year, and the three of us spent those first months of Kathryn's life in a languor of walks, feedings, and short road trips around the states of Washington and Oregon. When we didn't want to drive, we took the Amtrak to Vancouver, B.C., or to Portland. Emily's family invited us to join them on their annual trip to Europe. After Italy and France, we decided to cut it short and come home to be just the three of us again. Kathryn would pull on Emily's hair and I would pry her plump little fingers loose. In this little world of hair and muscle and helpless laughter, we believed that this was the way it was and the way it was to be.

Like Chesterton, I believed in the romance of everyday existence and drew mysticism from our trysts with everyday objects—the scratch of a needle falling on a vinyl record, the sizzle of onions when they first hit the butter in the pan, the feel of silk panties on my fingertips as they parted the warm flesh beneath. The hanging of a picture evenly on a wall, the slight surge in my soul when traffic lights turned green for us all and when the yellow heart of a poached egg burst open just for me.

Then I returned to work and found it grow more ridiculous by the day. Newer faculty came in, bringing with them all that newer scholarship, newer methodology, newer edges. These new assistant professors, fresh-faced though sleepy-eyed from having just submitted their dissertations, bear a slavish devotion to Theory. Where once the academy called for a plurality of voices, indeed, something I fought for, they now want to graduate English majors with little to no historical surveys of British and American literature. Where once we fought to include literature through Marxist, Freudian, feminist, deconstructionist, postcolonial lenses, they seek to now exclude all else.

I was appointed department chair. I quit that position within three years, during which my hair turned gray somewhere between mending faculty egos and assigning freshman composition to adjunct faculty. Oh, but I hired a lot of women, including the Nigerian one whom I mentored into the position of department chair, much to the resentment of Betsy MacDowell and the tawdry suspicions of Meyer, who is perhaps one of the last of the old guard who believe that women do not get ahead without bedding their senior faculty.

I will be the first to admit I had affairs. Not with the Nigerian woman but with others, mostly adjunct faculty over whose hire and dismissal I no longer held sway. I allowed myself also to be seduced by a student or two. This was back in the day, when the rules around such things were more nebulous. I betrayed Emily, who had grown distant for a while, absorbed only in Kathryn. But I never sought in another woman an emotional companion. That is not an excuse, of course, for my wandering. I should have pulled myself together. I should have been a better man.

Emily found out. She took Kathryn and went to stay with her parents for a while. I was devastated. I threw myself into work and got a book contract to write the biography of Chesterton. Emily returned. Kathryn looked different. Her hair was short, like a boy's, and her kiss on my cheek was cold. She had turned lean. She was attached a bit too much to her mother. They became a unit and I was in their periphery.

Emily warned me to mend my ways with the women. She

kept throwing the parties, with a foul intent now, I could see. She wanted to keep tabs on me, hear the gossip, keep herself familiar and foregrounded among my associates on campus.

She stopped having sex with me. Or at least it grew terribly infrequent. I must have been drunk that one night when I pushed her onto our bed and grew a bit desperate in my lovemaking. She kept talking and I wanted her to be quiet and I placed my hand on her mouth. I meant to remove it sooner than I did. In my intoxicated state, I perhaps left it pressed on there too long, all the way until I'd finished. Emily said she'd felt choked for breath, that she felt violated, that it was the 1990s and a husband had no right to ask this of his woman.

The things that had drawn people into our lovely home—the way Emily and I reached out for each other's hands, the way we danced around the room topping off their drinks, the way I pulled out this book or that from my bookshelves to lend to a student—all of those became practiced, mannered. The strain began to show not so much in our bodies but on our guests' faces. We played the wrong music. Neil Diamond, where Springsteen would have been their jam.

A man walked into the Seattle Art Museum and Emily fell in love. I knew before I knew. By the time Emily told me she'd been fucking someone else, I had taught myself to be alone and I had resigned myself to moving into a studio apartment. But she didn't want me to move. She wanted to move in with her man, Gerome. He was an architect and he lived in one of those modern homes in Leschi, built with eco-friendly material. I drove past the house one day, and though it had no spectacular Seattle view to speak of, I could see Emily happy, surrounded in skylights and southern exposure. She said she wanted me to stay back in our house so Kathryn would want to visit me often and see it as going home. She asked me if I wanted to keep Sylvia and I said No. I couldn't be trusted to remember to feed a dog.

I suffered for years. I threw myself into work and into bright young things who thought they could heal me, but I grew gaunt and cynical. In the early years after the divorce, I traveled, never on my own dime but on conferences paid for by faculty conference funds. I'd pick conferences on the basis of where they were to be held—not beautiful places but places where I knew no one. Scholarly interest in Chesterton had flagged in recent decades, but I still had a book contract, so I traveled to London to explore his friendship with G. B. Shaw. This alone yielded three papers and had me serve as panelist, moderator, and division head at conferences.

I did things Chesterton would never have done. But he had had Frances. The good Frances. And I had a flailing ego.

Beware the flailing ego of an academician at an academic conference. Any academician will tell you that conference sex is the best sex. Some young graduate student will walk up to you, hair freshly shampooed and creases not completely ironed out from her skirt suit, and she'll tell you that she's read your work and would love to pick your brain. She isn't interested in Chesterton but she's interested in learning how to be published. You crinkle your eyes and make a great display of reading her name and affiliation on the card across her chest as you hold her hand in a shake. If she seems friendly, perhaps you squint, look back at the hotel's terrible lights, then back at her name-card and reach out to adjust it so you can read. This achieves the dual purpose of (a) showing her that you care deeply about getting her name right and (b) letting your fingers brush against her chest. You always refuse an offer of coffee. You look at your conference schedule and say that you are in consultations and meeting all day but can perhaps meet in the hotel bar for a drink, say, at 9:30 p.m., if you're not too tired by then. That way you make sure she's attended her division meetings and her alumni socials and dined with her graduate student friends to whom she can show off that she's having a drink with Dr. Oliver Edward Harding, yes, *the* Harding whom she's cited for a year now and who she's terrified of asking to read her paper, but perhaps, after a glass or two of wine, she will.

After the drink, in which you listen with deep interest to her words while looking piercingly into her eyes and congratulate her profusely over the way her work will drive new theory, you look at your watch and ask her whether she'd like to join you in your room, and if she agrees, you are the Harding who moves from appearing multiple times in her bibliography to coming multiple times on her bosom.

Conference sex is the best because she is not your student and you never have to pretend to recognize her if you see her again.

Yes, that is how ugly I was. Even in those years, I wondered what would make me stop. I got a dog—Edgar—but I left him with friends and dog-sitters for long periods when I'd travel. I wondered what I sought, and in the absence of knowing the answer to this, I wondered whether something would find me someday and soothe me into a respectable solitude. Something more than just a dog or knitting.

Something did find me. Or rather, I stumbled upon it.

I was at our local outdoors store REI one Thursday night after teaching class. I was there to return a parka I had purchased online that I had believed to be the color of rust but ended up being a flagrant orange better suited to a different sort of man. I was frustrated at the store because they didn't have the color I wanted but said they would order it and mail it to me. I decided to walk off my annoyance and also fetch a loaf of bread. I took advantage of the parking spot I already had in REI's garage and walked south on Yale Avenue. Not too far down the street, next to a convenience store where I bought the bread, I saw a sign that simply read "Float." I peered through the glass doors and saw a young woman at the reception desk, with long strawberry blond hair, dressed in a silk kaftan that ended at her knees. She was deeply engrossed in a book. The rest of the reception area looked bare and seemed to lead to another area with a sofa and a few magazines. It all looked spotlessly clean and inviting. And empty, which is how I preferred spaces where I'd strike up a conversation with young women who had that precise color of hair.

I stepped inside and the young woman looked up. Her face broke into a large, fake smile. I liked fake smiles. The genuine ones terrified me. The genuine ones made for harder work.

"Are you here to float?" she said.

I chuckled. "I don't know," I said. "That's quite an outcome you're promising there."

She laughed, brightly. She had probably heard some version of that tacky line before.

"We have flotation tanks here. Are you familiar with those?"

I shook my head, disheartened at the mention of something

that sounded like it belonged in a bathroom rather than a bedroom, but then she jumped off her stool and for just a moment I saw the lines of the edge of the stool pressed into the flesh on the back of her thighs. I had the urge to trace my finger over them and so I mumbled in interest.

"There's no cost for looking," she said, walking toward me and then toward a door behind her. "Would you like to follow me? I'd love to show you around."

And so it was that I met the first pretty young thing I didn't pursue into a fuck.

Floating cured me of thrashing about in pursuit of sexual congress.

I would never have known that in order to go on sensing the real world, I would, for an hour every Tuesday and Thursday, have to deliver myself into a tank of sensory deprivation. When I lay on my back in a two-foot-deep pool of water in a system called Restricted Environmental Stimulation Therapy, which was basically a shallow bathtub of a thousand pounds of Epsom salts, I found my pulse.

In the buoyancy of the liquid, I found a vitality of the mind. In the weightlessness of my body, I found my temperature. But most of all, in the absence of suicide, thoughts of which I could not entertain ever since Kathryn had arrived kicking and screaming into the world, I could come the closest to simulating death by laying myself down in a samadhi of saturated salt.

For a better world, hold Harding in homeostasis.

CHAPTER EIGHT

"It's All Pretty Fucked Up, No?"

Today is November 5th. I had another fitful night of sleep, perhaps a result of eating nothing but crackers and cheese with whiskey as I wrote late into the night. No meal delivery from Janet. And what I thought was an approach from her on my porch in the wee hours of this morning was actually something more disturbing. I woke up to what I imagined was the shadow of a human, a head peering in at my window, rendered somewhat shapeless by the curtains. By the time I gathered myself and stumbled to the door, there was no sign of anyone, just a cold wind blowing in some leaves. Edgar ran out and I had to follow him, cursing and cold, onto the street. There, again, I had the sense that I was being watched.

One could dismiss such foreboding as paranoia, but many would agree that this isn't a good time for ordinary men such as me. A rage so much like Ruhaba's—albeit bereft of beauty such as hers—is bubbling up around us. Misplaced and blinded, it seeks to strike down everything in its path.

Not that I am afraid, but perhaps I could watch my step with these federal agents and their questions. Who knows how far their inquiries of me stretch and who knows what some disgruntled person from my past is now spurred on by our times to say or do? Ray Waters Jr., I sense, has seen some of this coming, is perhaps as troubled as the next man by the advance of hashtag marauders, but who is to say whether he will stick his neck out for me?

And so, perhaps, I should call and tell him now of the things I recall from the time I took the boy for a hike. The things the boy said about his family.

It had been three days since my coffee with Ruhaba, and I hadn't heard from her. To be fair, it was my turn to ask her out. I considered inviting her out to dinner, but I hesitated. Meyer promised me he was hard at work trying to find out more about the university committee's inquiry. I showed great restraint. Nevertheless, due to my solicitude for Ruhaba, I would make it a point to amble by her office window or—on one desperate afternoon—drive by her home to make sure that she was safe. Her neighborhood, by daylight, exposed a different kind of Pacific Northwest creature—the hipster with a man-bun, riding his bicycle with his cloth grocery bag, on his way to the farmer's market, in search of community art or small-batch honey. The man and his man-bun swept around to glare at me as I drove too close to the mandated bicycle lane in my hope of tipping him over and snapping his neck like the sugar snap pea that he'd set out to find among the Imperfect Produce.

The boy, meanwhile, had shown up on time to walk the dog

every day, twice a day, which was a whole lot of bus commuting. Clearly, he was reliable. It could also be a sign of a militaristic discipline acquired in some sort of training. His punctuality could be what those radical Islamists at the mosque had seen as precious in him; perhaps their role for him would have been that of a timekeeper for setting off serial blasts across Toulouse, or a getaway car driver arriving right on time to pick up shooters after a mass killing, or perhaps even a punctual suicide bomber himself.

I had started to swing into such darkness. On a whim, I decided I would invite Ruhaba and the boy to go on a hike with me. A hike would do us all some good. I could draw Ruhaba close. I haven't been on a single hike in which a woman didn't reach her hand out to me for a little help. And, whatever his role may have been in a terrorist cell, the boy had enough of the qualities of a good hiking partner.

Ruhaba didn't answer her phone. I waited. Then, I texted. She wrote right back. She said she couldn't make it. Some matter with her students, she said. I thought for a few hours and then texted again, asking whether the boy could still accompany me. I knew I was taking the risk of drawing him close to me, but perhaps I could get to know him better, ask some questions, get some answers that Ruhaba didn't seem to be seeking for herself.

"The boy is too much in his head," I wrote. "Being in the mountains will get him into his feet and his breath." And, it would get me inside his head.

I waited all day for a response from her but there was nothing. Instead, my eye was forced to an email asking for my signature on a letter. Mark Bauerlain, an English professor at Emory University, a guy I'd met at a conference or two, had joined Frank Buckley, a professor at the Antonin Scalia Law School at George Mason University, and other conservative scholars to organize the letter. It had more than 150 signatories from academicians on a one-sentence statement backing Trump's candidacy. The letter read: "Given our choices in the presidential election, we believe that Donald J. Trump is the candidate most likely to restore the promise of America, and we urge you to support him as we do."

In my boredom and anxiety over awaiting Ruhaba's response, I almost considered signing the letter, just so I could see what those fools would send me next. Nah, I decided. Not worth my attention, even though I was beginning to have a grudging admiration for Candidate Trump's campaign, for its raw, unbridled energy. And the man did have a sense of humor sans pretention. Did these things make him worthy of the American presidency? Certainly not. I did some idle searching on the prospects of this candidate and found, unsurprisingly, a drop in his support, especially among women. The election was barely three weeks away and a *Wall Street Journal*/NBC News poll showed Clinton with a nine-point lead and projected to win at least three hundred electoral votes.

A hundred years ago, Chesterton had excoriated politicians. "It's distressing to contemplate how few politicians are hanged," he'd said. Of course, one couldn't go about quoting such a thing during the Obama years, no matter how innocent it was and how equal in its opportunity. Not that I would be able to bring it back during the Hillary years, either. We are headed for some humorless years, although Trump and his absurdist wit are unlikely to lose favor. I imagine he would do better at the fringes and start some sort of small movement to radicalize the right or then leverage his wild attempt at the presidency into launching some sort of reality show.

I went back to ruminating about matters more immediate to my own life—I wondered whether Ruhaba thought it odd, this interest of mine in the boy. This was the second offer I'd made out of the blue. Perhaps it made her suspicious of this as a ruse for getting closer to her. To be true, yes, that is what it was for me, in the end. But also, aside from my growing suspicions and my determination to keep Ruhaba safe, the boy was far enough away from my world to be a wondrous and examinable being, not unlike the young poet Lucian Gregory was to Gabriel Syme. In fact, I found myself in a state of thrumming curiosity over so much these past few days, something stirred up in me as a scholar once again and I called my editor and told him to expect a few chapters from me soon on the Chesterton book. Perhaps my burst of productivity rose from the turbulence of the boy's story and my misgivings over his intentions, perhaps it was stirred by the meeting with Ruhaba after. Perhaps it was Ruhaba's own restless passion for her research. Perhaps it was just the primal instinct of the hunter in me roused to rescue my woman. Perhaps, and this thought embarrassed me then as it does now, if it turned out that the boy was harmless, I was the ancient gatherer, readying to bring a human or two into my fold.

I did not overthink it, I just showed up at my desk and faced a blank page and soon they were filled with not-insignificant writing. Passion is so good for a man's productivity.

The next morning, a response from Ruhaba flashed on my phone: "Oh, a hike would be wonderful! He fought the idea yesterday, but he said today that it was because he was worried about taking on a difficult hike with his bad leg. Doesn't want to slow you down. Could you pick an easy or moderate hike for him? And just let me know when. Should I buy 'The 10 Essentials' or something?"

I considered waiting out at least the morning before sending a response, but I knew I'd then spend the morning with words of response swimming around in my head. Best to get it done, seal the deal: "No need for 10 Essentials. I have everything we will need. Just a small backpack, a bottle of water, and something to eat at the summit. Tell Adil that Edgar Allan Poe will be joining us."

I picked the boy up at 5:30 a.m. that Saturday. The lights were on in Ruhaba's house when I drove up. The lights in the house adjoining hers were still off. The dog across the street still barked. The white Cadillac seemed to have dragged deeper into the mud beneath it and the windshield was clean gone, leaving it open for a raccoon infestation. If only Ruhaba would let me closer in, I would . . .

In the darkness, I saw the boy shuffle down the front steps and then bound over to my car. Ruhaba stood at the door, wearing a silk robe over her pajamas, furry slippers, and, Jesus, a headscarf tied not very firmly around her head, as if she'd done it in a hurry. I should have gone to the door. But she had said to text from my car.

We stopped off for breakfast, as I usually did on my hikes, at a diner in the small town of Granite Falls. They knew me there and always welcomed Edgar inside with a treat. I told the boy to eat a hearty breakfast with a good amount of protein. The boy ate an omelet, no ham. I ate my usual fried eggs and bacon.

I'd assured the boy that hiking Pilchuck would be no problem at all, even with his leg. To be sure, many hikers considered it to be a somewhat difficult trail, but if I were Adil, I'd certainly be ready for some challenges, some feats of sorts, to transition from boyhood to manhood.

It was a typical late October morning in the Pacific Northwest. It started to rain as we reached the trail. The boy gleefully took out a bright blue GORE-TEX jacket from his backpack. It looked new. Glancing at the boy's shoes, I noticed these were new too, perfect hiking boots, almost like my own. It gave me a spike of delight that Ruhaba had spent some time and money on this excursion I'd suggested. Why hadn't she called me, to escort her to the store and help her pick out the boots? Had she called someone else? Would I one day be afforded the casual intimacy of roaming aisles in shops, chatting in line at the cashier, making plans for lunch after?

The boy did well on the trail. The morning light started to trickle in through slivers and shafts between the thick overlay of evergreens, and he, silent and focused, grew more surefooted. The ground was slippery, and moss had begun to grow on the rocks. I kept a respectful distance from him. I wondered whether I'd see signs of his bad leg tiring, dragging perhaps, or slipping every now and then. I had crampons to give him in case he needed them, but I wouldn't bring them out right then. I noticed that he did not speak more than necessary. Every now and then, a hiker or two would overtake us. After a few of them had,

I noticed him quicken his steps to keep up. I chose my words carefully and said, “We have to find a rhythm—you, the dog, and me. It’s our first time hiking together, and we should err on the side of a slow to moderate speed.”

He seemed relieved and slowed down. Edgar seemed restless and threatened to betray my words of restraint, but the boy didn’t seem to notice. He was watchful of the trail, of the other hikers, of the wider terrain, and then, finally, of the glorious beauty around us. This was the part I always waited for when bringing along a first-time hiker to this part of the earth. Although it had been a while, hadn’t it? The last time had been some two years ago—Elaine, an angry little pianist I met on my brief stint on Match.com. That hike had been disastrous. We’d argued about something, I don’t quite recall what. I may have tried to offer some counsel around the bitterness that consumed her when she referenced her ex-husband. Then she had tried to blame me for a tumble she took on the hike, cracking her elbow. She was blessed with friends who, perhaps accustomed to her irrational and no doubt understandable divorce-trauma-induced flights of imagination, talked her out of taking her ridiculous little accusation too far. One of them even called me to apologize on her behalf.

“So . . .” I said, after it looked like the boy was flushed with the joy of the woods. “You mentioned someone named . . . Cammy? Sorry . . . Camille?”

The boy smiled instantly and threw a sideways glance at me. “Camille, yes.” He picked up a rock and threw it far up ahead into a puddle of water. “The French way make the ‘el’ silent.”

Edgar took the tossing of the rock as a signal of some sort and bounded ahead, but stayed within sight. Dogs were supposed to be kept on a leash on this trail, but I had never seen anyone dare say anything, really, not even the passive-aggressive folk of Nordic heritage with their faces as pinched as the cold tips of their REI hiking poles.

"What would you like to know?" the boy said on his own a few seconds later. "I don't have much things to tell."

"Don't you?" I asked, keeping a teasing tone in my voice. "It sounded like she and you were close. Hers is the only name you said more than once from among your friends."

He fought a losing battle in trying to hide his smile. "I like her. But I don't know if she likes me back. She is an artist. I mean, after school, she wants to be an artist. She is practicing with Manga right now. You know Manga? We are part of a group of five, sometimes six friends. Together in the same grade since we started middle school. Camille, she is different from the other girls. She is not all the time on Snapchat. She likes to read and she is in her dress . . . she dresses more . . . modestly."

Dresses modestly? So, the apple doesn't fall far from the Pakistani mango tree, I thought.

As if reading the nature of my thoughts, the boy glanced at me quickly. His smile disappeared. He missed a step and stumbled but caught himself and avoided a fall. "By modestly, I mean not too . . . how do you say . . . flashy? Not obsessed with fashion and style. She is stylish, yes, but not like . . . a follower of fashion."

"Were you dating her?"

"Oh no . . . no. I . . ."

Even from the quick sideways glance I gave him, I could tell the boy's face had fallen.

"*Dating* is not what we do in France. You ask a girl if she will 'go out' with you, but that means you are already asking to be boyfriend and girlfriend. We would have taken a kiss. Camille and I would kiss and then we would be together and people would know we are together."

"Saves a man a lot of money," I said. Could've saved me a fortune.

"I was planning to ask her on my birthday," the boy said. "To be my girlfriend."

The sadness in his voice hung around us in the silence of the woods. Birds and insects seemed to roar into the silence, cry out that they didn't care about his sad tale.

"She is almost a year older, and I thought asking her out when I was fifteen would be better than fourteen. I don't know. It seems stupid, no?"

I cleared my throat. "No, I think I know what you mean." Oh, to be sixteen, not fifty-six, I wanted to say. Oh, to feel the nearness of a sixteen-year-old girl's thigh.

"But I didn't know all the things that would happen. And now I hit myself. I mean I kick myself. I cannot even text her, not even email." His voice cracked with emotion.

"I bet that hurts. But perhaps she is missing you right now. Absence makes a heart grow fonder. She might be happy to see you when you return." I stopped myself before I came up with emptier and emptier platitudes.

The boy walked in silence.

I thought of something to say to brighten up the child, make him talk some more. "So, after she is your girlfriend, surely you will take her out somewhere? Where would that be?"

The boy answered instantly. "The Fondation Bemberg. It's an art museum. We went there on the school trip once. Then I see her there again one another time when my family took my father's cousin's family there on a visit. Both times, she goes to stand in front of the same painting. She stands very straight and so still in front of that painting." His voice fell almost to a whisper at that last line, as if he were wary of being overhead.

"Which painting?" I asked.

"*L'arlequin jaune*. By Degas. Camille stares at that painting. I can't be for sure if she finds it beautiful or . . . if she has fear of it."

"Why would she fear it?"

"It is a . . . strange painting. Of a fool. A masked fool."

And you're an odd boy, I wanted to say. A fool in love.

Instead, I said, "What if we decide from today that this dog is named for Edgar Degas?"

He grinned.

For the next half hour, the only sound we heard was our feet on the trail. Then we came to a stream of water that we would have to cross. I was surprised that the water, though not high, seemed so rapid at this time of year. Perhaps it had always been this way, perhaps I was only noticing it now because we didn't have four strong legs between us. The dog, of course, would wade and swim. He never seemed to feel the iciness of the water.

Our shoes were covered instantly in mud. The rocks around were loose. I was careful to offer a hand to the boy only when he stumbled. I was too late. He actually tumbled on his knees into the icy water.

"You steady?" I asked the boy when he picked himself up and let go of my hand. He nodded.

"You cold?" I asked, pointing at his jeans that were soaked below the knee.

"No," he said. But I insisted he dry as much of his pants as he could with the small towel I got out of my backpack.

The sun had risen now and peeped through the evergreens at us, adding a glow to a mist that still hadn't lifted. Smells turned fresh, views began to emerge and early snow from the approaching winter appeared underfoot. Here, on this mountain, when my breath warmed my lip and my heart pushed a steady and insistent beat in my chest as I approached the western ridge and knew I was close to the summit, I felt, each time, a crushing sensation of both hope and fear, of being close to the end of a span of something and yet too far away to let go.

Staring into the cloud for the beach-house-like structure on the summit, I slipped on the snow. The boy rushed up to me, and Edgar bounded back from up ahead. I waved the boy away, but I did take the crampons out of my backpack and insisted that both of us wear one each. He put it on the shoe of his good leg, not his bad.

"It's the one that does the hard work," he said, noticing my look. Again, a line that sounded like he had had to say it many times before.

At the summit, the boy's face turned to awe. I pushed him to climb onto the rock at the summit and then followed him. Edgar flopped on the ground not too far away. I took out a collapsible plastic bowl and poured some water in it for Edgar. I gave him some treats.

“Now, we eat,” I said to the boy.

I brought out the peanut-butter-jelly sandwiches and baby carrots I had packed. The boy opened the zipper of his backpack and brought out two medium-size Tupperware boxes that had plastic forks and napkins taped to them. “My aunt made lamb biryani for us,” he said.

My eyes widened. “You’ve been carrying this heavy load of food all along?”

He smiled, and then we ate. The delicious flavors burst into my mouth, and the hike turned new. Food always tasted divine at the summit of a hike that had drawn all your senses for hours, but the tastes of cloves, saffron, cardamom, mint, and cumin here, in the spectacular sweep of sun and trail and peak and crevasse of the Pacific Northwest, it turned almost too much for me to bear.

But there was more. The boy reached back into his backpack and withdrew a flute.

“A flute,” I said, stupidly. I had to blurt out something, to cover any other words that may have spilled from me about that time at the park, just a few mornings ago.

He nodded. “I have taken flute lessons for three years from an Indian music teacher in Toulouse. First my parents they were forcing me and then I start to love it. May I?”

As he cleaned the instrument and cleared his throat, I settled my head on a rock and let the sun dapple my eyelids. My ears were clear and ready this time. Whatever little tune he was readying to play, I would take in its squeak and its screech and would even attempt not to compare it to the classics of the West.

In a few moments, I stirred toward the boy, wondering what was taking him so long to get started. He looked back at me and smiled.

"I put you to sleep," he said. "How was your nap?"

I looked at him, incredulous.

"What?" I said.

I had fallen asleep. The boy had perhaps turned Pilchuck into the Himalayas, and I had missed it. Like a goatherd by the Ganges, the boy of the Garonne had played what he told me now had been a morning raga. Perhaps because the music was so unfamiliar to me, it left me in my slumber. I might have let it touch my heart. I could have sat up, alert, turned my face to the snow of a peak, and let a raga drape cool white lace upon my years of dusty contempt. Instead, I had slept.

He didn't seem to mind. He was silent for a while, in the manner of a human who had turned wind to rhapsody and was now spent. Then, he asked me this: "Is it possible to love something you fear?"

I had to struggle my way into thought, so stunned was I by my sense of loss and now this perfectly phrased query. I mumbled something like, "I don't know. They're . . . love and fear . . . incompatible, opposites, one would suppose."

But the boy was already far away.

"Why do you ask?" I said. He said nothing.

So I made a lurching guess at what he might have been referring to. "Does your father . . . does your father treat your mother as an equal?" I asked him. I had to return to a harder line of questioning. All this beauty and the strange innocence in his talk were compelling me toward tenderness.

At first, it seemed like he hadn't heard me. He had asked his question and then had sunk back into a state of bliss not too different from the kind I had enjoyed until a moment ago. The bastard.

I did feel also a sense of relief that perhaps he may not have heard my question. I suppose I regretted asking it. To bring the boy up here to a peak from which he could not possibly descend on his own and to lay a trap of such a question, it seemed too predatory on his emotions, even for me.

He had his face turned up to the sun. His long lashes were half open.

"I ask you that question about love and fear because I saw it written somewhere," he said. "Like, on the back of a book or maybe on the poster in the Seattle bus. It is in my head now. But what you ask about my father and mother—answer is Yes but also No."

I waited for more, silent.

The boy said, "My father, he is French outside the home and Pakistani at home. His parents move to Saudi Arabia when he was young. My father and his older brother grew up there and then went to study in England. Then they went to Paris and work at my uncle's Algerian friend's restaurant. My father says that his parents hold on . . . held on to the traditions of their homeland from the time they left Pakistan. They had been through the partition of India . . ."

He looked at me questioningly, to discern whether I knew of this history.

I nodded.

"So, you know, they go through all those things like horrors and massacres. Tradition, they make it important. And in Saudi Arabia, they grow more and more traditional in their new home of more hard . . . devout . . . Muslims. When their sons left home, they ordered them to . . . to keep the tradition. Then my mother's family in Pakistan heard through their friends about my father's family looking for a bride. They were excited that their daughter would marry into a big-world life with old-world Muslim tradition. It's all pretty fucked up, no?"

I was startled at the boy's use of profanity. I had never heard him use that word before. I waited for him to be flustered or at least pretend to be, but he sat slack with his back resting against his backpack, his eyes still half-closed. The mountains had a way of loosening your tongue. Now, the boy started to hum.

After a few minutes, he said, "My mother, yes, she believes in those traditions, but I think she wants them to go and die with her. I think she wants a European life for me and Naeema. She fought with my father and she keeps me home from the mosque since I was around eleven years old. I said I didn't want to go anymore because I met my Moroccan friend from school there. He feels then that he and me, we should be best friends so he started to come to my home but my parents didn't like him because he was renoi . . . Black. So even more fucked up, but I don't know all these things back then. And I was just happy to stay home from mosque. Now I learn about the Koran online."

The boy took a long drink of water from his water bottle. "My mother is like more religious in the past few years, I think ever since the stuff happened with my leg." As if remembering his disability, he rubbed his leg, massaged his quads. "I think it will change now, to set my sister back on track. My mother wears pants and long skirts and such, like any Frenchwoman, but she will put on a niqab when someone visits from Pakistan or Saudi Arabia. Recently all the ladies she knows have started wearing it everywhere, so she also joined," he said, shaking his head.

"But on the other hand, your aunt . . ." I said.

"Yes, that is confusing, no? She wears the hijab! My mother is not so much fashionable like Khala Ruhaba. She looks older than Khala, also, even though she's three years less old."

I was surprised to hear that. I had assumed that the boy's mother was Ruhaba's older sister.

As if reading my thoughts, the boy said, "The story which they tell us—the proposal from my father's family came first for Khala Ruhaba, like, when she was twenty or something like that. But she cried and begged. She threw the fit. She tells them she applied to study in the United States. My grandparents say okay because Khala Ruhaba was, uh . . . having excellent grades in school. They agree to let her go to NYU because my grandfather's sister lived in New Jersey and said she would take like the care of Khala Ruhaba. This part is funny—Khala Ruhaba told them she was going to study Islamic art history, you know. But then she went studying law and then also she is not an *avocat*."

I grinned and he grinned back.

He said, "Then she becomes a professor of criminal justice for African Americans or whatever."

"Racial justice," I said. Only to keep things straight.

"Yes," he said. "Anyway, back to that time. So, my grandparents do not want to let such a best marriage proposal go. So, then they tell my mother to get into marriage early. She says okay."

"And your aunt?"

"So, my grandparents and my parents kept finding marriage proposals for Khala Ruhaba for years and years they say. But she refused and refused, then she stopped the visit to Pakistan. She doesn't like my father—too traditional—so she never made a visit to us in France. My mother said that Khala Ruhaba would do visit if we had stayed in Paris. She would have come just to do her shopping, my mother would say. So angry. But then my father leave away from Paris to start his own Pakistani-Indian restaurant in Toulouse, I think just after I was born or something like that."

"Did your parents ever say why your khal . . . why your aunt never married?" I asked.

The boy looked at me. I looked away quickly. Too guiltily, I thought, trying to keep my face from flushing like an idiot.

"Because she is lesbian?" he said.

I stared at him. I couldn't tell if he was making an honest assertion and was curious why I didn't know, or whether he was asking me to answer a query. Ruhaba, a lesbian? That could not be true.

We both stared at each other. "Is she not that?" the boy asked.

"I don't know," I said, trying to keep my voice even. "I . . . I don't think I have heard that from anyone, well, on campus at least." It was all I could say with the wind left in me. "Have you seen her with a woman? In her house?"

"No," the boy said. "Maybe it was just like this and that *ragot* in my family. I don't know. Anyway, do they care if she was a lesbian when they go and packing me off to stay with her? It didn't matter if she was a witch or was being married with two Christians and three Jews."

I felt the blood on the tips of my fingers and toes turn to ice. The temperature on the mountain seemed to have dropped sharply, but of course, it could be that the heat in our bodies from the effort of the hike had fallen. With the tastes of the Spice Route still in the crevices of my gums and with flashes of a naked Ruhaba from my many imaginings of her face moaning beneath or above me, I gathered up my things slowly, threw another few treats at Edgar, and nudged the boy into action.

On the way down, he kept talking. I wanted him to stop.

He talked about this and that—an episode of a television show called *Touche Pas* that he was missing out on. The brutal sounds of the English language. The deliciousness of Seattle's coffee. None of this was of interest to me. My mind was singularly caught up with the possibility that Ruhaba enjoyed a completely different sexual life from what I had imagined, from what had flourished in my fantasies and dazzled my recent days.

CHAPTER NINE

The Boy Let Go of My Hand

An Idle Nazm, by Ruhaba Khan

To Whom It May Concern

Don't come to me

Don't seek me

I will find you

You will know you are chosen

I am no greater than you, no older, no younger

When you have pillaged what I gave at my call, my cry

Edgar was missing on the trail.

The boy was the one who noticed. We'd been walking downhill for a while, turning corners on the path.

The boy had quickened his pace, and I, irritated at this, asked him to slow down.

"Why didn't we caught up with Edgar?" he said.

We called out to the dog. The boy whistled. We quietened down and listened for rustles in the path.

Nothing.

I asked the boy to stay where he was while I ran up ahead a little. No sign of the dog. I hurried back and told the boy that we would retrace our steps. Edgar must have strayed off the track. He had done that once before and then run suddenly out to me.

We walked back up the mountain for a half hour, calling out to Edgar, then falling silent to listen, calling out again, scouring the track, the shrubs, the drops and falls all along the way. I tried to show no signs of panic, but I began to feel a little faint from the stress. The boy looked close to tears.

We heard a rustle behind us, but it was two hikers, a man and a woman, climbing up. I asked them if they had seen a dog off a leash. They shook their heads and wished us luck in our search.

"Maybe we just sit down right here. He can smell us and find us," the boy said.

I thought at first that this was his way of giving up because he was tired. The lost dog was perfect timing for resting a sorry leg.

But, finding no other idea of any merit, I nodded. We sat down on a rock beside the trail and kept still. Some ten minutes later, we walked another bit of a distance and did the same thing again.

The boy said he heard a whimper. "Shush," he said to me.

There was the whimper again. "Edgar!" I shouted. The boy jumped to his feet and whistled. We heard the whimper again. It was coming from below us on the trail, not above. We rushed toward it and called out to the dog again. A faint bark, this time.

We couldn't see Edgar anywhere. I didn't want to admit what was now becoming obvious. He had fallen into a crevasse. I knew exactly where the crevasse was. Hikers often warned newcomers to beware around it. A nudge or stumble and a person could fall to their death down that thing. Edgar was alive, but was he in a state that made him worth rescuing?

Breath is the slightest of things, and yet we give it all the heave we have. As if in indignant response to the possibility of abandonment by an owner prone to dismal self-preservation, the dog let out a stronger bark than before.

Before I could warn the boy about the crevasse, he had run down toward it with a reckless excitement. I thought I would now be witness to my first sighting of a human plunging to death. But he halted just in time, using the good leg and its crampon to brace himself against the gravitational tug of the rubble and leaves around the crevasse. I grabbed his hand and held on hard.

Fuck, the relief of not having to make that phone call to the bugger's aunt.

I beckoned to him to get onto his belly. The two of us then inched our way to a view of the crevasse below us, holding on to the ground and its mooring around us. We could not see Edgar, but the dog was now barking as furiously as he could in his fear.

"I wish he would stop barking," I whispered. "He may stir his body into a further fall. Goddammit."

"I will go down there," the boy said.

"No, you won't," I responded, annoyed at the silly bravado he was offering.

"Let me try," he said. "You won't fit in there. I will. You can be hold my hand and I will crawl down so carefully. Very slowly, I promise."

I couldn't see this working. The risk was too high. But below us was a poor dog barking his way toward a terrible death. I just wanted the barking to stop. Either way.

And perhaps the grip on the boy's hand would be a good measure of whether or not this was a foolhardy plan. We went ahead with it. The boy turned his body around, gripped my hand, and explored a footing with his good leg. Then, he had his bad leg follow, using his free hand to settle it down, not letting go of either his footing or his grip on my hand. So far so good.

Had I wanted the boy to lose his grip and fall to his death?

Had a small part of me wanted to silence the beauty of his flute along with Edgar's bark?

No. *I could never.*

"I see him," the boy said in a low voice, looking up at me. His black eyes shone.

All right, Aladdin. What do you propose next? I felt desperate, sad, antsy at all this imposition on my emotions. There was no way the boy could seize the dog without . . .

The boy let go of my hand. I felt the shock of grabbing on to air. Then I heard a welp. I couldn't tell if it was human or canine.

What in fucking hell had just happened?

I blinked furiously, looking down into the chaos of the crevasse. Within my reach, I saw a dog, clambering upward rapidly and awkwardly, struggling to find a footing, slipping, climbing again. I grasped as far down into the crevasse as I could, and on the dog's next clumsy attempt, I hooked one long outstretched finger on his collar.

I pulled with all my might. On the other end of the dog was a push. Thank fucking God the boy was alive. Edgar was upon me in one piteous snarl at the pain of being tugged upward from his throat.

I sat up and rubbed his back. He wagged his tail rapidly. Then he scrambled back toward the crevasse. Bloody hell. He couldn't possibly go falling down there again! But he stopped, sat down, and began to whimper.

I flipped onto my belly again, crawled as far as I could into the edge of the crevasse, and called out.

"Adil?"

"Je suis là," the boy said. He was speaking French. He was frightened.

"How far down are you?"

"Too far," the boy said.

"Do you have a firm footing?"

"Oui, mais . . ."

I waited.

"But what?" I said after a few terrible moments.

"But my leg is shaking. The bad leg. I am scared I will fall. Please call my mom."

I took a deep breath. "How bad is the fall?"

"C'est terrible."

"How hard is the climb up?"

"Nothing for me to grab," the boy said, his voice shaking. "And I don't want to move my legs."

Even if I let down a jacket or my pants or a dog leash, or the three things tied together, the boy would be dead weight. The risk that the clothes would rip and the boy would fall would be too high.

"Okay, Adil, listen carefully. Here's what I'm going to do. I'm going to fetch help. You stay exactly where you are. Do not move. Stay still, hold on to whatever you can, keep your legs strong. Breathe. I may be gone a while depending on how quickly I find someone. If I don't find someone, I will at least get into cellphone range and call for a rescue team. If I have just one or two more people, we can form a chain or something and come get you."

"Okay," the boy said. His voice sounded like he was trying hard to keep it steady.

"That's a brave young man. Remember, no moving."

With that, I put Edgar on his leash, tied the leash to a tree, and left to find help.

I walked for more than forty minutes down the trail—it was more likely I would find someone coming up, since we hadn't seen anyone pass us on their way up the trail in a while. When I finally heard someone approach, I ran down toward them, waving like a madman.

It was a skinny, frail-looking woman, not a strong man as I'd hoped. Well, fuck, she'd have to do. In fact, she might be better, if she had to crawl down into the crevasse a little, the way the boy had done. Jesus, why had I let him do that?

The woman agreed to help. The two of us kept checking our cellphones for coverage even as we ran back up the trail. I felt dizzy from the fear of what we might find when we reached the crevasse.

Please, God, don't let there be silence.

There wasn't. When we arrived at the spot, the boy was sitting there, on firm land, his back against the tree to which I had tied Edgar's leash. Edgar was in the boy's lap, licking his face. I stopped in my tracks and stared.

The boy was breathing hard, but he grinned at the woman and me.

"I manage to crawl up," he said. "I suddenly felt very strong. Too strong to be staying down. This happened before. I feel brave when I am alone. My muscles don't work when someone try to help. Best alone."

I was shaking. Edgar jumped from the boy's lap and ran up toward me, but his leash held him back. The woman was clapping her hands and making the polite whooping sounds that strangers make in the nothingness of the larger humanity's happiness.

On the drive home, the boy slept, his head lolling about against his seatbelt in the front passenger seat. The dog slept on a pile of blankets in the backseat. I still shook hard, every few minutes, from the aftermath of the events. I played over and over in my head the alternative scenario. Dead dog. Dead boy. Live dog. Dead boy. Live dog. Dead boy's body airlifted with a split skull and twisted leg. I wanted more than anything to stop at my usual bar on the way home, to get a drink. Whiskey would be like a mother's kiss to me right now.

I feel brave when I am alone. No kidding.

I looked over at the sleeping child. I felt a rush of tenderness. A man can no more love the thing he fears than he can predict who he will be when fear arrives.

The boy stirred awake as we arrived into the heart of Seattle. He shook his head, then stared at me.

I turned to smile at him. When I looked back ahead at the road, he still kept staring.

"You saved my life," he said. "Thank you."

I frowned. "I didn't. You saved your own life. And you saved my dog's life. I should be thanking *you*!"

The boy looked ahead into the traffic, as if moving these facts around in his head. Then, he chuckled softly.

I thought he was losing his mind. "What is it?" I said.

"Your face. When you came back and see me sitting there."

"I bet I looked like I saw a ghost."

"You made the sign of the holy cross."

It was my turn to stare at the boy. "No, I didn't."

"Yes, you did. You made the sign of the holy cross."

He laughed. I let him.

When the boy was quiet, I said, "Please let me thank you with a gift. A gesture of my profound gratitude for saving Edgar. And for saving yourself."

"Ah, no. No, thank you. I am grateful to be alive. But . . ."

"Yes?"

"But please don't tell my aunt what happened."

"Are you crazy? Of course, I have to tell her. I have been going over in my head the words I will say to her. I'll have to calm her first and then apologize, then give her the details and apologize again. I am just so glad we're not taking you home dead in an ambulance."

"Please. She is already too guarding of me. She will not let me go anywhere."

"Maybe for a few days, she will be that way. But then she will settle down. I will tell her that this is how boys turn into men. I will calm her as much as I can, but we must tell her."

The boy let out a frustrated sigh and fell quiet.

"So. Tell me what gift I may give you," I said.

The boy thought for a while. Then, he said, "It's not a thing. It's an action. An activity."

"Okay . . ." I said. "Please don't tell me it's hiking."

He laughed. "Can I please use your computer? I will not do email. I just want to see pictures and posts of Camille."

I think back to that day and that hike and the things that came before and after. I pick up the phone and call Ray Waters Jr. They want so much from me, these federal agents. They are leaning hard into my every memory, and yet there are parts of these people that are so closed to understanding the very things that will shed the most brilliant light on the whole matter of the boy.

They ought to understand all that I haven't thought yet. One does not fall asleep at night a sage. We tumble into our pillow with strained muscle and shrunken memory from all the concrete and grass and paper of the day. Few among us could claim that we reflect well on the words that were said, the looks exchanged, the suspicions risen, the emotions withheld. What do you offer a boy when you take him on a hike? Do you offer him a ready arm on a stretch of slippery rock? Do you offer him a view of snow-capped peak and bald-headed eagle? Or do you offer him a wing of friendship that flies past fear?

When Ray Waters Jr. answers the phone, I ask about the boy. How is he, how far did the bullet pierce his body, how likely is it that we will have him back?

He is somewhere closer to life than to death, but we can't be too sure, is the reply. What is it that you called about, the man asks, trying to keep impatience out of his voice. I tell him, as I must, about the family, about Saudi Arabia, about his mother turning more religious in recent years, about the devout father and uncle, about the desire to peer into the life of a young French girl with a name as sweet as Camille.

I don't know what to make of these things that float up in my memory, I tell the federal agent.

Leave that up to us, he says, sounding kinder now. Just call anytime you remember anything else of importance.

Which brings me back to the matter of the letter the boy wrote. I am holding it in my hand now. If it is indeed to reach sweet Camille by her birthday, I should mail it soon. If it is to help these federal officers come to the conclusions that best serve humanity, I should have handed it to them yesterday.

I have read the letter before, but perhaps if I glance at a single line in it now, the way we parse through things said during the day and make of one of them the precise thought that pushes us into the arms of sleep, the line would speak to me, tell me what to do.

I glance.

"I am scared of America."

Well. That was no help. No help at all.

CHAPTER TEN

Look What We Let In

I must take a nap. My head has grown steadily heavier all morning and it is now 3 p.m. I feel as if someone is pouring layers of wet cement into my brain and watching it dry. Layer after layer, all is turning to concrete. Airtight. A tomb. A mausoleum to comprehension into which I keep chipping to engrave fact. I must rest.

It was a mistake to rest. My nap lasted three hours and I missed some of our precious few daylight hours. I awoke to Edgar's whimpers for food. I rose from bed feeling dizzy and disoriented. Then, I made the mistake of catching up on the news about the incident of November 1st. Worse, I read some of the emails floating about on university threads. All these theories. All these questions flying at me after perfunctory inquiries into my well-being. If I don't gather my thoughts and write everything down now, I will be assailed by others' perceptions of truth.

When I dropped the boy home, Ruhaba invited me in but seemed distracted. She offered me water, and although I didn't need any, I said yes. When she was in her kitchen, I glanced at her bedroom. The curtains were drawn and the room darkened. The sheets on her bed were rumpled. Had someone made love to her in it? Perhaps she had seized the opportunity to invite a lesbian lover over, with her nephew gone for most of the day with her lonely old colleague from work.

I drank barely a few bitter sips of the water before she started to usher me toward the front door. At the point of leaving, I turned to her instead and described at length the incident in which her ward had almost fallen to a terrible death. She listened to me with a remarkable absence of outward emotion. After an initial sharp intake of breath, her eyes had turned expressionless and veiled. Her face was stoic and her voice so even, it sounded decidedly cold.

She didn't think the boy needed to go to the ER to be examined for any signs of shock or trauma. Although I agreed with her, for nothing troubled me more than the overmedication of America's children, I told her I was somewhat concerned about any residual impact on the boy's leg—the climb and descent alone would have been challenging; the quiver and push against the gravitational pull of death might have aggravated some nerves.

Where I wanted my words to cause a gasp from her lips, I was given a strong setting of jaw. Where I wanted a little widening of her world and a narrowing of ours, I found doors shuttering, one upon another.

Still, I may have been relieved, too, with the sense of closure that Ruhaba laid on the medical end of things. I didn't want overly meddling hospital staff asking questions that may give the impression that I had endangered the boy's life or worsened his polio-weakened limbs in some way.

Ruhaba turned to me and dismissed me quickly, with an arid "Thank you for bringing him home safely." She glanced toward my car, as if she wanted to alert me to the vehicle calling out to me or something. She pursed her lips into a smile and stepped back from her door so she could shut it behind me.

Yes, she was afraid of creating some sort of paper trail on the boy at a hospital. Yes, she may have been biting back her rage against me for endangering her nephew's life. Yes, she could simply be callous, self-absorbed. But in that moment, what I could tell was that she certainly wasn't a lesbian.

The way she leaned against the frame of her door. The thrust of her hips in those jeans. The lace on her hijab. The smidgen of lip gloss that looked too fresh to have been disturbed by a lover's kiss (I imagined she may have rushed to rub it on before she opened the door to me). The flicker of glance away from my face when I gave her that look I knew women liked—wrinkling my eyes through my glasses with the suggestion of a smile that didn't fully settle on my mouth. The musky scent she wore. The long, manicured nails that would make the work of a lesbian, well, difficult.

My little study may sound tawdry, but in the end, things do come down to skin and nail and flesh. The certainties of the body trump the mysteries of the soul. Surrounded as I was by people who lived in their heads, I had found ways to retrieve myself and live by hair and scalp and nerve endings.

I walked away with the comfort of my knowledge mixed in with the discomfort of thoughts of that messy bed and the brusque dismissal meted out to me. When I turned to wave from my car, Ruhaba's door was already shut. This felt needlessly cruel.

The chill that hit my chest when I opened my own front door felt warmer than the reception I had had from a woman, an aunt whose crippled nephew I had delivered to her childless bosom. The scurrying of my dog to his feeding bowl, the worn edge of my rug against the hardwood, the scent of old and newer books, the acidic nutty scent of years of coffee brewed, spilled, and breathed into the fabrics and woodwork of this home of mine—all this drew me deeper in through my very soul. Or so I told myself.

Without putting my things away or taking my clothes off, I flopped onto my large brown leather couch. The mud that was caked on the front of my jacket fell in small clumps through the cracks in the seats. The grass on my boots found slivers within the fibers of the rug. In all these ways, over the years, I had brought in and carried out bits of myself—my living, cellular, cerebral self—from a home in which, for almost fifteen years now, I had felt the kind of contentment for which others went to their graves yearning.

But that night did not bring contentment. I considered going to the flotation tank, but I was too tired. I toyed with the idea of knitting, but I hadn't touched it since the brunch with Kathryn.

Just before I fell asleep, I wondered if Ruhaba's coldness had less to do with me than with her. Was it something to do with the ongoing inquiry against her? Had she heard something that put her employment or her presence on American soil in jeopardy?

The reason became clear to me the morning after. A matter at the university had me bolt out of my house at 7 a.m. that day. I left a key under the mat and a note on the door for the boy—"Emergency on campus. Please walk the dog as usual and feed him—cans of dog food in the kitchen." I wasn't sure if he would come, if he and his leg had recovered, if Ruhaba's taciturnity had been based on some reason to distance herself and the boy from me, but I took care to shut down and password-lock my computer and lock the door to my study. Doing one or the other would have sufficed, but these kids had their hacks these days. Any cyberstalking of sweet Camille would be done under my supervision.

The students of the College of Humanities had occupied the premises and were staging a sit-in. A cryptic email from Dean Walter Cummings in my inbox—sent to a select few whom the Dean was summoning to form a Core Advisory Team—had said nothing more than that. On my way there, I wondered what he meant by "occupied," and I feared the worst—something bad-smelling and bedraggled, like the Occupy protests that had lined the Seattle streets a few years ago, forcing me to drive on several evenings through a colony of cautionary tales—men and women for whom I had at first had charitable thoughts (ranging from "this is what happens to you when you don't value a liberal arts education" to "there, but for the grace of thee, go I") but who had forced me back into my wisdoms when the stench of pot and sweat and the dried palette of sexual deviance had assailed my senses.

Sure enough, these student occupiers had drawn their inspiration from that same social movement and its tactics. When I entered the Dean's offices, some fifty to sixty of them were sitting in the lobby with protest signs. They had piled up sleeping bags against the wall that displayed the hall of fame portraits of past deans. A sign with a roughly drawn arrow read, *See something wrong with this picture?*

I didn't. But I knew what they saw—each of the deans was white. Although, to be fair, there were three women in the mix. My buddy and savior who had brought me here years before—Walter—was the current dean and had been for several years. His picture hadn't been changed since he took over. He was now sixty-two years of age.

Sleeping bags. So, this would be more ambitious than a sit-in. It would be a sleep-in. They had erected a shrine of some sort in the middle of the lobby, books and flowers and incense in a gaudy heap, so that you were forced to go around it even to meet the Dean's administrative assistant.

I recognized a few of these troublemakers. Not all of them were minorities, but an overwhelming number of them were. That girl Conscience or Essence was there. An Ethiopian girl in a burka handed me a pamphlet even though I had deliberately avoided eye contact as I tried to make it past her toward the Dean's office. She was a good student, a hard worker, and I wanted to say to her that this was not the way to go, but there seemed to be a new steeliness to her gaze. I decided I would keep an open mind.

I shoved the pamphlet into the pocket of my jacket and waved at the protesters on my way to the Dean's office. I recognized a few more students. A couple of white males, too. I was surprised to see among them young Cunningham, a boy who'd hung on to my every word and visited me often in my office until a few months ago. I would not have expected him to have a friend in this lot, let alone join in their protest. Not because he wouldn't have sympathies, but because I would not expect someone like him—all-American blue-eyed blond colonizer-type—to have earned their trust. Odd, these new alliances.

I had only to look at Dean Walter Cummings once and we both knew: we have been here before; we survived these wars once. But this time round, it was different. Back then, it was faculty pushing to ring in mediocrity. Now, the students were leading the charge. In these times of a country questioning the value of a college degree, the student dollar served as gift or guillotine. This time, our heads would roll.

Look what we let in.

Four other faculty members and a couple of hacks from university administration were present. David Meyer was among them, and he looked relieved to see me. Each of the people in the room was holding a mobile coffee mug close to them like some sort of symbolic reminder that America still had recourse, if all else failed, to nuclear weaponry.

The Dean's office was in the newest building on campus. Three sides of his office walls were glass, with rounded edges, facing outward into the city, part of the university's new strategic vision to interface with our tech metropolis and the endearing chaos of Seattle's diversity. From the streets outside, people stared at the soundless anguish of men and women toppled from an ivory tower to dart about in a fucking fishbowl.

"We must prepare a statement," said a small-breasted blond woman whom I didn't know but recognized from other events where faculty were forced to break bread and frame sentences with staff (such things are best when they happen organically). She looked and dressed like she was from the offices of University Counsel but dreamed of being from Paris.

"We must listen before preparing a ham-fisted statement," said Regina Powers, the Black full professor from the Department of Sociology whose words always shut everything the hell down. I had heard from many that even the other faculty of color did not trust her performative ways. Seriously, no one ever spoke after she spoke, for several minutes. She was always the one who spoke up after the silences that followed her having spoken.

"Any statement we attempt to craft right now will only be made up with words from our echo chamber," she said. I looked around the room for anyone who might have seized upon the irony, but if they had, they didn't show it. Their lips were on the rims of their coffee mugs, their eyes were on the rug. We were at war, we had the weapons, but our new generals were speaking already of disarmament.

I slumped into a brittle, late-modern chair and waited for Regina to use the term microaggression; I knew that I would at least see a flicker on my buddy David Meyer's eyelid then. But, despite going on for a bit, Regina didn't, and I was somewhat crestfallen.

"They're calling a press conference," the Dean said. "Will the reporters come? I mean, these are a bunch of . . . undergraduates . . . aren't they supposed to be distracted by their Facebooks?

My benefactor's last nap must have lasted about twelve years. Sure enough, a chatter arose among the best minds in the room, about whether students even used Facebook anymore, or whether Instagram or Snapchat, YouTube . . .

"Well, let's not be disdainful of the undergraduate," Regina said. "Nor of social media. Where do you think they *organized*? They have a Facebook page called . . . pardon me for being the bearer of bad news, but it's called "Down with the Living White Dean and His Dead White Dudes."

The Dean blinked. Everyone else stared into their coffee mugs as if expecting a fortune to appear written at the bottom.

"What does that even mean?" the Dean asked.

"Well, look at their demands," Regina said.

The Dean gave her a look that said, "And whose side are *you* on?"

She read the look correctly and added, "If we are to push back . . . if we are to negotiate with them . . . we will have to take that charter of demands seriously."

"We will not negotiate with terrorists," someone said. It was Meyer.

"Let's be careful of the words we use," the small-breasted woman said. "We don't want anything to be misconstrued here." She cleared her throat. "Let me point out that a good number of the student protesters are Mus . . . Islamic . . . of the Islamic faith."

"*Jesus!*" Meyer said.

"God almighty," Regina said. "Am I hearing this right? Someone uses the word 'terrorist' and we immediately jump to an association with Muslim students?"

The small breasts started to cave in on themselves, like a poorly chosen hideout in the terrains of Afghanistan. The woman cleared her throat again and shook her head so hard, her French chignon came undone. "That is not what I was . . . my responsibility here is to avoid any . . ."

"Let's all calm down," I said. This was my moment, if any. I had no idea what I was going to say next, but I knew my voice soothed these people, even Regina, if she'd care to admit it. My elocution reminded them of a safer, less complicated time.

"With regard to the Dean's query about whether the reporters will come," I continued, now that I had everyone's attention. The small breasts seemed to perk back up, or at least halted in their implosion. "I reckon they will. The *Seattle Times* recently launched, as you, my dear well-informed, print newspaper–subscribing colleagues will be aware, a race and equity initiative of some sort. You should see what some people are saying about that sort of thing on some subreddit forums."

If the people in the room understood my reference, they did not let on. I didn't bother to educate them. I continued, "In any case, the spectacle that is playing out past the locked door of this office is just the kind of thing that would continue the employ of scribes who are scrambling to keep their joys in a dying vocation."

"So," I said, "whether we like it or not, the insane are running the asylum, and we must listen with a patient ear and speak with a gentle tongue and smooth all these ruffled feathers, no matter that some of these . . . students . . . barely ever speak up in class, even fewer can use a correct comma splice on their press release, and perhaps the whole *99 percent* of them, if congratulated on their chutzpah for turning the lobby outside into their agora, would probably think you are referring to a sweater."

The small breasts shook with muted laughter and the rest of the room was quiet. Regina was scowling in her seat and the Dean was leaning in.

I said, "What are their demands?"

Highest on their petition was a complete overhaul of the humanities curriculum. These radicals wanted not just to add to the body of the curriculum but to molest the very heart of an American education.

So. This was what Ruhaba had been trying to warn me about. And I hadn't paid heed. I perhaps could have nipped this whole thing in the bud. These people were coming for my job and the jobs of so many of my own kind. They wanted to render our universities unrecognizable, our education puerile. Ruhaba knew and had tried to tip me off, but not strongly enough.

For a few years now the highly paid vice presidents of this or that on the university administration had been in what these iGen students themselves referred to as "a clusterfuck." They rose up at every event to congratulate themselves on the rising numbers of diverse populations in the student body. Meanwhile, these contaminants—and by this I will say I was referring to *ideas*, not *people*—had taken issue with what they referred to as a Eurocentrism in the learning being handed down to them. They sought to "decentralize whiteness."

They were wailing for "a critical focus on the evolution of

systems of oppression such as racism, capitalism, colonialism, etc." Across America, young people want to take down all that is good and wise and learned. They wanted to topple statues. Seattle just happened to be at the forefront of this preposterous uprising. We all knew this nonsense wouldn't grow or last. They would sit in, sleep in, march, shout for a bit, and then we'd all go back to the pursuit of truth and beauty and a good, strong meritocracy. But, these outbursts always did their damage and left a few adjunct faculty unemployed.

If it weren't for University Counsel and the growing sway it held over every word uttered in the halls and malls of this campus, I would have stepped out into that lobby and asked the formerly colonized peoples and their American-born progeny to go home and talk to grandma about oppression. I'd be damned if she didn't pull the hair from their scalp and tell them to be grateful to be reading Plato.

The Dean was speaking now. "What concerns me . . . what ought to concern us all . . . is their new demand that the revamped curriculum be taught by . . ." He referred to the pamphlet on his desk, around which he had cleared out space, as if this single sheet of bright yellow paper with photocopied bullet points carried the only commandments to which he would hereafter need to refer. "Taught by qualified faculty from marginalized backgrounds, especially professors of color, professors from recently immigrated communities, and queer professors."

All the coffee from the room had been sucked up by now and there was nothing to suck but air.

Or, as it turned out, dick: "Those of us who have served on this faculty for years have no doubt you will steer us through this with your consistent and calm stewardship," Meyer said to the Dean.

I was afraid I might laugh, so I spoke quickly. "Recently immigrated communities? What, an African American faculty member doesn't count for shit now?"

Although I wasn't looking at her, Regina gasped. "*Professor* Harding. This is not the first time, but this had better be the last of your microaggressions."

Now that I had gotten *that* out of the way, I felt the need to sit down. "I'm on *your* side," I said to Regina as unconvincingly as I could.

"Now, now," the Dean said, taking care not to look at anyone in particular. University Counsel looked at him like the proud owner of a circus monkey that had just jumped neatly through three rings of fire. The Dean continued: "They're also calling for a curriculum that urgently does a radical examination of what it means to turn its students into agents of social change. They want us to prioritize dialogue about racism, gentrification, sexism, colonialism, imperialism, global white supremacy, and other ethical questions about systems of power. They want us to lead by example and set a standard for students here in our college before doing service-learning or studying in other communities or countries."

"Jesus. In my day, we just went on a study abroad," I said. "That's where some of us finally got laid."

"Quite specifically," the Dean said, speaking quickly over my last remark before someone could express disdain, "they are asking for the establishment of a new major in Critical Whitening Studies."

"Critical *what*?" said more than one of us.

"Sorry . . . Critical *Whiteness* Studies it says here," the Dean said, squinting at the paper in his hands.

We sat there, looking at each other, uncertain of what the fuck that was and whether it might hold out some promise for us after all. The word "whiteness" might have implied that they needed white faculty or white expertise, perhaps? But the word "critical" kicked that idea in the balls.

There was a sharp knock on the door. It was "Sindy-With-An-S" Greere, who taught classes on global poverty with a special focus on Latin America, although she also dabbled in the poverty of South Asia. She was part of the Core Advisory Team (CAT) the Dean had summoned. She apologized for her lateness. Then, looking around the room, she said, "We need more people of color in here."

Everyone turned to look at Regina. Several of them then instantly looked away. I kept my eyes on Regina, and when she looked at me, I rolled my eyes. In solidarity. She smiled a tight smile and shook her head just a bit. There. I'd built bridges and it wasn't even 9 a.m.

"With your permission," Sindy was saying, "I'd like to invite Dr. Ruhaba Khan to join us."

"Don't bother," I said. "She's busy."

Now everyone stared at me. I felt foolish. I'd spoken up in panic. I didn't want to have to work with Ruhaba on all this. This kind of thing was where sex came to die.

"She excused herself from the Space Committee already," I said. "She has a nephew in town who's going through a rough time. He . . ." I stopped myself. What was I about to say? I imagined the boy's scared little face holding on for dear life in the crevasse just twenty-four hours ago. I pursed my lips and stared out the window. I felt Meyer's eyes boring into my skull.

"Well, it's a bit complicated with . . ." the Dean began.

I met Meyer's eye. He squinted at me. The Dean was probably wary of including Ruhaba while an inquiry was in process against her.

"It doesn't hurt to ask," the Dean said. So, he was desperate. He nodded at Sindy, who made a call on her cellphone. Ruhaba answered instantly on the other end. I knew Sindy had been cozying up to Ruhaba, probably to leech onto some collaboration and coauthoring on the poverty of Pakistan, to travel there using Ruhaba's contacts and put that wretched place on her poverty-whoring résumé.

Don't take the bait, Ruhaba, I said with all the might in my head. Think of Adil. Spend time with Adil.

"Women of color get asked to do disproportionately more service," I said to the room, speaking over Sindy's cheery greetings to Ruhaba on her phone. Regina's head shot up and she stared at me, as if seeing me for the first time and seeing there not a whole man but a man with a goat for a head. The Dean, too, was looking at me with confusion, but also with some fearful indignation, like a man on the *Titanic* watching women and children being offloaded into the rescue boats and wondering if his turn would come at all.

The room went back to straining to hear the conversation on the phone. We watched as Sindy's face fell and she hung up. Looking at the floor, she said, "The woman says to give you all her regrets."

How quickly Pakistan had slipped away like a mirage from Sindy's horizon, and how quickly a Pakistani had gone from being a Dr. to "the woman."

I sighed. "I told you she has her hands full with . . ."

Sindy threw me a look. "She says she is outside, joining the protest with the students."

Gasps went up in the room.

"There you go," said Meyer, still looking at me.

"Unbelievable," said Regina.

"In violation of the Faculty Bylaws," said the small breasts.

The Dean slumped in his chair and covered the pamphlet before him with the length and breadth of his hands, as if trying to snuff out its breath with the sheer size of his masculinity.

I felt an odd sense of relief mixed in with . . . arousal. And then I was relieved at my arousal. I hadn't felt it much these past three days, what with the boy dampening my stalled interactions with Ruhaba with his full and urgent presence and his declarations of lesbianism. Now, I imagined Ruhaba sitting cross-legged on the floor with the lesbians outside, her skirt riding up, her face defiant with demands. I had to lean across my knees so my faint erection wouldn't grow into the line of sight of University Counsel.

"She says she's not alone," Sindy said. "More faculty have joined in solidarity. She says to come outside. The press is here."

CHAPTER ELEVEN

#ImNotRacistBecause

To: Khan, Ruhaba

From: Khan, Ruhaba

What was it the gynecologist said the other day? That she didn't expect the word "fuck" to come from the mouth of someone who looked like me.

What did she mean? Is "fuck" not worthy of me, or am I not worthy of "fuck"?

Hell, that pap smear was rough. Did I imagine it, or was it rougher than last year?

Don't be paranoid, babygirl. Not everyone is out to get you, ffs.

And lordy, *had* the press arrived. The Dean opened his office door and television cameras marched right in, along with a stream of protesting students. The administrative assistant had disappeared, fled perhaps. As the fishbowl filled, people in the streets outside peered in and aimed their cellphone cameras. They had no idea what was up, and even if they did, it would mean so little to them, but cameras beget cameras.

The television crews broadcast a sharper image to the world, or at least to a one-minute click-and-share audience in the city. The white reporters from the *Seattle Times* were there, looking unhappy because they weren't as cool and were instructed by their establishment to not even try to be as cool as the kids at the *Seattle Weekly*, which had turned into a socialist rag lately while *The Stranger* lost its moral high ground when the use of "fuck" in its headlines became predictable.

Reporters rushed at the Dean, who looked so beleaguered, I felt sorry for him and went to his assistance.

"We are here to listen," I said to the gathering.

"It's too late for that!" one of the protesters shouted.

This response made the reporters ask me my name. I refused to give it to them. What I really wanted to say was that we were living in an age of reaction masquerading as an age of reform. But I shuddered to think of the many ways in which they'd misquote me on that. I craned my neck past them to scour the lobby for Ruhaba.

She was standing in a corner of the lobby, not sitting with her skirt riding up, but leaning against the wall, neutral in expression, distant from other faculty, watching it all with a steady and beautiful eye. As if sensing my gaze, she glanced over at me. I expected an icy glare, but instead, I got a neutral nod. This was why she had been cold last night. All of this was being planned. This was the way things were going to be.

All was lost.

The students were now holding forth on their demands.

Someone asked about what Critical Whiteness Studies meant. A whole lot of words flew up around us.

This one would not go away easily, I realized. Everything was slipping away.

Before we knew it, we'd have yoga classes for credit. I'd be asked to team-teach a class with Fugly, demonstrating the Kama Sutra. That's how they'd come for me. I could feel them closing in.

And then they practically pulled off a mugging. They said they wanted a "Day of Absence," when all the white students and faculty would leave campus.

Shouts broke out among the crowds. Cameras clicked so furiously, it sounded like the shattering of glass all around us. Reporters shouted their questions, halting and stumbling over words like "privilege" and "inclusion."

Deer in the headlights. Deer with bad knees in the headlights.

When I think back to that morning, I think of how I could have been a better ally . . . to David Meyer. I had forgotten the man even though he stood close up next to me. I hadn't heard his heavy breathing in the cacophony around us. I hadn't seen the froth at his mouth. So, when Meyer shouted, "*That's racist!*" I jumped out of my skin. I could have stopped him, been a sounding board, said some soothing words, perhaps just shared out loud with him the acute observations I had been making in my own head. But I had been remiss and he had hurled out one of the two words we are never to hurl.

Naturally, gasps went up around us. Meyer went red in the face. A student asked loudly, "Who defines racism?"

Another answered, "The white man is defining racism."

Meyer went redder. He lurched toward the front of the room. I tried to grab him. At first, people thought he was about to assault a student. But he simply wrenched the mic from someone's hand and sputtered into it: "You call me racist? Read the student newspaper from June 1996. I led a campaign against racism on this very campus. Have you heard about the fraternity rush event that employed Black strippers? Do you know who protested that the event was racist and sexist? Do you know who investigated the incident and contacted the press? *I* did! I was only a young man myself. I was asked by the administration to be quiet, that the whole thing would go away. But I risked everything. I risked *tenure*."

He paused. Titters went up in the audience. I felt bad for my friend.

But my heart sank as Meyer looked straight at me. He beckoned to me to join him. I shrank back into the audience. That didn't stop him. He spoke my name: "Dr. Oliver Harding remembers this. We were both in the same cohort. He will vouch for me."

Thankfully, no one wanted to hear another word about that story from the grave of injustices past. The mob had listened to him more out of the ecstasy of witnessing a train wreck. Unbeknownst to Meyer, in the past four minutes since he began to speak, his meltdown had been recorded on cellphone cameras and tweeted out with the hashtag #ImNotRacistBecause.

Someone stood up from the floor in the front row and reached for the mic. Meyer dodged the hand. I could see Meyer standing there, beads of sweat on a bald head where thirty years ago had been a full crop and a keener pulse for reading a room. He couldn't see me. He looked over at the Dean, who quickly glanced away. It was a thing that would keep you up at night, the look on the face of man who believes he is leading the charge but turns around to find the troops behind him gone. Truly the thing of nightmares, the broadcast breath of a man who learns he's been abandoned mid-battle.

He didn't go down without a fight, though. He said, "To my faculty colleagues in this room—you could be next." He was looking right at me.

It would have been what the kids these days call a mic drop, except that the mic was wrested out of Meyer's hands, and he and his life's work were instantly rendered irrelevant.

Let them have this moment. It's no movement, this. The tiniest of ripples of manufactured discontent have no real enemy, no oppressor to speak of. All around these people are, indeed, their benefactors. Here we are, educating them with nary an ounce of discrimination or prejudice. They will tire of it, these screen-eyed rebels, when they realize there is no whiteness to study, at least none that is whole or imbued with any voice, let alone violence.

For, look now, the white voice in service of color. The student who had snatched the mic from poor Meyer was young Cunningham. I thought he was going to speak, but no, he gestured at a Black girl. Essence. She went up to the mic and said a few things I can't recall now, I was so troubled by what had happened with Meyer. After a bit, she gestured for Ruhaba to speak.

Ruhaba stepped up to the mic and said: "I request the press

not to take my pictures. I am stating things here only for consideration of those associated with this university. My comments or any oblique mention of them will not be published or broadcast. Students—I say this with love. I do not believe in calling out people as racist and leaving it at that. I believe in calling out institutions and structures. We are part of a racist institution."

Hoots and cheers went up in the office of the once formidable Dean Walter Cummings. I watched Ruhaba as she spoke. Ungrateful. Unreachable.

Unforgettable.

CHAPTER TWELVE

A Fortunate Man

I suppose I am a fortunate man. Sometimes, when I feel like all is lost, things turn around, look up, sort themselves out. Perhaps fortune has nothing to do with it. Perhaps I have worked my way to this fortune. Stepped in, stepped up, stepped to it. Fortune favors the bold and all.

I had spent the rest of the day wondering whether I had lost Ruhaba now, given that we were on opposite sides of the picket line. I had to endure Meyer spewing all over my office. He asked if I would coauthor an op-ed with him on the nature of racism. I tried to talk him out of it. He looked injured, so I gave him some talking points, some guidance. I said I did not want coauthorship, that he could go it alone. I didn't tell him I was certain no one would publish it. I excused myself and walked him in a convivial fashion out of my office because I had to lend an ear to the Dean, edit his statement to the press, which came to me after a round of edits from the woman at University Counsel. Her grammar would have been the last straw for me, but there was another straw waiting.

Someone had slashed my tires in the faculty parking lot. It was late in the evening and the light was dim, so I didn't notice until I tried to back the car out. A rage I hadn't felt in years tried to form in the ashen gray cells in my head. If my brain had been on a scan, it might have shown a purple haze light up and then fizzle out. I stood there, leaning against my car, wondering whether to first call Public Safety and lodge a complaint or call AAA roadside service (ah, but my membership had lapsed) or to finally download the Uber app on my phone. These choices, these solutions of modern life, crowd out the purple hazes of rage and turn us into white sheep.

A car drove past me, stopped, reversed, and a window rolled down. It was Ruhaba.

"Goodness," she said, squinting in the dark past me at the tires of my car. "That's a shame."

I shrugged. I didn't know whether she was being sympathetic or sarcastic. It didn't matter. She looked beautiful, end-of-a-long-day beautiful, her makeup gone a bit adrift as if she'd been in a tussle under the sheets rather than leading a pedantic protest.

She pulled into the spot next to mine and got out of her car. "What do you want to do?" she asked.

Make wild love to you. "Call an Uber," I said instead.

She shook her head. "May I offer you a ride?"

I let my surprise show on my face.

"I know, I know. You're a CAT and I'm a mouse," she said.

Baby, you have no idea. "Ah, no, no," I said. "No such thing. The university has a way of pitting us poor faculty folk against each other," I said. "We have a fable in the Western world about the monkey getting the cat to burn its hand in doing the monkey's bidding."

She smiled. "In the Western world, huh? You can narrate it to me as I drive. Jump in," she said. And then, she paused and slapped her hand on her forehead.

My heart fell.

"I forgot. I have to go to the grocery store. And then I have to pick Adil up from the movie theater. I had him go to a movie so I could . . . you know . . . all the things that happened today."

"Ah," I said, shuffling my feet now, stepping back from her car.

Then, I added, "Actually, I don't mind accompanying you on those stops. I have to pick some eggs up myself."

"Oh, good. That's perfect, then. Hop in."

Over my years with women, I had become attuned to the many signs they give off, overt or covert, of interest. Ruhaba wasn't one of those who asks you to drop something off at home and then lets you see her in a bathrobe. Her "reveals" weren't intimate to her alone but involved the boy. Her advances left me dizzy not so much with expectation but with wonder at whether they were advances at all. So, why was I here, in her car, like a lost little boy in an adult's care?

Will she ask me to vote in favor of the protest demands?

She drove in silence for a while. KUOW was broadcasting the day's local news on her car radio. I was relieved when the first segment ended without any mention of the campus protests. I thought I sensed her relief, too.

I asked how the boy was feeling. He's well, she said.

I tried again. I asked about his leg and watched her closely to see if she'd forgotten. She hadn't. She had given him a warm compress and a hot water bag last night, she said. And ibuprofen. He'd awoken this morning before her and slipped out to go walk Edgar. The mention of my dog's name on her lips. The casual leash between her world and mine. Could it be stronger than the clash at the college? Or the clash of civilizations?

She navigated the late evening traffic to Whole Foods and we remarked on what one remarks on now in Seattle in that quarter of the city—everything was crowded, these Amazon tech wizards had invaded the town with their hypermillennial desires. Here was the Tesla showroom, there the hipster pizza, here the Whole Foods, there the craft brewery, all of it dizzying, controlled, geniused. An electric madness darted within the aesthetic sameness of the gleaming glass buildings around us.

Ruhaba's homespun academic gaze out the windshield made her more familiar to me than foreign. Her faint perfume mixed in with her leftist-liberal day-long sweat, which in turn mixed in with old-car-smell, all of them offered up together a warm protective blanket around me as we rode through this planet of cloud-computing whiz kids.

So many things happened on that short ride and that brief stop. Or was it that I was alert to everything, straining into each moment as if to penetrate it or have it pierce me in turn?

I will mention just two of those many things. The first one happened as we walked past the cashier line at Whole Foods, on our way to the produce section. A little girl shrieked, "Look, Mommy! A Muslim!"

Ruhaba and I glanced at the little girl. She was pointing at Ruhaba's headscarf. Her mother looked stricken. She pulled her girl's pointing hand roughly down and at first tried to shrink back into the anonymity of the line of waiting customers. But those in line were now looking at her, at her little girl, then at Ruhaba.

The woman realized that a swamp of expectation had gurgled up around her. She stepped out of the line toward Ruhaba and said: "I'm so sorry. She should not have shouted that. It was so rude. I had no idea . . ."

Ruhaba waved her hand vigorously at the woman and smiled broadly. For good measure, she stepped up to the little girl, who was now hiding behind her mother's legs. Ruhaba crouched down to the girl's level and put out her hand. "Yes," she said. "I am a Muslim. You are a smart girl!"

The girl shrank farther back. Nothing in her young life, orchestrated and curated by the adults in it, even in a rapidly diversifying Seattle, had prepared her for a *close* encounter with A Muslim. Perhaps she had never imagined that a Muslim spoke. Here was this apparition, separated as a Muslim by a scarf, similar to a walking, talking woman by a crouch and a strong-jawed smile.

The mother yanked the little girl's hand, the one that had been used for pointing, and stretched it out toward the Muslim hand. Someone took a picture.

Ruhaba stood up like a bolt of universal lightning. "Please," she said into the crowd of watching people. "No photos. Definitely no posts. Give a Muslim woman some privacy?"

The crowd shuffled, some people nodded, others hastily put their phones away.

Ruhaba waved at the little girl or, rather, at her mother, because the girl was now stretching her body away from her mother's grasp, toward her next exhibit, a puppy.

Perhaps that was the first moment in which I felt the jab of an invisible elbow in my chest. All those ridiculous things Kathryn had talked about. Was it possible that all this time, this *work* I was putting into Ruhaba wasn't merely in pursuit of skin upon skin? Was it the pursuit of something greater? Something one-big-greater?

Ruhaba's guileless moment with the snotty little girl followed up rapidly with her ramrod-straight request from the surround of strangers. One never knew where one stood with her. Perhaps that's why I didn't just want to sleep with her. I realized that I wanted to *walk by her side.*

It's a frightening thing when a casual obsession turns deeper. Perhaps it's an emotion reserved for men like me. What do I mean? Well, let me explain. In my rummaging around in news stories this afternoon when I took a break from writing all this, I saw that same photograph of Ruhaba from the grocery store, the one she'd forbidden. That pure gesture, that candid moment of Ruhaba's spontaneous handshake has today gone viral on social media. And I felt the same sensation I felt that day—like an invisible elbow daggered its way so deep in my heart. I saw the photograph today and thought I would shatter the screen of my computer and send a howling message to the "Alan Frye" who posted the picture. Some Alan Fucking Frye, standing in line with his goji berries at Whole Foods that day, had decided this morning that Muslim or not, request or no request, Ruhaba's image was now fair game for bringing some liking and sharing and angry emojis into his sorry little life. He had blurred out the faces of the little girl and her mother. But all bets were off when a Muslim stepped from the grocery line into the headlines. My Ruhaba's beautiful head, scarfed, smiling at the girl, now haunts me via the scumbaggery of social media strangers.

The second thing that happened that evening is even more important to this story. It wasn't an episode—with a beginning, a middle, and an end—like the episode with the little girl. It was an unremarkable encounter that left me oddly bereft.

Ruhaba pulled into the pick-up zone of AMC Pacific Place Theater, and the boy bounded toward the car. He beamed when he saw me. He put his hand up for a high-five. I glanced at Ruhaba and she looked pleased. My heart soared.

I offered to jump out of the front passenger seat into the back. Among the many things I turn over in my head as things I shouldn't have done, this is one.

Ruhaba nodded at my offer and suddenly I was in the back, with barely a view of the side of her face. The boy told me he had walked Edgar before heading to the movies. I asked him how he was feeling. I didn't speak specifically of his leg, and I thought I saw some relief on his face. He asked about what happened at the university that had brought the bounty of a movie his way. Ruhaba gave him a quick update. Sensing her discomfort in talking about it around me, I jumped in to change the subject.

"Which film did you see?" I asked the boy.

"The new Jack Reacher movie," he said. "It was awesome."

Well, that was the end of that. There was nothing to be said about Tom Cruise these days that hadn't already been said.

Apparently, I was wrong. There was a lot to be said about Tom Cruise and Jack Reacher, and the boy then told us the entire plot.

Ruhaba smiled and asked questions through it all. When there was a lull, she said to the boy, "I forgot to tell you. Your mother called last night to say that you are to discontinue your online classes with Noor Academy for now."

"Yes!" said the boy, pumping his fist.

Ruhaba laughed. "Do I want to know what Noor Academy is?" she said.

"You don't know Noor Academy?" he asked, looking at her with wide eyes. "If you had children you would know."

Ruhaba glanced at him. I peered at her from my space in the shadows. Had the boy hurt her feelings? Did she nurse regrets at not having had a child yet? Did she often tense at sentences that began with "If you had children"? But the boy was looking at the road in front of him, grinning and shaking his head. Ruhaba half-smiled now. She seemed to have decided that his remark was not any sort of jab. It did seem rather matter-of-fact.

"Tell me about this Noor Academy," Ruhaba said. "I take it you didn't enjoy the lessons."

"Not at all one bit. You are kidding? Two times a week, Naeema and I had to go online for thirty minutes and we learn the Koran from these guys in Pakistan. Naeema had a lady tutor and all. They gave my mom a discount for two kids, so then instead of thirty euros each, it was twenty-five euros. If my mom just gave me that money, I would be a good Muslim forever."

Ruhaba laughed. I had heard her laugh before, but this sound was something entirely different in its levity, its tumble and its flight. This child made her laugh like a girl.

She laughed like she had forgotten I was in the backseat. They were speaking of the Koran and Pakistan and mullahs like I didn't exist.

No, not like I didn't exist. Something else. Like their words need not be interpreted for my benefit. That I either understood or I was irrelevant.

"Those people are so entrepreneurs," Adil said.

"Entrepreneurial," Ruhaba said.

"Yes. So, it's this online thing based in Pakistan. They teach a basic course to learn to recite the holy Koran with proper tajweed rules. You know tajweed rules, Khala?"

Ruhaba nodded, still smiling.

"Anyway, we get on Skype, we use screen-sharing software, and then we learn both tafseer and hifz."

"Which one do you prefer?" she asked.

"Tafseer, of course. You know for that it has stories and interpretation. Understanding the Koran is much more fun than making it into memory . . . memorizing. No?"

Ruhaba shrugged.

They fell silent. After a few minutes, the boy said, "Actually, I think if you had kids, you would not teach them the Koran." He was watching her.

Ruhaba looked at him and shrugged again. Then, as if deciding she owed him something without taking something away from her sister, she said, "Perhaps having children makes you want to deepen your roots. So, I may feel today like I would not raise my children to be Muslim, but who knows? If I had had children . . ."

The boy nodded.

"Moving away from home does that too, right?" she said.

"How?"

"We start to see home from far away and we start to either hate the things that happened there or love them, or both. I long for the food and the songs—the phirni, the jalebi, Noor Jehan. So I cook in all the traditional ways and play my old songs over and over, as if stuck in a time warp. Your mother and father probably want to give you all those gifts from home. It's a common phenomenon."

"But they also hold on to the . . . bad stuff. You are not holding on like that."

"What bad stuff?" she said. Then, as if suddenly remembering me, she jerked around to look at me in the backseat. I smiled at her, quickly.

The boy was already speaking: "They say Naeema and I must only marry Pakistanis. Not just other Muslims, but other Pakistani Muslims."

Ruhaba kept her eyes on the road. Was she suddenly wary of my presence? Had I turned relevant again? Or was she simply imagining the weddings of these children—Adil and Naeema—imagining herself there, the unmarried aunt, stepping into a freakish twilight zone of food she loved, with everyone speaking in a mix of world accents but playing with their children's lives like marrying off their dolls?

"What do you feel about that?" she asked Adil.

"I think it's gross," Adil said. "They keep pushing Naeema to our cousin Fawad. Already! Our cousin!"

"And what if Naeema . . ." Ruhaba stopped herself. She seemed wary of the boy now, of perhaps overstepping the fault lines of relationships embedded by her sister and brother-in-law, in which Ruhaba would not simply be "the cool aunt" but the infidel.

My Ruhaba, in her solitary world, seemed to be lost in her thoughts of a greater unknown. Whatever was going on in that French town of Toulouse, with a mother insisting on wearing a headscarf as political protest or private oppression, it seemed, to me, entirely different from what Ruhaba was doing with her own scarf over her head. This piece of fabric was a means to an end, it wasn't the end in itself. Ruhaba's sister was fighting a radical fight of some sort with those Europeans and their secular ways, but she was pushing outward while still chained to all that was swampy, profoundly swampy, underneath and around her. Yes, push against the French, but first find your way among them and out of the Islam that will claim you as its hero while turning you into its slave.

I was trying to think Ruhaba's thoughts. But she seemed to have forgotten again that I was sitting barely inches away from her.

"Why do you wear a hijab, Khala Ruhaba?"

The boy's question startled both of us. Perhaps he was emboldened in asking her because I was present. Perhaps our conversation at the hike had brought this up and pulled it front and center for him. Perhaps he wanted her to answer the question in front of me so as to seem less foreign to me, for her to seem more American. Or, perhaps, I was simply, irrelevantly, privy to a conversation in the universal phenomenon of teenagers speaking to adults about the deepest things in the passenger seats of cars, when no eye contact was required.

But she didn't answer him. She didn't dismiss him either. She said: "Maybe I'll tell you all about the mystery behind my hijab some other day. But for now, I want to tell you that I love the way you address me. Khala. I have never heard the beauty in that word in all my years of addressing my own khalas. But I think it's also so pretty because your accent is so cute! A French boy saying 'Khala' seems to . . . seems to create less distance between a nephew and his khala, no? And when you say 'Ruhaba' with your French accent, it makes my name sound even more open."

She grinned at him. "Am I embarrassing you?"

"No," he said, frankly. "Your name means 'open,' no? Ammi told me."

"Open. Expanding."

I was disappointed that she wouldn't speak of her hijab. And then, these sounds between them, drawn from some old world but turned distinct, untarnished, in their new speech, how much it all pushed me away. And yet, like some sorry liberal fool, I strained my ear and craned my neck, a soggy old pretzel, I, a days-old pretzel-man forgotten in the backseat, who would later Google these sounds and names to taste the salt and sugar of things that didn't feel my tongue.

They went on that way for a while, breaking their banter every now and then to include me, out of politeness. How did Edgar sleep after his trauma, the boy asked. And how did *you* sleep, I asked in return. He said he was fine, he had a good story to tell his friends back home. He told me his aunt had given him a hot water bottle to comfort his leg at night. She clicked her tongue in a way she sometimes did, a little sound of protest against needless praise. They went back to talking to each other, about some musician now. Ruhaba told the boy he knew nothing about Nusrat so he should stop pretending. He challenged her. She rummaged through her playlist and turned on some music so cacophonic, I almost said something. I wondered at how they could like the sounds—a man with a raspy voice howling over tinny musical instruments woven in with orchestral grandeur. The boy began to sing along in what I suppose was Urdu. Ruhaba laughed in surprise. In joy.

I watched the side of her face as she looked at him. At one point, she threw a glance at me in the back, as if expecting me to have a look that mirrored hers in wonder.

Despite my status of a negligible speck, this single hour in her domain had done more to quicken my pulse than any other company I had kept in years. Nothing was boring in Ruhaba's world. Nothing was irrelevant. I possessed a weary knowledge of established narrative and literature. Ruhaba possessed the currency of a story taking shape. The scale of her hours was in stark contrast to the shrinkage of my days. She was loved by her students and feared by America, and she walked in the knowing of this. She was othered, tokenized, pathologized, yes, but never gripped in anything resembling my own ocean of ennui.

Never invisible.

Something made me ask Ruhaba to pull up and drop me off at LifeFloat. Perhaps because it was my sudden urge for relief from the day, from the slash of words and slash of tires. Perhaps it was because I wanted her to know of a little eccentricity of mine, turn myself exotic. Perhaps it was simply because we were in the neighborhood. I would still have to Uber it home, but it seemed worth it.

Sure enough, when Ruhaba pulled up outside LifeFloat and I got out, she peered at me from behind her wheel, squinted at the door to the business, and laughed. "You pay good money for this?" she asked.

She didn't look mean-spirited. She was teasing me. I warmed to it.

"Yes, I'm afraid I do," I said. "Would Adil and you like to try it? Come on in. Join me!"

Adil started to get out of the car, but Ruhaba put a hand on his shoulder and pulled him back in. "Perhaps another time," she said. "It's been a long day. And *my* place to drown myself is my bed." She smiled.

I wanted to say something about not drowning but floating. But then, she clicked her fingers and said, "This floating thing reminds of a verse by an Urdu poet. His name is Mirza Ghalib. It goes, *Duboya mujhko honay ne . . . Na hotaa main toh kya hotaa*."

For a moment, it was as if she'd disappeared into herself even though she was smiling and looking at me, leaning over and past the boy, her neck crouched so she could speak to me. Then, realizing I had no idea what she'd said, she said a wordless "Oh" and then, "Let me translate: *Being* has sunk me . . . If I hadn't been, what *would* be?"

She waved at me and drove off. I stood there, watching the car pull away. When she stopped at the stop sign, I saw her glance at me through the rearview mirror.

And she hadn't asked me for my vote.

I clasped my satchel and my single grocery bag that carried a carton of six eggs, and entered LifeFloat. When I laid my body in the salt water, I imagined Ruhaba's bed.

What would be? *If I hadn't been me, would I be with her?*

I wanted to float into the pure pleasure of her imagined presence with me here, with me there, but instead, another question came crowding into my head, unformed, then half-formed, then unformed again. It was the boy, on the mountain, asking a question. Then it turned into an image and voice from a car window just before its driver plunged it into a crevasse so wide and deep that they'd never hit the ground. I fought against that image, tried to return to Ruhaba's bed. In the end, I gave up. I kept alert and restless in the brine, letting crusts of salt form on my belly as I made a mental note to send an email to Public Safety as soon as I got home, to complain about my slashed tires.

CHAPTER THIRTEEN

Un-American

To: Johnson, Essence
From: Khan, Ruhaba

Dear Essence,
Good news! Our paper has been accepted in the *Journal of Criminal Law, Criminology, and Police Science*.

We did it! YOU did it! Thank you for the impeccable research assistance. I want you to have first authorship on this article, OK? Apart from the fact that you totally deserve it, it will boost your grad school application. We'll discuss that when we meet.

Would you like to join me and Adil for a celebration? My treat, of course. You pick a restaurant. Pick a fancy place. What's somewhere that we can show off to Adil so he will think Seattle is the best place on the planet?
Cheers,
Dr. Khan

I awoke this morning to rapid knocks on my door. I had fallen asleep writing at my desk. I startled from sleep and was stunned to see I had slept almost seven hours, just slumped at my desk. I had drooled onto the pages of my journal. My back ached as I stood up. I was cold and I needed to piss even more badly than Edgar did.

I hurried to open the door to a cold draft and some icy looks from the federal agents. What were they doing here? Wasn't it a Sunday? Didn't I get an extra hour from daylight savings? But I will write now about this conversation that just transpired with them.

The federal agents have found my porn. I'm surprised it took them this long.

I have been waiting for it. They have been poring over my work and home computers. Yes, I shouldn't have looked up porn at work. But that's not what they wanted to talk about. And they didn't reveal this "finding" of theirs right away. They said they worked Sundays, that they were here for anything else I'd like to share with them, and then, in the middle of my telling them all the insistent questions Adil asked of his aunt and her hijab that night in the car, Sarah Kupersmith slipped in, "We'd like to clarify the nature of your relationship with Ruhaba Khan. We came across some . . . images on your computer."

I was startled to hear her address me after these past few days of Ray Waters Jr. doing all the talking.

"Yes," I said. "I know what you are referring to."

"We should begin by saying that human sexuality is a complex thing," Ray Waters Jr. said.

I fixed a blank stare on him.

"We don't act on all our fantasies," he said. I wondered how much more he would elaborate until it was clear that I am entirely off the hook even before the questions are posed to me. Clearly, this line of questioning had been pressed on by his female associate.

I may be a contributor to the multimillion-dollar Muslim Women porn industry that blossomed after 9/11, but I was certainly not a prime customer. And this is not only because I cannot afford the premium stuff on an English professor's salary. No, it's because I simply do not enjoy the bulk of that genre—hijabi porn.

I told the detectives this. Yes, I was attracted to the Muslim woman—she was a professor and my colleague, an attractive woman who just happened to be a hijabi Muslim. Yes, I had imagined her naked, imagined her in bed with me, searched for women of her color and her set of eyes in images online, imagined her to be the woman in the videos I watched, but I never meant to act on any of it.

I lost my marriage owing to my past indiscretions, I said to the man. I lost custody of my daughter. I have been done with inappropriate relations—well, relationships at work, relationships with an unequal power dynamic—for some years now.

He nodded vigorously and took notes. Why had the agents reversed their roles for this interview?

Sarah Kupersmith cleared her throat and said, "Since you bring up the matter of your ex-wife and daughter . . ."

I stared at her.

"We spoke to them," she said.

The color might have drained from my face, because Ray Waters Jr. jumped in with, "Just a routine thing we do, Professor Harding. We fan out far and wide."

Sarah Kupersmith continued, "Your ex-wife—Mrs. Emily Decker now—spoke of an incident of violence toward her by you. Sexual violence."

"What does this have to do with . . ." my voice fell away.

"Emily and your daughter felt we should inquire into your relationship with Dr. Ruhaba Khan."

"My daughter? Kathryn said that? She was present when you . . ."

"Yes, she was. Your daughter asked to be present when we met your ex-wife and her current husband. Your daughter seems to have known about the incident of sexual violence. She seemed to urge her mother to talk to us about it."

We were standing in my study. I sat down at my desk. The agents remained standing.

"That was so many years ago. It was nothing. A bit of rough role-play. If it had been something more, Emily would have filed something with the police. Gotten a restraining order. Yes?"

Sarah Kupersmith stayed silent for a moment.

"These sexual games from the past," I said, "these private moments from our bedrooms, they have all been given a new glare from the lens of our current times. Now we're outraged about everything. If you go looking into every bedroom, soon we'll have a witch hunt!"

Ray Waters Jr. put a hand on Sarah Kupersmith's forearm. She stepped back.

He said, "We take the statements of ex-wives with a grain of salt. And you're right, there was no complaint or restraining order. We dropped that line of inquiry. As I said, we have to follow all leads. You are not under suspicion of any sort, Professor. You have been very helpful."

He asked if he could have a cup of coffee. I offered to make him one. The three of us walked into my kitchen. The conversation shifted to the weather. The election—not the candidates but the voter turnout expected in Washington state. Neutral subjects. Dogs.

As we leaned against my kitchen counter and sipped on weak coffee, Ray Waters Jr. asked me if I wanted to say anything else of relevance to my relationship with Ruhaba and the porn they found.

"I would like to point out one thing," I said. "I do not view pornography that involves women with hijab. I find that to be demeaning. It's also un-American."

"Could you elaborate?" he said.

Of course, I didn't tell him that in all my fantasies, Ruhaba's hijab is the first thing that comes off. I have spent the better part of my lust imagining the sweep of her hair alone. But the federal agent before me did not need such details.

"Most American men who pay for porn featuring Arab women want to imagine them in scenes that demean these women. It's repugnant. She's begging forgiveness for her community. She's begging a policeman to let her go. She's begging a visa officer to let her in. Some of these women are not even Muslim. Almost all of those who are Muslim are Arab. I could not find Ru . . . I could not find Dr. Khan in those images."

He nodded. The idiot. He had no idea what I was talking about. He can't tell the difference between an Arab woman or a

Pakistani. He does not know of the precise shifts in beauty, in the contours of distances. Mountain ranges move the size of chin. Rivers and seas lend lashes on the eyelid, valleys set into place the shyest of overbites.

"The vile Muslim porn videos—and you won't find those on my list—force the woman to keep her hijab on all through the act. If you know what I mean. To put it crudely, the hijab often is the receptacle for the ejaculate."

I let him swallow that. I watched as imagined images flickered before Sarah Kupersmith's eyes. She looked away from me and at her colleague. Seeing that he was no longer taking notes, she took out her own note pad and scribbled something into it.

I said, "Perhaps men who pay for such porn are imagining revenge upon women from the Muslim world. Perhaps they are just sick. Perhaps they aren't patriots. Please don't count me among any of them."

The man looked back at me and watched me for a few long seconds. I could see that he was looking for my custom irony. I looked back at him, dead sincere.

"There you have it. I was attracted to her. Make of that what you will. She was not attracted to me. Never laid a hand on her."

"Well," he said. "Did you know anything about who she did sleep with?"

"No," I lied, after the appropriate half of a second. "And I don't believe that's any of my business. But if you must understand that complex woman, here's something that she said to me once—'Morality is like a river. And no man ever steps in the same river twice.' Make of that what you will."

They left. I won't think more about them for now. I will

return to the story. I must shake off their terrible intrusion upon my account here.

The morning after the campus protests and the ride in Ruhaba's car and my gradual returning to a state of being no one but me, I found myself longing for a state of being nowhere and nobody else. Few people I know had the riches I had acquired, fewer the delicious temperament of solitude, and fewer still the lush inner life to which I had limitless access any time I walked into this space called my home. And yet—what was it—social conditioning, perhaps, that led me outside, outward, in a mindless series of nods and smiles and synchronizing of calendars with the cretins of my world? Was their need for emotional comingling such a compelling quagmire that I eventually slipped? Was their fear of anything but cohabitation—vulgar cohabitation—so unquestioned, that I fell in step? What was I doing?

The nadir between their sense of human longing and my own had been the time when I had let them persuade me to go to therapy. The "them" at the time had been Emily. I had let her in, for years, suspecting she would be one of mine, but she had stayed one of them, year after damned year. It was likely that even through the time we met in college, and at that time I had felt the strange stirrings of attachment of a kind I had sworn I was incapable of, she had been sizing me up for a therapist's couch. And now, it would seem she had poisoned Kathryn against me and tried to throw me under the scrutiny of the FBI!

One may as well think about Emily now.

Emily was the prettiest girl in college, and I had not had the nerve even to imagine setting my eyes on the sweetest peak of pink nipple on the warmest swell of breast in all of Wisconsin. But there she'd been, smiling at me through the thinnest, wettest film of lip gloss after a math class we were both required to take. Over pizza in 1984, she asked me the kind of questions I could deftly avoid on a date in this century but back then just seemed like the quickest way to get to bang her in her dorm room while her roommate giggled outside.

If you could meet your father today, what would you say to him? Will your mother think I'm pretty? Why don't you like Byron; okay, I'll hate Byron, too. Why do I feel so safe with you?

Emily was the one who had convinced me I was handsome. Look, she'd say, that girl is eyeing you right now, how can't you see it? Look, Prof. Cynthia Marshall was leaning over your paper so you could examine her cleavage. After sex, Emily always wanted to know more about my boyhood. Her own upbringing was quite unlike mine. She was raised in an incorrigibly happy, WASP-y family in Massachusetts.

She'd fill her eyes up with tears and let them flow down her cheeks as she goaded me to talk about my mother and father, but I really had too few stories to share about them. They were just plain old middle-class folks, and I'm loath to write about them even now. It would annoy me when Emily asked for photographs of them and had me find a dusty old shoebox under my dorm room bed so she could pore over pictures of my family and our home in Queens. She was endlessly drawn to the stories that I had buried away. She liked to ask questions like whether my parents ever flirted with one another. They didn't.

The singular memory from my childhood that I shared with her was one that needn't have stayed with me at all. It was of my father sitting at the kitchen table, reading the newspapers, on the morning after my tenth birthday party. He had been working late at his job in middle management at IBM and hadn't made it home on time. He smiled at me from the top of his newspaper and motioned to me to step up to him. He ruffled the hair of my head.

"Are you happy to be nine?" he said.

"I'm . . ."

"Good. You're such a big boy now."

Emily held me tight when I recounted this inane story and told me she was the space in which I could come to cry. I told her I didn't want to cry, but I held her hard. In later years, Emily told me I needed to raise the matter of my parents with our marriage counselor. What matter with my parents, I'd asked. Their lack of emotional expression, she said. That I was an only child in a neighborhood with families of three and four children per household. I refused to talk about these pointless things with the therapist. She told the therapist about them anyway. I didn't say a word, not even when she got the details wrong. "On his ninth birthday, his father . . ."

What would Emily have said about my affinity for these Muslim people now? In the early years, she would have turned her face up to me with adoration, loved me for extending myself. In the later years, she would have mocked me. She would have brought up some nonsense about my parents leaving me seeking love from impossible places. She would have said something similarly unimaginative about my outgrowing easy white girls for repressed brown harem stock. Emily and her fine group of friends who signed petitions for letting Syrian refugees into America or letting Black teens into pool parties in white homes in Texas used such imagery to hold up a mirror to men like me. Then, after their virtue-signaling shares on social media, they'd go back to summering in Martha's Vineyard or "recovering from the toxic divisions in America" with rituals of self-care at yoga retreats in Mexico. The use of filters in their photographs made them flawless; the use of irony in their updates made them faultless.

CHAPTER FOURTEEN

Before All Hell Breaks Loose

To: Harding, Oliver
From: Khan, Ruhaba

Dear Ollie,
Here's a link to that poem I was referring to the other night. Adil asked me more questions about it, and I'm so happy he loves it. I thought you might enjoy it, too. Not a very good translation, but as a literature professor, perhaps you are able to read beyond translations?

Would you like to join me and Adil and a student or two on a walk one of these days? Perhaps sometime before the big vote, before all hell breaks loose?
Warmly,
Ruhaba

A couple of days after the protests on campus, contrary to my predictions, *The Wall Street Journal* published that op-ed David Meyer had written. As one would have predicted, it was shared widely across campus.

There was a punch in the op-ed for everyone. If anyone would have asked me, I would have said that I had not imagined that Meyer could have summoned such chutzpah overnight.

We are living in an age of reaction masquerading as an age of reform, he said.

Other sentences that drew much sharing on social media:

"Offices such as that of 'Multicultural Solidarity' have been created to make us look busy doing the good work of diversity and inclusion. But the insane start to run the asylum. To be sure, as a lifelong learner, I embrace the cadence of a word like heteropatriarchy. But I do not embrace the drumbeats of feral mobs.

"At an institution of learning, when last I checked, there was work to be done. The work of learning. The work of challenging one another. The work of listening, of discourse and debate. Perhaps if one abandoned all these ideals, there would still be the work of studying, taking exams, and graduating. Have we lost focus on that? Have we entirely lost our minds?

"I am in the crosshairs today for using the word 'racist' on those we should consider 'precious.' But I warn my fellow academics, and, to be sure, anyone who speaks an uncolored truth to power—You could be next.

"They are asking white students to leave campus as an act of solidarity. Nobody should be asked to leave campus. I call that being racist, yes, but I mostly call that being absent. I will mark you as such. Black or white."

Barely had I picked up my car from the auto shop early that morning (the new tires set me back $450 . . . that's $450 I would not be donating to the Black Student Union, the Muslim Student Association, or the Office of Multicultural Solidarity), when a text alert went off on my phone. I hoped it was Ruhaba. But, then, I had begun to have that hope every time my phone buzzed.

It was, instead, something that threatened to place a chasm the size of hell between Ruhaba and me. It was an automated text that went out on the emergency alert system from campus: "Campus on lockdown following threat of shootings. The campus community is advised to stay away from the premises until further notice."

The threat had been posted on 4chan. A garbled voice had also placed a call to the main campus line and said that if white students were forced to leave campus on this "Day of Absence" thing, a shooter would be delighted to have a perfect aim at the feral herds of the monkeys and pigs left behind.

Jesus.

The next call I received was from Meyer. "*What have I done?*" he said.

I told him to pull himself together. Do not, under any circumstance, take on any blame. Repeat after me: "I am a thinker. I think and I write. The action of others is not my fault."

When I got home, I was surprised to find the boy sitting on the Adirondack chair on my porch. Had I forgotten to leave the key under the welcome mat?

Where was Ruhaba?

He had walked the dog, he said. But he was bored and didn't want to go home yet. "Khala Ruhaba has a huge group of students over at her house."

I sighed. "Plotting my erasure, I suppose."

The boy chuckled. "*You could be next,*" he said.

I punched him lightly on his arm. It was delightful, his quick wit. Not always easily on display, but charming when it found its way.

"So, you read the newspaper."

"How to avoid? Khala Ruhaba and the students, they are talking about how that newspaper article invited the shooting threat."

"Nonsense," I said.

I shouldn't have. The boy shrank back a bit from my doorstep.

"Crazy people will find something to instigate them," I said. "The shooting threat is not serious, you'll see. I wouldn't be surprised if it's actually coming from the protes . . ." I stopped myself in time.

"Didn't I tell you it was possible here also?" the boy said. "That first time we meet. When I talked about the campus shooters? I told you I was correct for to be scared of your campus."

He looked more sad than smug. This wasn't a "I told you so." It was a "This is what I was afraid of."

"Well, let's have a large breakfast," I said. "Do you like poached eggs?"

He took a while to get to it, but eventually, after nearly eating me out of home and hearth, the boy asked if he could see what Camille had been up to. I had forgotten about my promise to him.

There wasn't much on Camille's social media feed to slake the boy's thirst. A few pictures of the streets of Toulouse, teeming with tourists. An update about a music concert she'd enjoyed. A poem she'd written. He read that anxiously, looking for himself in her verse. But the poem was about a pigeon. He sat up straight, though, at a picture she'd posted of her favorite painting of the harlequin by Degas. He drew my eye to it. The image of the man filled my room with a dread that grew and grew around us. I wondered whether the boy felt it too, as we stared at the man's masked face and his wooden staff, all seeming more ominous in the shadow of threats from men with guns.

I asked the boy if he'd like to go shoot a gun with me. As soon as the words left my mouth, I realized how odd it was. I was accustomed to spontaneously inviting a colleague or a minion here and there to go to the shooting range with me, for sport. But here I was, transferring that sense of casual and rare camaraderie onto a wholly different creature. I was inviting a Muslim youth to learn to shoot a gun. Putting a gun in the hands of the Muslim World, someone like Meyer would say.

But he's the boy who rescued Edgar. He's not the Muslim World.

"What?" the boy said. "Certainly not. No shooting for me," he said, smiling a little at me as if to invite me to say I was joking.

"I want you to shed your fear of guns and gunmen," I said. I was sincere now and he could see it.

I continued, "If you ever encounter a man with a gun—and I believe that sooner or later we all will—you will know his next move. You will know about timing and reloading and whether he knows what he's doing. All this is important information. You will know his mind."

"I don't want to know his mind," the boy said.

"Then know your own. Or, know that a gun is a tool and you are its master. Trust me."

He protested for a little, said something about his aunt not allowing such a thing. We wouldn't tell her, I said. Yes, I broke all the rules of conduct with a minor. But it was perhaps my nonchalance about precisely those rules that drew the boy in. With all the adult world going crazy around him, with his little pigeon-girl homing away from him, carrying too few messages to his aching heart, with a crazy middle-aged white man pressuring him in ways not quite the same and not quite different from his peers at the mosque, the boy acquiesced and we were on our way.

CHAPTER FIFTEEN

The Stupidest Man in America

I shot them a message and the FBI wants to know why I took the boy to shoot guns. Of course they do. To ready myself for their questions as they circle back to my home for the second time today, and to rest my back still aching from sleeping at my desk, I went to LifeFloat this morning. I had a sensation, a half-waking vision of myself as a lobster, grotesque, sitting in a chair like a human, with a large, distended tongue, like no crustacean has, nor a human. This vision was the same and yet also different from one I'd had before. I am sitting at a cafe table with the boy, who soon turns into a lobster himself, but with a young lobster's body and so much of his boyish human face still visible in the lobster. I pin down his arms and start to eat that face. All the while, he keeps smiling at me with that flash of guileless query that his aunt and I would often see on his face.

For the first time in my floating experience, the pool started to close in around me until it was filled with two thrashing lobsters. The water turned warmer as if with blood, and I tasted metal on my lobster tongue. I found my head thrashing from side to side, and soon the high-density salt water was in my eyes and I was in the real world, with little clarity except that I ought to spritz my eyes with the dainty spray bottle of clean water provided on the edge of the flotation pool.

I left the tank and told the young woman at the reception desk that I wanted to cancel my membership. She rattled off a list of other options with reduced fees. I grunted at her and left.

I need to be two steps ahead of the federal investigators. What could they be looking for? Oh, Harding, look at you, old man with sweaters smelling of mothballs, trying to outsmart the police.

When they arrived, I wanted to tell them that I had had that feeling again, of someone hidden from my view, in a neighbor's yard and then crouched behind a car or lurking behind a tree near my home, watching me come and go. Edgar didn't bark. But I didn't have the occasion to tell the agents this. They wanted to know of the boy's demeanor that day when I took him shooting at the gun range—Did he ask to go? Why did I agree to take him? Why didn't I suspect anything? The subtext: What kind of doddering old fool wouldn't be suspicious of a Muslim teenager asking to learn how to shoot a gun?

It was my idea, I told them over and over again. All mine. But then they had questions about why I had the idea. Could I have been led to that idea?

Certainly not, I said. I offered to take him to the gun range because he was afraid of campus shootings.

Why not just take him to Public Safety and let them talk about their training and procedure in the event of an active shooter on campus?

Because the campus was closed due to a shooting threat, remember? Those guys were sort of busy. Also, I didn't think that teaching the boy about the new Run-Hide-Fight plan in the case of an active shooter would help him feel calmer. Certainly not the kind of calm that comes from being on the right side of a gun.

Look, I thought he needed to get over his fear of guns, I said to the federal agents. I told the boy that in the event that he was confronted with a gun, perhaps he should know what it could and couldn't do. Be at the better end of the tool. I don't suppose the federal agents appreciate my kind of thinking. It doesn't hold up with their belief that guns don't kill people; people kill people. Why show a boy that guns are safe things when he is afraid (claiming to be afraid, they reminded me) of the man behind the gun? Perhaps I believed I could show him his own image as boy with a gun so he wouldn't fear a mirror image of another boy with a gun.

They looked at me, today, as if I were the stupidest man in America. The stupidest man alive.

They rained question upon question. Did he look uncomfortable at the gun range?

No.

Did he seem to know his way around guns?

No.

Which gun did he choose?

A 9mm pistol. Mine.

They recorded everything. On a recorder and in written notes.

What other kind of guns did he look at?

Nothing I particularly recall, I lied at first. Then I remembered the CCTV footage that Northwest Armory always had on. The agents had probably already viewed it.

I sighed. I had pointed out an AR to him at the armory that was part of the gun range. I wanted his eyes to be a little less wide, a little less wild as he looked at the array. I wanted to show him that the people there were friendly, that they didn't see him—a Muslim youth—as different from the white geek behind us.

I told Ray Waters Jr. all he needs to know.

The twenty-something sales clerk at the counter had said, "How old are you, buddy?"

Adil responded nervously and the man said, "Well, I don't know a fifteen-year-old boy in the world who doesn't want to hold one of these." The boy held the AR and tried to look nonchalant. The young man pointed at a sign on the top corner of the store wall that said, "Aim your gun here, please," for safety. The boy held it there rigidly, studiously. He wanted to know whether AR stood for assault rifle.

"That's a name given by the media," the shop clerk said, unblinking. "AR actually stands for Armalite, the company that first manufactured these rifles."

"This is the one that shooters use . . . on campus shooting and movie theaters?" the boy asked.

The young man shot a quick glance at me and said, "Any such shootings, which happen all over the world by the way, have been done with different kinds of guns, even shotguns that are used for hunting ducks or even the 9mm pistols you guys are shooting in the range today."

I gave Ray Waters Jr. a lot of details and yet as little as I could get away with. I didn't tell him that the boy had looked afraid. I didn't tell him that the boy's hands shook when he held the AR. These people will never know that child the way I did.

Oh, the boy had listened to me with such interest about the guns. But I know there was not a bone in his body that meant large-scale harm, I told the federal agents. Yet again Ray Waters Jr. looked at me as if I am an idiot.

As we'd driven home from the shooting range, the boy didn't look me in the eye, and that might have been because I was driving, but he didn't look over when I looked at him, either. Am I reading too much into that, in hindsight? I won't let these investigators get under my skin.

I told the boy about the flag-waving divide in the gun-owning community between 9mm pistols and 45s, about the preference for power over quantity of rounds. Now I wonder—Had I gone into too much detail about how 9mms can carry twenty-one rounds in one magazine and it would be the gun of choice for a shooter in a situation where people were running panicked? You want more bullets in that kind of situation, I told him, although the 45 guys would say that power was more important since it could do more damage—kill a few humans versus injure several. What makes it higher on the next day's news—death or injury? Why did I tell him that? I wonder now. What macabre part in me wanted to either fuel his fear or put him in the mind of a madman? No, no, I had merely sought to exorcise fear by summoning up the worst.

Another thing I don't tell the investigators—the boy had

asked me what kind of human it would take for *me* to shoot to kill.

Who are you afraid of?

I'm not afraid, I told him. But perhaps you could ask me what kind of people I feel justify their being shot.

He shrugged. His shrug hid a squirm.

"Scum," I said. "Like ISIS. Burglars. Intruders on your property. Car thieves, rioters, graffiti artists, vandals. Freeloaders. People threatening to take your property and invade your way of life. People who want to take your place."

Graffiti artists? the boy repeated, incredulous. *That* time he really looked at me.

"Like Essence?" he asked.

"Who's Essence?"

"The student. The African American student of Khala Ruhaba? She is that one? Like of the organizers of the protests. Quiet girl. And amazing. You don't know Essence? She's my friend."

"Your friend?" I said.

"She shows me pictures of her graffiti art all over Seattle and I play for her my flute."

"I see. A budding romance there."

He stared at me. I looked at him and frowned in question.

"No. I love Camille," he said. "Remember?"

He'd flinched when he heard his first gunshot—well, at least his first gunshot on American soil—when he filled out the waiver in the store, which I had to sign for him, owing to his status as a minor. As we put on our protective eyewear and earmuffs, I found him looking through the corner of his eye at a pimply faced white boy, probably a year or two older than him, wearing a Temple University sweatshirt.

When I asked him what he was looking at, the boy whispered to me. I had to take my earmuff off to hear him. "That's the kind of boy of whom I have fear with a gun. Look at his bad haircut. Those campus shooters, they all have bad haircuts."

I should have responded with mirth, but I didn't. I told him the people here were friendly and of all races—white, Asian, Black, and the ethnically ambiguous. Everyone here was about peace.

The boy flinched when he took his own first shot. He had picked his target from the sheets offered—he didn't pick the picture of a zombie threatening to eat a big-breasted blond woman, nor a figure of humans' "vital organs," but "perpetrator," a man in a hoodie, not dark-skinned, not racially profiled, just urban-looking and menacing, in every culture.

He'd listened carefully to my instructions on how to load the magazine, keep his finger off the trigger, keep a bend in his knee and his shoulders hunched forward. Relax. Put the gun down on the table in front of you, point it away, never anywhere but away from all humans. On his first shot, the boy was startled by the shell that sprang back and grazed his ear. Still, in spite of being shaken, he instinctively followed my instructions and put the gun down, facing away, before rubbing his ear. He shot twice and then put the gun down and said he was done.

Because the FBI will probably soon ask for my iPhone as well, I had to tell them about the cellphone video I took of the boy shooting his first gun. I had meant to delete it from my video library but had forgotten.

They want the video. Dear God. I expect to see it on the news tomorrow. I hope people see the boy's laughter for what it was—nervousness. I fear they will see it as sinister.

CHAPTER SIXTEEN

You Said You Would Dance

We never told Ruhaba about that excursion to the gun range.

Why didn't I tell her? Because, when I dropped the boy home after the shooting range, she told me the federal agents had come calling again. They had made inquiries about whether the boy went to campus. She had said No. They asked whether she knew anything about the threats to the university. She said No, that she was on the other side, working to protect the threatened. They had seemed satisfied by the responses to the threat but also looked disapproving about her activities. Then, a bunch of sweet-faced white students had arrived, to make posters. The FBI agents waved at them and left.

Ruhaba looked shrunken, drawn, like someone had taken the wind out of her sails. She lived in America on a green card, she said. What was she willing to risk for the sake of a student revolution? Was her work threatening her nephew's world?, she wondered, standing there at the door. I decided this was not a good time to tell her that the boy had been at a shooting range while the FBI inquired about him with her. She would have driven me out of her life.

In any case, she didn't seem to have noticed that the boy had been gone awhile. I felt sorry for him and for myself. Was she so much of a woman leading a revolution (that, frankly, would go nowhere) that she could never be a woman who sat in waiting for a man?

It all didn't seem to bother the boy. He breezed past her into the house.

I turned around to leave, but she said, "Ollie . . . would you like to come in?"

I had promised David Meyer that I would meet him to craft a response to the deluge of jeers and threats he had received after the op-ed and the shooting threats. He was probably buried under interview requests by now. Well, he was a big boy. He could manage this on his own. Or he could go shoot himself. He'd already shot himself in the foot. A bullet to the brain wouldn't be a bad idea now that the remainder of his academic career was fucked.

"I'd love to," I said, crinkling my eyes at Ruhaba. "If you don't think it's suicide, with you building my guillotine and all."

She managed a laugh. That was the first note of music I had heard in a long time.

She threw her front door wide open. There's something about a woman standing in a doorway and throwing it wide open. If one steps aside from the lurid imagery that comes immediately to mind, one can see it as something far more stunning to the heart—her exquisite form before her hearth and the possibilities of a hundred poems between the stretches of bone and concrete. What if I were to abandon my old manners of seduction and show up for her as nubile, awkward of limb and sincere of face, an unbroken colt?

Of course, there was little possibility of much happening, for many reasons, not the least of which was the presence of the boy. Still, I took that gulp of air and stepped inside.

Until then, despite that stark first evening with the FBI, her home, her rooms, her spaces, the things she brushed against, the pictures that looked at her, the objects that told stories of her, had felt obscured, formed and floated only in my imagination, somewhere between cliché and mystery. That afternoon, I saw them for the first time.

If I had imagined her home as dark and cozy that first night, and it seemed disheveled that brief second time, I now found it quite the opposite. It filled me with light. It was one of those coveted homes in Seattle that brought in afternoon sunshine. The light on that afternoon was dazzling beyond measure. She didn't just have the view of the Cascade Mountains from her bedroom but also, partially, from her living room. A ficus plant grew strong and healthy there. A floral-patterned sofa faced the large windows in the living room. She ushered me to it and took the loveseat across from me, the one on which the FBI agents had sat.

The sofa was new, she said, seeing me look around for the overstuffed chair in which I had sat a few nights ago. "I want Adil to be comfortable in every way," she said, pulling on a little lever to the side of the sofa to demonstrate to me that it was a La-Z-Boy.

She had literally discarded the seat I had sat on.

Barely had she sat down when she stood up and slapped her forehead. "Oh, I am a terrible host," she said. "What will you have to drink? And you must be hungry. I had a sandwich ready for Adil and I can rustle one up for you," she said.

I acquiesced to a glass of rosé, the wine I detested with a passion. I declined the offer of a sandwich.

"Are you sure?" she said. "My sandwiches are a thing of legend."

I laughed in as casual a manner as I could as I watched her, more comfortable than I'd ever seen her, because she was in her own space. She was wearing a silk skirt, one of those things that women wrap around, decidedly hideous on some frames and unbearably arousing on others. I would have to keep my arousal in check.

I was conscious that I felt like a boy. I didn't want to eat an unwieldy sandwich right then despite the fact that I was ravenous. I didn't want her to disappear into the kitchen for too long, especially since she hadn't asked for me to follow her. I wanted her before me and me before her.

I had my wish in moments. She and her skirt rustled back into my view, bearing two glasses filled with rosé. Oh, Ruhaba, you were a vision that afternoon. I would have drunk venom from your hands.

She must have caught my naked gawk, for she looked down at herself the way women sometimes do when they are reminded suddenly of their feminine form in the presence of a male. No, pinned down in the gaze of a male, I am certain.

She said something I can't recall now, about students and clutter in her living room and what a terrifying day it was.

It was a beautiful day.

"How afraid should we be?" she asked, leaning toward me from her loveseat, which was at an inconsiderate distance from the sofa I was on.

"Afraid? Why should we be afraid? We are permitted to keep each other company," I said.

My heart lurched in my chest when I saw her forehead jump into a frown. At first, I couldn't believe I had said something so ridiculous, had been burrowing so clumsily in my own desire that I had lost track of the day and its events, the context of her words.

Then one thought struck me again: *Was she going to ask me to vote in her favor?*

In the next second, though, her face burst into the most pleasurable of giggles I have heard in a woman over twenty-five. Oh, her laughter. My heart almost stopped as she stood up and walked over to me. She leaned down, revealing a flash of delectable flesh at the neck of her faded round-necked sweater. I sat frozen, unsure of the moment, until she raised her glass to mine and clinked it and said, "You shouldn't make me laugh but you do."

I ached to reach out and touch her, pull her down to the sofa and be done with it all, win something or lose it all, for losing everything could not possibly be a fear now. Risking everything carried exquisite hope.

But again now, she had stepped away and my arms and lips and flesh had stayed in place, stupid, placid.

I pulled myself together. "I was joking, of course," I lied, not too awkwardly I thought.

"Of course," she said, but her face held an unmistakable dance of mischief on it. I am sure of that. It held mischief.

"I know you mean to ask about the safety of you and the

boy," I said, softly. Could I speak of such matters as danger and still be seductive? In the light of an October Seattle afternoon, could Harding offer comfort and still be a devil?

This question held me that afternoon in a delicious grip. Every word we exchanged loosened or tightened this grip and I was in a thrall from which I never wanted to emerge into the remainder of the world.

"You should stay vigilant," I said. "Call me instantly if you have the slightest suspicion of danger."

She nodded. The mischief that had lingered for so long on her face was replaced with a wistfulness. "I am a woman who walks in a headscarf every day of my life in a country that hates and fears and fetishizes this piece of cloth around my head," she said. "I have learned to be unafraid. But now I am a woman with a child to care for," she said. "How do you people manage this terrible fear?"

I was relieved that I understood instantly that by "you people," she didn't mean Americans but parents.

"I am sorry," she said in the next instant. "I know things are difficult with your daughter. With Kathryn. I shouldn't have . . ."

"She has been misled by her mother. Kathryn will be back someday."

"Oh," she said. "I am so glad. I wish a swift arrival of that day for you."

The lilt of sentences structured quite like that one. They would make me want to bite down gently on the lip that carried them to me, dear Ruhaba.

We sat in silence for a few moments. I could sense we both wondered where to take our conversation next. I swigged down my rosé and she walked up and poured me more. I could have sworn she leaned in closer this time. At the closest point, she let her gaze linger on mine. Scents of musk and flowers threw their lot into my sensory overload.

She said something about David Meyer then. It was so out of place in that moment that I cannot recall it at all.

"Ah, Meyer," I said. "Meyer is a fool. The only meaningful thing he has ever said is that you are beautiful."

Her eyebrows jumped up. She sat back in her loveseat with a languor that either my words or the wine seemed to place there. Her eyes sought mine and pierced through the tumble of my words.

"Did he?" she said almost in a whisper.

I watched her. I wonder now if she'd said this next thing or whether the wine sang it into my ears or whether my memory now is toying with me.

"And you? Do *you* think I am beautiful?"

She had summoned the Harding of old. "I find you beautiful," I whispered. "Radiant. Mesmerizing. You are a mesmerizing beauty, Ruhaba."

A pulse—hers or mine or both of ours beating each to each—throbbed in the air of that room.

She kept her eyes on mine for a moment and then let them roam over my face. As if drawing herself out of her reverie, she then said, "I ask because I sometimes wonder how white Americans *see* me."

Is that what she'd said? Perhaps a version of it.

I was saddened by this way of yours, Ruhaba, of dancing on the edge of your sensuality and then standing at attention to your intellect. It would break my heart, your swift journey from wiles to wonder to question.

She went on: "In Pakistan, my kind of looks are nothing to swoon over. I am darker-skinned than the maximum grade of pigment considered beautiful. Words like 'lovely' and 'beautiful' aren't used on women like me. 'Attractive,' yes. Perhaps *striking* on a good day."

I was shaking my head now, crinkling my eyes again, readying to perhaps stand up and walk over to her, run a thumb over her cheekbones, *do something*. It excited me that she was talking about her looks, *her* body, not incarcerated bodies in distant prisons.

She lifted her legs onto her chair and crossed them under her. I sat back. Her knees were visible to me—their dips and curves and sweep were strong and shone in the light of the sun dappling her loveseat. I could have spent an hour nuzzling against those knees, kissing the caps, whispering on their insides, biting the softness in the back.

Instead, I said you were the most beautiful thing I had seen in my life, dear Ruhaba. I said you should believe me. I said I spoke for all American men and spoke most sincerely.

She nodded as if taking in a data-point provided to her in a meeting. A data-point from the other side. A shutter slammed over her eyes. She reached out and looked at her phone. She let out a whistle and swung her legs off the loveseat.

That's when I noticed that the artwork on the wall behind her, above the loveseat, wasn't a piece of metallic art representing the white waves of an ocean. It was some sort of lashing of Arabic words.

"What's that?" I asked before I could stop myself.

She glanced at the piece, frowned, and said, "It's wall art. It says *La ilaha illa Allah Muhammad Rasulullah Kalima*. I got it on Etsy."

She didn't bother to translate. It was my clear cue to leave. I stood up, awash in a bitterness that surprised me.

Perhaps sensing this, Ruhaba set her phone down and walked up to me to take my glass from my hands. "I don't mean to be brusque, Ollie," she said. "But I am getting anxious texts from students. Frightened, even. I should respond." She looked sincere.

"Is there anything I can do to help?" I said.

"Mmmm . . ." she said, frowning.

I hadn't meant to be sincere. I hoped she would let me off the hook, with that wave of her hand that often set me adrift. Please, please let her not ask me for my vote.

But she said, "Could we do something fun? For us all? Some faculty and students? Our CAT-and-mouse battle lines could still be drawn—the fight must go on, but it does not have to be with violence or even coldness. We could perhaps do something symbolic between your side and mine. A party! I'll bring some of the student protesters. A ceasefire of sorts. Let the FBI have that."

"Symbolic?" I said. I did not want to address her comment about us being on opposing sides, not when I wanted her on the same couch as mine.

"Like the ceremony on the Wagah border," she said.

I looked at her blankly, of course.

"It's the border between Pakistan and India in Amritsar in Punjab. Every evening at sunset, the Pakistani and Indian military perform a ceremony in which they lower their flags and do a sort of dance—a military pirouette . . ."

You pirouetted when you did this, dear Ruhaba. It may have been the wine, but I'd like to think it was my company that made you dance.

Dance. I almost buckled at the knees not from the wine but from the weight of desire. I had always known that I would recognize love when I yearned, more than to see her naked, to see the object of my desire *dance*.

I yearned, with every fiber of my miserable being, to see you dance.

". . . and then they go back to being enemies the next day."

"If you will dance at this ceremony, this truce . . . this party . . . I will organize it."

"Then I will dance," you said. Dear Ruhaba, you said you would dance.

I smiled. Where she spoke of borders, I saw bridges. Chesterton loved bridges, not for their own form, nor for what they brought together, but for the chasm for which they were built. I felt an intensity in this chasm between Ruhaba and me. I felt a danger in this chasm, and it was delicious. Did I want to close the chasm? What would come after, if I closed in and lay on the other side?

Before I could follow my thoughts beyond all caution, Ruhaba clapped her hands. "I know! Rumor has it that you used to throw the best Halloween parties. Is that true?"

I was flustered. "Well . . . that was back when Emily . . . it was more my ex-wife's thing . . ."

Her face fell. "Oh," she said.

I should not have mentioned Emily, at least not taken her name.

"I will throw the Halloween party," I said quickly. "Why not?"

I could think of at least thirty reasons why not right then, but my words were out there and it was decided.

She yelled out to the boy in childlike excitement. He emerged from his room, earphones inserted, sleepy-eyed.

He mumbled something in French and then tried to look gracious. Ruhaba said something to him about learning American things through American festivals.

And it was decided. Amid the race tensions, shooting threats, and terrorism suspicions, Oliver Edward Harding, the idiot in lust, the fool in love, would throw a Halloween Party and serve Bloody Marys in the hope of a truce between tiny bloodthirsty nations taking root in his soil.

CHAPTER SEVENTEEN

Look for Me in the Songs

The matter of the Halloween party hit me like a ton of bricks as I drove home, aided by my lightheadedness from drinking wine on an empty stomach. I didn't want to miss Emily, so I had avoided until now the things of which she had been the keeper in our lives. Now here I was, seeing flashes of her hands setting out pumpkins for my students to carve, her frown as she stood over the oven looking at a pie that she'd just pulled out and wasn't satisfied with. The oven had seen little to no baking since she left.

"Here, try some, Ollie," she'd say. "The crust must be flakier than last year's." That same line had twisted itself into bitter jabs in our final years together. She'd perform the same actions but her words would be, "Your tongue will recall last year's flake? She was buttery. Perhaps this year's will crumble at the slightest touch?"

Emily was so much fun in the early years planning our Halloween costumes. They would be coordinated at first, quite predictable even. Scott and Zelda, Scarlett O'Hara and Rhett

Butler, Gatsby and Daisy. Then, separate in later years, up until the year when she'd just pulled on a robe, mussed up her hair, worn no makeup, shoved her feet into slippers, held a stained coffee mug in her hands and declared herself "a tired academic." The women from the English Department laughed icily and took it as a barb, rightly so.

And I'd have to make polite guesses at people's costumes. The pretty girls would be dressed as slutty this-or-that. The plain ones would dress up as Emily Dickinson or Virginia Woolf. That shit never got old. I could hardly recall what the male students dressed up as except that they used the opportunity to present themselves as some version of a bad boy or a male who could afford to pay for a slut. Everything they did was tinged with irony now, but underneath it all was still an earnest ache.

Holy hell, I'd have to figure out a costume for myself. What could I possibly go as? A provost. I'd wear a badly cut suit and clip a university-branded pen into my pocket and declare myself a provost.

We sent out word for the party to be held at my place on Saturday, October 29th. One knew, of course, that young people would have their own, more fun plans for the actual Halloween on Monday the 31st. I feel such a chill now, when I think of all that happened between those three days and then the day after. Was it really all just less than a week ago?

The boy came over early, to help out with preparations for the party. I noticed immediately that he was looking a little sheepish, distracted. I wondered if it had to do with Ruhaba. Why hadn't she come, too? Would she feel awkward to be helping, to appear as a cohost of sorts? I wished we could be done with those damned protests and such. I wished we could return to the matter of love and desire.

"Is all well?" I asked the boy as he put his costume in my study to get into later.

"Yes," he replied.

"Come on. Out with it."

That's when the boy gave me the letter. That's when he gave me the letter for Camille.

"Will you please read it and tell me if . . . if it is stupid?" he said.

He had placed it in a Ziploc bag, to protect it from the rain. I felt something ignite itself and fizzle in me instantly, the ignition intended precisely for the misery of the fizzle. What was it that I felt? Embarrassment for him?

No. Envy.

I envied him the flush of a first love.

I pitied myself for everything he had in that moment. To love someone from a distance. To hold a memory, nurse it into a longing, kindle it into a yearning. To love someone with the consuming fear of one's love going unrequited. To be unafraid of attachment. To be nakedly afraid of rejection. To stand in the center of uncertainty's storm and yet feel certain of one thing as sure as a raindrop on one's lip—that you love someone.

I didn't want to read his damned letter.

I took it stiffly from his hands and said I would read it later. His face fell.

We worked quietly on readying for the party, me setting tablecloths and plates out, him picking books up from the floor in different rooms and arranging them in neat piles on the corners of end tables, since the bookshelves were full. We moved at a good clip and were ready for the party before we knew it. The boy offered to take the dog on a long walk to tire him out.

As he clipped the leash to Edgar's collar, I looked at his earnest little head and said, "Young man?"

I waved his letter at him. "I will read this now over a cup of coffee."

His face lit up and then he looked sheepish again. He nodded and shut the door behind him and Edgar.

The letter was in French. Goddammit. But of course it was in French, for Camille. I sat down before my computer and found translations when I needed them. I will translate it here now.

Dear Camille,

How are our friends? How is school?

I will go straight to my main point. I am writing to tell you that I love you. Let me say it again in a short and simple sentence: I love you. I should have told you before I left. But maybe you knew it?

I must also tell you something that a boy should maybe not tell a girl right after he tells her he loves her. I want you to think I am strong and brave, but more than that, I want you to know my thoughts and still love me. So, here it is—

I am scared. This fear is different from the fear I felt when my mother was humiliated in the park that day. After that day, I was scared of my anger. I was scared of how quickly it grew. I was scared that I was like those young men whom I followed into the mosque. I started to understand them. I started to feel for them. Even when they spoke of the death of people, I understood them. And then I was scared that my rage would become bigger than all the poetry and all the paintings and all the places in the world that I wanted to travel to. I was scared that the anger would be bigger than the fun.

Camille, did you believe anything those policemen said about me? Did you believe I could want to harm people? If you say you didn't believe it about me, I will be less scared.

I am scared of France. I am scared that France does not love my Abbu and Ammi and Naeema and me the way I thought before. I am scared my parents may not be able to keep loving France. I am scared my sister will be married off to our cousin. I am scared that my parents will begin to love more and more their old ways from Pakistan. What if they begin to love Pakistan more than they love their children? Is this thing possible, Camille?

Now I am scared of where I am. I am scared of America. In America, they are more scared than anywhere I can imagine in the world.

Here, they keep guns inside their homes.

I shot a gun a few days ago. My hand still shakes a little from it. My ears still ring. My friend Oliver—Professor Harding—said I was a "good shot." He took me there, to the gun range, to shoot his gun. He said it would help me get over my fear of guns. It didn't. I will never pick up a gun again.

When I write to you next, I will send you a photograph of me and Professor Harding and his dog. He is actually my aunt's friend from university—he respects my aunt and she said she respects him.

So much madness is going on here, in this city of Seattle. I hope one day I will be able to tell you about it myself. But now I think the madness is because they don't have kebabs here. I miss Kebab McDo and instead I eat at Dick's Burgers. Khala Ruhaba, my aunt, loves to laugh at me and my food choices, but mostly at my accent. She is such a smart professor. You would like her and she would like you. She is fierce and she is very focused on her research about Black women in jails. It is a big problem here. Khala Ruhaba talks a lot about how people with darker skin are thrown into darker prisons. She is very Americanized in so many ways. She loves to watch stupid reality TV shows like *Say Yes to the Dress*. She works out and does hot yoga. She even has a bit of an American style under her clear Pakistani accent. But she loves me like an aunt from old stories. She worries about me and thinks I am a small child. She believes me about my innocence over that whole thing with the mosque. It is such an odd thing that she wears a hijab, not even a loose dupatta or niqab like my mother, but a hijab like the Arabs. I don't want her to wear it, but I am proud that she wears it like a political statement, to educate people about choice for women in Islam.

I love Khala Ruhaba. She is a feminist, like you and like me. She will be sad when I leave, but I hope to keep visiting her and have her visit us in Toulouse. I know Naeema will love her and she will love Naeema, probably more than she loves me, because Naeema is a girl. But also, Khala Ruhaba trusts me so much that she has given me her debit card and enough cash so that I can go for films and go into the cafes here. I mostly just take the bus or ride my bicycle all over the city to explore.

But I miss riding our cycles around the Garonne. Remember that photograph you took from the bridge, of the little girl chasing a pigeon below? I still think that photograph belongs at a gallery. I wish I had a copy of that photograph, and also one of you. When I look at you, I don't feel the way I usually do when I think of who I am in France, or Pakistan, or America—a boy on the outside, looking in.

Will you write to me? A letter. You can send it to this address of the professor. You don't have to say you love me back. But if you don't love me back, don't tell me that. It will make me lonely so far away and it will change the shape of home in my mind.

I hope to come back home soon.

Did you go to the museum recently?

I hope that you are having fun but I also don't hope it. I hope that you are missing me and that your fun is a little less because of that.

Give my love to Place de L'Estrapade. Give my love to our homeless friend Philippe and his mangy dog. Do they still sit outside Imaginères?

I know that one of our friends also loves you. I pray that you don't love him. I am writing all this down foolishly, from the heart, like an old poet, a bad one. But Camille, please wait for me.

Please don't forget me.

Please look for me in the songs we listened to. Please find

me in the pigeons at the Garonne. Most of all, please believe in the goodness of me.

I love you, Camille. I will come home soon and love you much more. Have a very happy birthday.

Your friend,

Adil

I sat slumped in my chair. *Please believe in the goodness of me.*

What could I have said to the boy upon his return from walking the dog? What *should* I have said? Was that letter destined to do good for the boy's love for Camille? Or harm?

A more practical and urgent matter—What should I say now, to the federal agents? Which parts of this love-soaked letter will do good and which will do harm?

When the boy returned with the dog, he looked at me with a forced nonchalance. "The letter *is* stupid," I said. "But that is a good thing. Stupid is sincere. Sincere is moving. If Camille doesn't already love you, I know she will be in love after she reads it."

I believed in some of what I said. I didn't tell him that he was right in his instincts not to tell a girl about his fears. Perhaps I felt that same envy, of a self-awareness the boy possessed that allowed him to pour the untarnished truth onto a page.

He beamed at me. "Thank you, sir," he said.

"It isn't merely a love letter to your young love," I said. "It's also a eulogy to your aunt. You do worship her odd way of life, don't you?" I said, turning away so he couldn't see my face.

I noted down Camille's address and told him I would check with the post office to find out when would be a good date to post it so it arrived by her birthday on December 1st.

Let's get back to the party. A lot happened at that party.

Essence arrived first. She was dressed as Rosie the Riveter. Her jeans-shorts hugged her curves, and everything on her sweet little body looked tight, well-toned, well out of my reach.

I asked if she was twenty-one. She nodded, so I handed her a beer as the boy went into my study to put on his costume. He emerged looking not very different from himself, apart from pink and blond streaks in his hair spiked and gelled into a cowlick and some roughly scribbled tattoos on his forearms.

"Zayn Malik?" Essence squealed.

The boy grinned. Before I could ask who that was, other guests started to arrive. We had four Donald Trumps that evening and six Hillarys. I began to feel tired, and the evening had barely begun.

I grew restless waiting for Ruhaba. I checked my phone every few seconds. I vacillated between worry and annoyance.

I divided my time between the three rooms of the party, the way Emily and I once had—the kitchen, the living room, and, for those who wanted to sit down for a bit of a quiet now and then (it struck me that these were the exact words Emily would use), the study. A good amount of noise and music started to rise up around the house. I thought again of Emily and how she would lay her hand on my forearm in the middle of parties and say, "Hear that, Ollie? We are giving people good memories."

The boy seemed to be having fun. He stuck close to Essence,

I saw. Again, often, he'd fall into the periphery of the clutch of kids talking animatedly and showing each other things on the phone.

Outside, looking in.

But a soft smile was playing on his face and I felt an odd contentment at that.

Ruhaba arrived. She was almost unrecognizable. She was Captain Jack Sparrow from *Pirates of the Caribbean*. I would have thought the choice odd, but then it made sense. It was a clever way to be both feminist and to keep her head covered. The moustache, though, was a boner-crusher.

Not for the gender-sexuality kids, it wasn't. They whooped with excitement as Ruhaba performed a Jack Sparrow stride and flourish of the sword. Fuck, I missed Virginia Woolf.

The party began to fill up. Conversations grew loud. I paused at this one or that, never too far from Sparrow.

In a corner of my living room, a group of faculty and students were playing some sort of game using idioms and popular phrases where they'd replace the word "day" with "gay."

"I want you gay in, gay out!"

"Thirty gays hath September!"

"It's been a hard gay's night!"

"Tomorrow is another gay!"

"I'm having a bad-hair gay!"

"It's just not my gay!"

"Another gay, another dollar." This one drew the most raucous laughter.

"Save the gay!"

Die another gay, I almost said. I bit it back and roamed closer to where Ruhaba was holding forth to a group of wide-eyed faculty and one male student, that Cunningham boy again, who was probably hanging around in this group to save himself from the gay game.

"We Pakistanis . . . we will suck on the seed of a fruit till its juices are dry and its veins stay hidden around our tongues to taste in secret for hours. You Americans want your apples sliced by a kitchen gadget made of steel. We want to pinch our lychees between our fingers until our lips hurt from longing. Seriously. I have never seen an American push his nose into the wettest part of a rose. Smell it where the scent can stop his heart."

Her words could not have been innocent. From the look on Cunningham's face, I would have wagered he'd agree with me. It irritated me that he was standing there, lapping up these delicious words of Ruhaba's.

A commotion rose up in the kitchen. A single voice louder than the others. Voices in the living room fell as people tried to listen. Ruhaba and I walked over.

Zoe Hallin, a sociology professor I had believed to be mousy enough to plug into my party, someone who was likely to offer help in the kitchen, which she had done earlier, took offense with Essence's costume.

"I should tell you, young woman, that your costume is a slap in the face of African American history."

"Oh, now it's . . . *why*?" Essence said. Her voice was low even though Zoe's volume had been at the level of a pronouncement.

"Well, Rosie's image celebrates ableism and white supremacy. She was born in the wet dreams of war-mongering propagandists and capitalists sending women off to work in factories.

Did you pause to think about the history of Black women in US labor?"

Zoe was white.

"Yeah, well, I'm appropriating that," Essence said, sounding less convincing than she usually did.

"Leave Rosie to the silly white feminists, sister," Zoe said. Don't just wear a white woman's costume over your skin and take on their work."

What was going *on*? Did no one know the world as it existed anymore? Everyone was jumpy. And everyone was jumping on a fucking soapbox.

Essence looked crushed. Adil looked over at me and asked whether we could bring out the pies. Ruhaba clapped in loud agreement and asked me if she could help with slicing them. I didn't want her to be this way. First, the Jack Sparrow costume. Now, the keeping of the peace.

Alicia, the other Black girl at the party, scowled at Zoe and put her arm around Essence but said nothing. I felt a soaring gratitude toward Alicia. She had come in with another student, Wade, a mixed-race kid who did well in my classes, a mix of Latino or Filipino and Black. The two of them had made a statement with their costumes—they were a couple now and they announced it to their friends "subtly," by dressing as Beyoncé and Jay-Z. I had earlier heard Zoe congratulate Alicia for dressing as a feminist icon.

And then, Betsy MacDowell arrived. At first, no one noticed. Students were in the kitchen, close to recent drama, the pies, and the fridge filled with beer. Faculty stood around the living room in their half-assed costumes, trying to sound more animated than they actually felt about the elections, barely ten days away.

Carrying plates of pie into the living room, I looked at Betsy and instantly had the sensation that I must do one of two things—(a) throw a blanket over her and bundle her out to her car, or (b) flee my own home. Before I could do either, someone shouted, "Holy fuck!"

It was Alicia. I took my gratitude back from her. People turned to look at what she had thrown her curse at.

Betsy McDowell stood there, blinking, with one black eyelid and one white. This was because she had painted one side of her body—the parts that were visible—black. She had left the other side untouched. She was a redhead and had left the untouched part of her body with her graying red hair and the other side . . . my jaw fell. The other side of her hair was dyed, temporarily, I supposed, black. It was somehow curled into as much as an afro as she could have achieved.

She was wearing a white T-shirt with the words "Whose Life Matters?" painted by hand on the front.

Her husband was dressed as a policeman. He was a white policeman. I never thought I'd long so much for his taupe suit.

The other kids came in from the kitchen and crowded into the room.

I need to pause here to say that at that moment, on that day, I was sure the world had gone to hell in a handbasket. I could not fathom why the citizenry around me was in a scramble to align *so personally* with the Blacks. I ached for White Silence.

I should also say a thing or two of the way things play out these days, between real life events and the constant awareness of the fact that nothing is simply real life, nothing is here and now. Few things can simply *happen*. Few moments can simply emerge, grow, and reach a resolution within the walls of a home and within the words of people gathered, present. Those far away, in their homes, on their computers, are present here, and they know it. There's no fear of missing out on a live event that you hadn't planned to document anyway. If it ends up being significant, it will find its way into pictures and videos. The only place to fear not being present is on your device. That's where you are either in or out of sight, in or out of mind.

So it was on that night, too. Even as the young and old among us drew in around Betsy, we knew, somewhere in the dull terror of our alcohol-laced minds, that we were becoming part of a story that would extend far and wide out of here, that the words we said now, the corner we stood in, with drink in hand or hurriedly set down, the sides we took, the shape and smile or frown of us, all were being assigned by some imaginary film director speaking a script directly, live, into our minds and limbs.

So it was now that no sooner had Alicia said "Holy fuck!" the smartphone cameras had come on and you were either with this moment or against it.

Betsy thought she was *with* it. "You get it?" she asked Alicia.

"Oh, I *get* it," Alicia said. Jay-Z swung his phone camera toward her now and jumped away so he could get both Betsy and Alicia within a single frame of boxing ring. Alicia pulled herself up and put her hands on her hips, and then Jay-Z crossed the room for better light.

Betsy kept speaking. "It's provocative. It gets people to think of why one side of me seems to matter more than the other. Why white lives matter more than . . . you know?"

Alicia was shaking her head, grinning. "It's *provocative*? To *who*? It's *blackface*, is what it is."

Betsy shook her head calmly, as if she were responding to Alicia's incorrect use of "who." But what she said was: "Clearly, I thought of that. The blackface business. It's not blackface because half of me is *white*. I checked about this with a Black friend—my best friend from college—and she told me it would be okay because I am not trying to dress up as a Black person. I'm here as a white *ally* making a point about white and Black lives. See?"

The room was silent now, except for Jacques Brel singing "Ne me quitte pas" on my vinyl player in my study.

Into the stunned silence, someone spoke. "Don't be so sensitive," Jim said in the worst voice one could insert into this growing situation. Betsy turned to her husband and said, "Shut up, Jim." The policeman crossed his arms across his chest and stepped back.

I was awash in relief that Meyer hadn't come. He was lying low. He disapproved of this party, thought of my hosting it as a betrayal. He was right about it all.

I looked over to see Ruhaba standing with Adil standing with Essence. Both the kids had their mouths open, staring into the arena. Ruhaba, despite her costume, looked nothing like Jack Sparrow . . . she looked frailer than I had ever seen her.

She had wanted that party to be a success, a truce. Such sweetness I found in you, Ruhaba. You promised me you would dance.

I wondered whether I could say anything at all that would shut this whole thing down. I couldn't. No. My home, my party, no matter what it was now, would be "an incident" tomorrow, and all I could hope for was that I'd be a footnote, a marker of place and time, not a quote. Not a word, Harding. Don't say a word.

Zoe Hallin now weighed in again: "Professor MacDowell . . ." She cleared her throat. "Professor MacDowell, I believe what we are all feeling is . . . is that in the attempt to *exhibit* your understanding of what it means to be an ally, you have appropriated the pain of Black bodies. And you have done so in a . . . if I may . . . a clumsy and insensitive manner. I hope you can feel not merely the disapproval in this room but the pain. At the sight of the . . . the . . . black paint on your face and your representation of Black hair, which itself is a location of much historical . . ."

"I *teach* about cultural appropriation, young lady," Betsy said. "You people don't even know . . ."

"I didn't say anything about cultural appropriation," Zoe shot back. "And please don't refer to me as . . ."

Alicia's icy voice cut in. "Did you just say *you people*?"

Betsy blinked and looked around the room. "What? Oh, *come on*. I mean *you students*! And you *young faculty* people. Not you . . . you . . . not anything else. Please!"

Something far more ghoulish than any costume could have achieved now bore down and sucked all the air out of the room. The audience was divided into those who knew a microaggression when they saw it and those who wouldn't if it came and bit them in the ass.

The only thing left for me to do was throw open the front door. Some people walked out.

Some people stayed. Ruhaba was among those who left. She

told me quickly that Adil would stay behind to help clean up and Essence would drive him home.

Your glance at me as you left was so weary, Ruhaba, I forgive you.

The man in the policeman costume led a woman away by the arm, and from the way she kicked and scowled at him, no one could be mistaken that she was anything but white.

The party cleared out swiftly. Only the boy lingered, with Essence, who now stood in the middle of my living room with tears running down her cheeks. Looking at her, one had the sense that something had cut deep and there would be no asking her about it, no unearthing of a Black pain, no posting it on social media, no profiting from it.

She and the boy sat in silence for a while on the steps leading out into my backyard, even though temperatures had dropped and rain was falling down a few feet from them. Edgar lay with his back pressed up against their behinds. From where I finally sat in my living room, I watched Essence's shoulders quake and quiver and I watched the boy stare into the darkness of the night beyond them.

I don't know how long I sat like that, unwilling to disturb the boy and girl sitting on my stoop, separate beings united in their unspoken pains of far away. I felt myself turn into fog. If I'd rushed up to them with an embrace, I would have fallen on them cold and thin and empty.

This evening, as November 6th turned dark, the federal agents asked me about that night. I told them they were right: the boy was angry about that episode, but it wasn't like he knew exactly what was going on. I got the sense that he didn't quite understand the politics of blackface and whatever pain Essence may have been feeling. Any anger he felt in that moment was impersonal, born of empathy.

Empathy, Ray Waters Jr. said.

Is that a question, I said.

The agent regarded me in silence.

I sighed. Empathy is the ability to understand someone's emotion and share it because you have felt something similar sometime somewhere, I said.

The agent said he wasn't looking for a definition of the word. He wanted to know why I felt that the boy's anger was anything but anger.

A businessman feels anger, I said. A poet, empathy. I was drawing on Chesterton, but this man wouldn't know it.

The agent pretended to take notes, because he still needed to treat me like a national hero, but he had a tick in his jaw, which held back either laughter or words.

I wondered about the notes he was making. I asked him.

I just want to know your impressions of Mr. Adil Alam, he said.

One could hardly refer to the child as "Mr." I said. Ruhaba would want me to say this.

You feel empathy for this boy, the agent said. Despite everything that happened.

I had to be careful what I said next. What did I want them to believe? Did it matter what I wanted? Their minds were made up.

I had read about Ray Waters Jr. and his ambitions. Seattle had never had a real terrorist episode. This one put us on the map, in a way. It put Ray Waters Jr. on track to run for public office or simply get that transfer he so wanted to DC. Perhaps if I looked in the agents' notebook, I'd see a template with predetermined lines to fill out, questions that were predetermined, answers even more so. A rubric of expectations. A tame matrix to be filled in with the touchpoints of terror. Perhaps I had never even needed to try, with these people. Perhaps I would wreak havoc in this man's algorithm, in the nation's sense of all that was right as rain if I didn't play my part.

Were I to play with fire, how much would I burn? Would I burn here or in hell?

As the agent snapped his notebook shut and started to stand up to leave, I said, looking past this man at my kitchen table, past to the point where Adil and Essence had sat staring into the night. And I said words that the detective would not recognize, words he would not know to be those of Chesterton and not mine, words that would perhaps not provoke this smirking man into naked anger but that he would feel as something he shared with others of his kind, a pain of someone's else's from sometime somewhere. I said: "The man who throws a bomb is an artist, because he prefers a great moment to everything. He sees how much more valuable is one burst of blazing light, one peal of perfect thunder, than the mere common bodies of a few shapeless policemen."

I may have said it too silently, or I may have mumbled, because Ray Waters Jr. did not seem to hear. It is for the best.

CHAPTER EIGHTEEN

"Is She Safe Here?"

The blackface incident did what it had to do. The video was in the hands of the student activists and had been shared around campus—and beyond—by the time I awoke with a piercing hangover. I had silenced my cellphone, in anticipation of the madness, but even I was shocked at just how mad everything was, and how quickly that madness had descended, even on a Sunday.

A local reporter had left a message on my phone, asking to talk about what had happened at my party. Betsy MacDowell had called, sounding stricken, begging me to talk to people, provide some perspective, some sanity.

I thought of climbing back under my blanket, but I was woefully behind in my grading. One had hoped that classes would be canceled for the coming week, but the Provost had decided that we needed to put students back in the classroom, protests and shooting threats be damned. I had also wanted to spend the day writing, working on my Chesterton book. I mentioned earlier that I was beginning to find a new rush of thought, an arousal of creativity, so to speak, and my editor had responded with much enthusiasm to my offer to send him fresh chapters. The world needed the wit and reason of the likes of Chesterton more than ever, and I intended to be an obedient conduit.

Edgar started to bark. I peered out the corner of my curtain window. It was the boy.

I opened the door, squinting, then looked past him to make sure no reporter was here yet. Thank goodness for electronic communication. Newsmen only showed up in person as a last resort these days. But I would have done anything to see Ruhaba there with the boy, like that first time.

He had come to walk the dog. I grinned at him. "You could have slept in a bit this morning, given last night's . . ." I didn't want to find a word for last night, not until I had had some coffee.

"Edgar don't give a fuck about last night. He still needs a shit," the boy said.

It warmed me to think of how he had come to feel comfortable enough to use profanity around me.

"The world has gone to hell," I said.

"Khala Ruhaba told me to keep a low profile today. She said I shouldn't talk to anyone about what happened, no matter what."

"Ah."

"I should not have my name in the paper or social media."

Of course. These past few days, I had forgotten that amongst us was this pleasant young man who may or may not be a member of a terrorist cell.

"She asks me to ask you for a favor," he said.

"Anything," I said. Jeez. I shouldn't have opened my mouth before coffee. The vote was coming up tomorrow, and I had to hold my cards close to my chest.

"She said I should just hang away in your house if that's okay with you. She said you could know how to keep out the media type people. Or at least you will know that don't give them my full name."

"Of course," I said. I should have known she wouldn't ask me for political support at work. When would I just go ahead and believe that? I was getting warmer and warmer in my quest to be in her life. Ruhaba trusted me with her family. What else might she trust me with?

"Not that they want my name and all that, I told her," the boy said. "But in case anyone wants to know who else was here last night or something."

"Where is your . . . Khala Ruhaba?"

The boy grinned, clearly at my pronunciation. "She's with the people protesting on campus. About what happened here last night."

Of course.

"Those people . . ." I said. "I mean the ones who are taking offense without knowing the details. Not people like your aunt, but the others. The snowflakes. The sheeple. The misled masses of college students. They have to learn that you can't let people's behavior and their stupidity trouble you. Someone can only make you feel small if you give them permission to do so."

The boy gave me a queer look. "You don't believe she was doing the wrong? That professor in blackface?"

"She is a twit. Dim-witted. But I expect more from young people. What if someone—a white woman or, let's say, a *Hindu* woman—had shown up in a headscarf and burka? I wouldn't want you to scream 'cultural appropriation!' I would want you to say, 'That's stupid and these people are ignorant.' Then just shake it off."

The boy stared at me.

Had I gone too far?

"Look," I said to him then. "What I'm trying to . . ."

"I don't *like* hijab. I'm not . . . sensitive . . . about it. Honest, I think it *is* stupid to wear one. I don't like when my mother is wearing one. I have nightmares. Sometimes my mother is drowning in the Garonne. Sometimes she is jumped off the bridge and falls down, down, down to the ground and her blood splashes on the pigeons there. Sometimes she doesn't fall straight proper—her headscarf gets caught on the wall and pop! . . . it snaps her neck. Other times it gets round and round her neck in the water and she can't breathe and I am swimming not far from her but I don't swim to save her, just watch her drown and she is still try to find me in the water."

We stood in silence for a moment.

"What about your aunt?" I asked. "What do you think about her wearing it? Why don't you ask her not to?"

"I don't know. Do you know why she wears hijab here? She still did not tell me."

"What do you mean *here*?"

"She never wore it in Pakistan or even first for few years in America."

"She didn't?" I tried to sound nonchalant but had to sit down.

"That's what my mother said. My father said it gives him anger that she broke not one but all rules."

"Is that so?"

The boy's face grew guarded. He seemed to realize he might have said too much.

Then he asked me something that left me slain: "*Is she safe here?*"

When I think back now, I wonder why my response was so quick. "Everyone is safe in America," I said. "Safer than she'd be in Pakistan, surely? Or even France, right?"

The boy shrugged, not looking at me.

"People are especially safe here if they assimilate," I said quietly. "We have room for everyone."

The boy turned away from me then. His shoulders were stiff.

"How is Essence?" I asked.

The boy seemed glad for the change of subject. "I texted her. She is not going to the protest. She is staying locked up herself in her room."

"Poor girl," I said.

"I hope she stays off the social media," he said. "They are saying terrible things."

"What kind of things?"

"Just stupid things about Essence's past. And saying how all these protest students have mental disorders. Black kids, Muslim kids, gay kids, trans kids . . . we're all this thing . . . pumped up on pharmaceuticals and have mental disorders, according to them. Essence used to be a boy."

I took a deep breath. I thought of the girl and her ass in the jeans-shorts.

"Let's not have you go out and walk the dog today," I said. "He can go in the backyard. Toss him a ball there to tire him out."

The boy agreed quickly.

Just how bad *was* it out there? Bad enough that even *I* couldn't tell the girls from the boys.

I drank a leisurely mug of coffee and watched the boy play with the dog in my backyard. After the last sip of coffee had scalded my throat and the sludge at the bottom had coated my tongue, I went to my desktop and let the world rush into my face in a full, hot blast.

That was when I gave the boy a key to my house. That was when I made it possible for him to come and go as he pleased. I have told that to the federal agents and I have endured their looks of contempt.

My house was closer to campus than his aunt's. I wanted the boy to know that if he ever felt that he was in danger, he should let himself in. Also, of course, it would help if he didn't need me to open the door for the dog walks.

The sleep-in protests about curriculum on campus had morphed overnight into race protests of a new kind. An intellectual kind, they'd have you believe. Naturally, the demand for Critical Whiteness Studies and the Day of Absence had gathered strength after the blackface incident. Students of every hue and gender joined in. More and more faculty joined in. From what I could discern, no one was trying to blame me. My name showed up on this Twitter post or that, but all references were to me as the host of the party where things became ghastly. Oh, thank goodness. I was the venue of the madness, not the avenue to it. I felt a twinge of disappointment. A part of me could've done with a good fight. But it would have driven Ruhaba away forever.

The university President sent out a message. The university was neither responsible for nor endorsed off-campus events, it said, but since the matter was related to faculty, the university was thoroughly investigating the incident. The university community should rally together in this moment of pain and should not be divided, the President said. If anyone needed counseling through this trauma, if the incident had left anyone in the community triggered, they could approach counselors who would be stationed at several safe spaces on campus for the coming few days. If faculty felt it best to cancel class so that students could gather to grieve . . . blah blah blah.

Safe spaces. They never really listed the locations of these. The triggered knew where to land. How come nobody ever told *me* where these were?

My inbox was also flooded with email from colleagues expressing their confidence that I would vote "no" on the Big Vote on Monday, the one that would render a good handful of us obsolete. Their expressions of confidence expressed their lack of it.

I wondered about my vote. Of course, I would vote "no." But what was the strategic thing to do? Denying the mobs would fan the flames, yes. How far did I want the flames to spread? Perhaps they would be snuffed out as students got distracted by another season of *Game of Thrones*. Perhaps the distraction would come from the election, and Candidate Trump's Proud

Boys would go rampaging in the streets in their loss and pain, take all these matters off-campus. Or these flames on campus would hide, burn as embers and sparks, until one day they'd reach my office door and lick at my carefully filed syllabus for Literature, Thought, and the Politics of Observation that I hadn't needed to change in millennia. But there was the possibility that the flames would need to be fanned by faculty, and I saw Ruhaba stepping up to do that, getting burned, engulfed, roasted alive. Whatever inquiry they had going about her, they would intensify it and take her down.

I put the matter aside. I had to make a more urgent decision this morning—I could choose between the shit happening within the bricks and mortar, in flesh and blood on campus, or stay here and be virtual, make some calls, put some posts out there of my own. Why go smell the stench of tires burning? Besides, did Sunday not mean anything to anyone anymore?

But I hadn't sat down with Ruhaba in days. I missed the nearness of her skin. I ached for the intoxication of her living room.

I didn't trust that she wouldn't grow completely apart. These were big issues for her, and several people would rally around her. I needed to be a face somewhere in there. I could tell her that I had given the boy my house keys, that I wanted Adil to feel safe.

By the time I arrived on campus, strips of bacon had been found hanging on the doorknobs of the Muslim students' dorm rooms. I read that a meme on 4chan had issued a more specific threat than before—if the university voted to cleanse the campus of its whiteness, blood would flow in the classrooms. And a life-size doll of a Black man was found hanging from a noose outside the student center, from the window of the Black Student Association.

Remarkable, what the student body could accomplish by dawn even as they complained about classes that began at 7:45 a.m.

The biggest furor, of course, was over the Black doll on the noose. The midmorning hours were consumed with messages flying about.

Someone zoomed into the photograph of the mock lynching and noticed a macabre detail. In the foreground of the photo, overshadowed by the dramatic image of the hanging noose, sat four students with their backs to the photographer. The students were clearly white. In fact, they were dressed in summer clothes, bizarre in this weather. Why? Because they were at a picnic. They sat on a blanket on the campus greens, their bodies resting on their elbows or palms. They were all looking over at the noose. They were simulating the picnics that white families would have at the lynchings of Blacks in the southern states after the Civil War.

If it hadn't been for the fact that some of the people's clothes looked damp from the rain, it could have been argued that their inclusion in the frame was an accident. It could have been argued that this was the handiwork of a clever and troublemaking photoshopper and that the picture of the picnickers was from months ago. After all, that was exactly the spot where the prettiest cherry blossoms bloomed in the spring.

Such an unfortunate action.

I didn't see Ruhaba that morning. Or I should say that she

didn't see me. I watched her from my office window, which had a direct view of the quad, where a sea of students had turned out to stand under umbrellas in the pouring rain. Faculty and students were taking turns speaking. The campus police were there and so were the city police.

When Ruhaba took over the mic, waves of cheers tore through the crowds. I could feel them rise up toward me in a tsunami that threw me farther away from her than I'd been in the past weeks.

I spent two hours alternating between reading news reports and tweets online and staring at my phone, sometimes starting a sentence in a text message to Ruhaba, then deleting it and staring at my blinking cursor. Her last text to me, sent on the afternoon I had taken Adil shooting and then texted to tell her I was on my way to drop him off, was a thumbs-up sign. Impersonal. Not from the world of Faiz Ahmed Faiz nor from that of T. S. Eliot, but a brown thumbs-up from the world of a Syrian orphan by the name of Steve Jobs who had had the last laugh on Americans.

I spent that evening longing for Ruhaba. Cold, listless, unable to devote myself to the writing I had intended.

Late Monday morning, I arrived on campus three hours before heading in to the Big Vote. I squeezed past the faculty outside my office who had lined up to lobby with me to vote either this way or that. I took the back stairs and avoided my protesters, some of whom were dressed in grotesque costumes, for Halloween, but it may as well have been their representation on any ordinary day.

I was once again possessed by a restlessness, an impending

sense of my own irrelevance. I drove to LifeFloat and pushed my way into a last-minute opening. The young woman at the reception desk, dressed as a slutty nurse, did not look happy at being asked to stay back over her lunch break, but these were the perks I enjoyed as a frequent customer, one who had threatened to cancel his membership.

I surrendered my body upon the salt water and waited for the calm to take over. My right calf started to sting from the salt on the scratch that Edgar had inflicted recently. I pushed against the sting. I followed my breath, imagining it as a cloud of pure and holy prayer that I drew in from the world and pushed out back into it, to soar over the tip of a mountain and disappear to the left of the peak and reappear to its right to travel back to my nostrils.

I saw the boy eating an ice cream float. I saw him through the refracted light of an ice cream shop window. He was seated with a man, a dark-haired man with brown skin. The man laughed and threw his head back, and I knew what he had laughed at. It was a joke the boy had made about Edgar. The only reason the man would laugh with such delight and attention to that would be that the man was none other than me.

Indeed, the man turned around and looked at me. It was I, with brown skin and black hair and black eyes. I looked terrifying.

So it was with some relief that I soon turned again into a fat, hideous, lobsterlike creature and started to eat the boy's arm. At first he found the lobster's act peculiar and funny, like a tickle. When he saw his arm disappear and his blood gush over the table, the boy started to laugh and snatched his arm away, waving it toward the people in the ice cream shop—hot mothers and hipster fathers with cute children in raincoats. They watched the boy's fleshy stump of an arm and stared or looked away as if he were no more curious an object than a bearded foreigner embarking their airplane.

I, the lobster, had at the boy's arm again. This time he snatched it and dunked it into his ice cream float. Seeing him take action, everyone in the ice cream shop stared at us, at me, daring me to bite again. I turned back from the lobster into the dark-haired, dark-skinned man. Then, I turned white. The people stood up and walked to the boy and took him away, somewhere safe. Everyone left. I stepped out. Everyone was gone. No one told me where to go.

Then, the lights in the flotation tank came on and I wasn't sure if I had slept. I had no way of knowing if the world outside this tank, outside the lobby and past the scowling young woman behind the desk, was the same as I had left it.

It wasn't. Someone had left a printout on my desk—a picture of Ruhaba without a headscarf. In all my searches of Ruhaba, I had never found this one. A stalker more resourceful than I had found a photograph of her with her curls shadowing half her face as she leaned over what seemed to be a library table. There was nothing candid about the photograph. Ruhaba had posed for it. A cocktail of emotions surged through me as I stared at the image. Ruhaba was wearing a white cotton shirt in the photograph. The buttons were undone deep into her cleavage. She was leaning over the table and smiling seductively into the camera, pointing the tip of a pen at the photographer.

For the briefest moment, I wondered whether Ruhaba had

sent me this picture of herself as some sort of ritual of seduction. I kicked myself for my giddiness. No, no, this thing was a tasteless prank.

Chesterton once said that there was room for wrath and love to run wild. And oh, did those two unbridled beasts run unshod within my heart then.

Whatever it was and whoever had sent it, it was an excuse for me to go see Ruhaba, alert her, express my concern. I went right over to her office and was told she was in class, teaching. I went over to the classroom indicated by her department assistant.

I peered into the door of the classroom. There she was, the unblemished object of my desire, lecturing animatedly to her students. Even under the harsh lights of the classroom and even standing in front of the great leveler that is a PowerPoint presentation, she commanded the grace of a dancer. I watched her for a while and then stepped into the doorway and stood there until she noticed me.

She excused herself from the class and stepped outside with me. She was unsmiling and looked worried. I hesitated over adding to the frown that already crinkled her forehead. But it was too late.

I showed her the printout of her photo. I was stunned at her reaction.

I had expected her to be perturbed. I had imagined she would seek my counsel on how to deal with the photograph. Instead, she said, icily, "What do you intend to do with this?"

She seemed not to notice the shock on my face. "Oh dear, no . . . goodness . . . Ruha . . ."

"I can't believe you would . . ." she continued.

"Someone left it on my desk! I would never . . . I have come to alert you. To offer help. I'm on *your* side!"

Her expression was unchanged. She held out her palm. I swiftly put the printout in her hand. I said, "Please trust me. I don't think the photograph is a big deal in itself, but if you feel we must get to the bottom . . ."

She turned around and walked back into her classroom. She tucked the printout into her purse. I stood there and watched her for a bit, but she went right back to where she had left off in her lecture, less animated now, but with nary a glance toward me in the door.

She did appear, though, at the meeting for the Big Vote. Fifteen of us—chosen from among the CAT and the raging mice—walked into the Provost's conference room, and the sea of protesters parted. The noise, the click of cameras, the swirl of anger, the hapless stare of Dean Cummings, all pulled at me, but my eyes were riveted on Ruhaba. Her own eyes were lowered as she took a seat quietly beside no one she seemed to know. As the Provost and the Dean said words and words and words about things we already knew, the stakes of voting this way or that—the end of the humanities as we knew it—I willed my Ruhaba to look at me.

And she did. For just a moment, a fraction of second I will hold in my heart forever, she raised her head to look straight up and into me. Her eyes were swollen red from tears, her jaw quivering so slightly that I was perhaps the only one who could see, her sweet mouth open as if fighting to suck in whatever air would be granted to her. All of this balled itself up into a clean bullet of clear thought and tore through me.

She looked away faster than I could exhale.

And now, all eyes were on me. I was asked what my vote would be. All others had voted. Mine would break the tie. I voted "yes."

CHAPTER NINETEEN

"*These* Women Don't"

From: Khan, Ruhaba

Dear Faculty Inquiry Committee,
I am in receipt of your email regarding an inquiry about which you seek to ask me some questions. May I be given the benefit of some clarification as to what this may be about? I do respect, of course, the protocols you must follow. However, in order to prepare to best answer for your . . .

When we left the President's office, someone shouted out the result of the vote to the waiting crowds. A raging wave of madness welled up around us. I walked with rapid steps toward my office building, fully aware that Meyer was in hot pursuit. The rain had stopped and a rainbow stood across the sky like a trite sign of victory over . . . what was it now—"the emotional, rhetorical, and ideological projections that center White identity and belief systems." There.

I heard someone call out to me. I ducked into an approaching surge of students and skulked my way into a corridor in the deep recesses of the second floor of the law school building, the last place that Meyer would think to look for me.

The only thing worse than protests is celebration at the victory of protests. The people of color had been unprepared for the vote to go in their favor, but they never came up short when it came to festivities. From my quiet spot, I had a good view of the quad below me. All manner of flags arrived, all sorts of musical instruments, all sorts of expressions of glee. Student leaders, faculty fools—all burst out in speeches on a mic crackling from the mutiny of multiculturalism.

What had I done.

My eyes scoured the crowds below me for Ruhaba so I could steady myself. To my delight, she was standing not too far from me, her face partly hidden, but close enough for me to sense whether or not she was awash from head to toe in relief. More importantly, whether or not she was bathed in adoration of me.

But I could read nothing from the way she stood. People urged her every now and then to take the mic, but she shook her head, quickly waved away their requests, and shrank back into the periphery of the crowds.

A young man stepped up to her and squeezed her flesh at the waist. A student. The male student from the crowd around her at my party. Cunningham. My heart stopped. She turned to him and jabbed him in the belly with a finger.

A jab. Not a push, not a slap, not a slam of the heel of her palm to bloody his nose.

She stepped away from the young man, and he walked away. Had I read too much into this? Is this what they talk about when they talk about male privilege? Did this happen to my Ruhaba often and all she could do was jab so as not to attract more attention to herself? She had already been sexualized by the photograph that was sent to me and god knows who else. Did all these young men on campus think they could . . . ?

Just then, a fight broke out in the madness. A young man was being pushed and dragged out of the crowds. He was white. The people dragging him were white, too, or white Latinos or whatever else. Campus police swooped down and, with the briefest inquiry this side of Hillary's email server, the young man was politely ushered away by the police.

There go I. Vote or no vote.

The crowds started to sing John Lennon's "Imagine." I was just glad that the rainbow had faded by now. I would have hurled myself from the second-floor window into the crowds below. I would have broken an ankle from the discontent in my chest and the maudlin rapture of the scene before me.

I drove home through crowds of hideous monsters—only part of this was owing to Halloween—and took a nap. I awoke to a rapid and urgent knock on my door. That's how I recognized where I was. I quieted my panic. I was in my bed. I had come home, darkened my windows by drawing the curtains, put in ear plugs that they handed out at LifeFloat to keep salt water out of one's ears.

I imagined it would be the boy at the door, but it was David Meyer. He looked livid. I had forgotten all about him. Or rather,

I had forgotten about the predicament, his and mine. I imagined that our friendship, if one could call it that in its thinned-out, desiccated, undernourished state over the past few years, had been given a death blow by my vote that afternoon. I had probably sunk our careers, or at least our current jobs, the ten years or so left before retirement. But, rather than let this one die out in frigidity, the man had chosen to have it out.

"I don't have the energy for this," I said, leaning an arm across my door and wiping the drool of sleep around my mouth with my shirt sleeve.

"You owe me an explanation, Harding," he said. He looked younger in his rage. Huh. Who would have thought.

I sighed and let him in. I walked into my kitchen to put on some coffee. This was a bad move, I knew, because Meyer would think I was inviting him to stay a while. But with the float earlier that day, the encounter with Ruhaba in which I was grossly misunderstood, and then the whiplash of the vote and protests and victory dance of death, I could barely stand without caffeine, let alone be at the receiving end of the ire of an academician whose career was rapidly turned extraneous.

"I really have nothing to say, but you may have your moment," I said, flopping into a chair at the kitchen table. I still hadn't done the dishes from the night of the party. I did not motion for Meyer to sit down, but he did. Rather, he leaned and half-sat on the table, towering over me.

Was he capable of turning violent? Not in a million post-apocalyptic years. Like most academics, he would use his words.

"What made you do it?" he asked. I was surprised at how calm his voice sounded even as it came from a tunnel of fury.

"I don't know," I shrugged. "It's the times. You and I are past our prime. Let them have it, I suppose. The marauding moors. Have at it, I say to them. Dig your graves. Take the academy and turn it into a hellscape of underexamined ideas."

"You're lying. I know why you did it."

Did he?

"You did it for the woman," he said.

I stood up to fetch the coffee.

"I have stopped doing things for women," I said. "You should know I don't believe it gets us anywhere. And these days, it's as if all the arts, literature, and politics are in a conspiracy to cockblock me."

"I don't believe it gets us anywhere with a classy woman, no. But it may get you somewhere with *this* one."

I turned around to look at him. I chuckled. "You should know better than to think this will get a rise out of me."

"You have lost your mind, Harding. Throw your stupid kumbaya Halloween party, sure. Did you even notice I didn't come, by the way? But now . . . changing the course of the university—of *the life of the mind*—for a woman who won't even let you close to her little finger?"

"I will let you run the course with your silliness," I said. "And then I have a lecture to prepare."

"Well, enjoy those while you still have a class to teach," he said. He pushed himself off the table and readied to go.

"Besides," I said. "You are being presumptive, aren't you, in imagining that she won't let me in?"

I shouldn't have. I should have let the imbecile head home to cry. I should have been a grown man.

When I recall it now, I did hear Edgar bark and scuffle around in the living room. At the time, I imagined he was growing impatient for his walk. Later, I would find out otherwise.

"If she hasn't let you in after these past two years of your soulful looks at her, she never will, Harding. Keep it shriveled in your pants," Meyer said. He seemed to be trying too hard to rile me up.

I snorted. "You know nothing," I said. "You with your marriage of twenty-seven years. You couldn't get it out of your pants if you tried."

"A tragic thing, to be mocked for marriage by a man in a prolonged state of dismal celibacy."

I stayed quiet. I imagined myself in salt water.

"Did you know she is sleeping with a student?" he said.

Now he was being ridiculous.

Whatever he saw on my face, he seemed pleased with it. His voice drew upon a new lease of animation. "Yes. With a student *or two*. That's what the university investigation is about. She sleeps with the boys and she sleeps with the girls. I heard a young man say that boy or girl, she'd rather have her pussy eaten than plowed. You might have what it takes, though, Harding. Minus thirty-five years."

I wanted to throw the mug of hot coffee in his smug, fat face. He almost seemed to be straining toward me so I would.

"Did you see the picture I left on your desk? It was taken by one of her lovers," he said.

I must have gone ashen. He looked pleased. Strengthened.

"Has she ever posed that way for you? Taken off her scarf for you? Poor, lovelorn Ollie. Throwing us all under the bus for . . ."

He went on and on. I wanted to fetch my gun and put a bullet in his head.

I was in bad form. I had to be careful. There. Naming the feeling is conquering it and all. My mind wasn't to be my cruel master even though my Ruhaba had turned Rahab!

"I will be in her bed by this weekend," I said as calmly as I could. "What would you like me to bring you as a memento?"

Okay, so I slipped. That would be the last of it.

"Oh, you will?" Meyer said. "And what, be accused of sexual harassment the next day? Be accused of exoticizing a brown woman? Be accused of rape? Oh wait . . . will you ask for permission? What do they call it . . . *consent*? Will you beg for consent? 'Just the tip, please, dear esteemed colleague' . . ."

I kept my cool. "I will need no permission. I will ask for none. She will do as I command. She asked for me to vote 'yes' and promised to sleep with me if I did. There. See? We're still doing things the traditional way. No asking for consent. It's a given in the rituals of mating. In fact, I will call her to my office tomorrow and fuck her on my English Department oak desk."

He looked taken aback. "In your dreams," he said weakly.

"Well, I invite you to stand outside and listen to her moan," I said.

Meyer turned around to walk away. I had no idea what I had set in motion. But I wanted him to be gone before the boy came by to walk the dog. Meyer was unpredictable in this state. Who knew what he might say?

And he did say something, just as he shut the front door behind him. He said: "Don't do it. Emily might have taken it without going to the cops. *These* women don't."

I didn't see the boy that evening. I let Edgar out into the yard to do his business, but he seemed lazy, too. I got a text from Ruhaba. I looked at it with some shame as I thought of the things I had said about her to Meyer. And I felt the footsteps of rage upon my chest. The inquiry and its findings. The student squeezing her waist. Could it be true, what Meyer had said?

CHAPTER TWENTY

Dishonorable

Today is November 7th. Tomorrow, the country will elect a new president. The air is thick with the chatter of a bumptious citizenry wielding its vote. The tragedy that happened six days ago in my office is a matter that needs wrapping up, for the FBI. A distraction for the nation. A searing gash in my soul.

But I have to push all pain into the airless, soundless space I have made in my chest. Too many other sounds are pounding into me, thanks to some information the federal agents just brought me that turned the world around me shrill.

I knew there would be consequences of my uncontrolled scorn toward Ray Waters Jr. at our last meeting, yesterday. I didn't know it would come back to bite me so swiftly, though, and in this manner. But I can see the beautiful precision of this revenge. Inflict pain to the psyche, not the physical form. I am just surprised that the FBI should possess the sophistication for such a craft.

They had gone through Ruhaba's cache of unsent emails in the folder I had tipped them off about. They wanted me to read a few and tell me what I made of them. What do we learn of Ruhaba through her rumination? What do we learn of her honor?

In whose imagination? I wonder. "Honor" means different things in the two parts of the world in which she had feeble claims to a home.

In which one did she invade? How do we invade Ruhaba?

I had to tread carefully. I felt trapped. I had to read her words, her private words, that were perhaps intended to die under her ritual of twenty-four-hour email forbearance, or perhaps to fly and pierce like no bullet could, from her brain, from the boy's cries, from my imagination.

Ray Waters Jr. brought Sarah Kupersmith with him, to take notes, ostensibly, but it seemed to me that her glare was sharper than it had ever been. I settled Edgar down, put on a cup of coffee, dried myself off and put on a fire, tried the federal agents' patience as far as I could before I looked at the printed pages they placed on my desk before me. After page after random page, there was this one:

From: Khan, Ruhaba

To: Khan, Ruhaba

Tues, Oct. 25, 2016. 1:20 p.m.

I don't give a shit about the Muslim world.

[A smile escaped me before I could stop myself. By the light of the fire and my dim table lamp, I saw Ray Waters Jr. cross his arms over his chest and lean toward me. Sarah Kupersmith made a note in her notebook. I had to be careful].

I don't give a shit about the Muslim world. I give even thinner shit about the presidential election. Yes, yes, please reassure me that this is my home and no one has a right to make me feel like an outsider. Yes, grab my gaze and I'll hold yours, sure, until you have smiled at me wide and hard enough to convince me that you truly forgive me and the other handful of Muslims you personally know, for 9/11. And I'll #NeverForget all over Facebook when the day comes around each year and wait for you to <3 it.

Yes, tell me once again how much I look like Huma Abedin. And I'll tell you I trust this candidate or that to negotiate peace. Peace, peace. Peace, peace, peace.

You don't give a dick about my peace. You couldn't bear to have me educate you about the horrors that all American presidents have inflicted on the Muslim world.

The sheet of paper was close to my face. I gradually pulled it in to attempt to conceal the grin that had grown thick as scar tissue across my face and also because I was leaning in to read all of Ruhaba's delicious words.

But yes, take a picture with me every now and then and post it on Instagram with #Humbled, #GiftOfMyLife. Yes, write about your encounter with the Muslim owner of the newsstand you go to or the Uber driver who just took you to watch the Seattle Opera at McCaw Hall, and tell your friends how afraid you are for these people if Trump wins. And I'll try not to feel too bad that none of you invited me to join Pantsuit Nation.

Yes, of course I have the connections to bring Malala to campus, Dr. Sindy Greere. Next year, for sure. Just a couple of phone calls, no worries. In fact, I think her mom and I went to school together. There's just that few of us. I know it doesn't seem like that at all when you're seeing us pop up all across the world like whack-a-moles, but it does seem that way when we need to connect you to another one of our kind, doesn't it?

And yes, I'm fucking your son, Dr. Lisa Cunningham. You must be so proud.

I drew a sharp breath. The paper fell from my hand. I felt Sarah Kupersmith's piercing gaze on my face. I knew these facts of Ruhaba already, I suppose, but I turned hot from seeing it in her words, in cold print, under another woman's watchfulness.

Sarah Kupersmith leaned over to spot which line I was staring at. I flitted my eyes all over the sheet of paper.

"Something seems to have startled you," she said, quietly.

I was taken aback. Her voice was still unfamiliar to me.

"All of it is startling, wouldn't you say?" I said, looking at Ray Waters Jr. My voice was so devoid of tremor and tone, it sounded like a tape I may have made in another time to play at an opportune moment such as this. That was enough. I was now able to meet Sarah Kupersmith's eye, trained as it is in the rigors of her vocation, with my own, trained in mine.

I picked up the sheet of paper again, shook it once, and continued to read.

I will have to do something about the young Mr. Cunningham, for now, while that inquiry is on. When he graduates next year, I won't care who knows. I'll have tenure and they'll have a rude awakening about the sophisticated Dr. Khan. She's not dating the white scholar of Islam? Or that sweet Jewish professor, what's his name? That would have been so heartwarming. She moved in on a student? That's just dishonorable.

I paused. "Dishonorable," I said, looking past Sarah Kupersmith at Ray Waters Jr. He nodded slowly and smiled a half-smile. A sneer?

Maybe the young Mr. Cunningham will move on by next year, although I hope not. He has an intensity, an intuitive manner of finding his way around my body that is hard to come by. But yes, the young Mr. Cunningham also has my heart. He's loving, innocent, tender. I will have to find a way to let him go. Ease my talons, turn them upon myself, rip out a bit of my heart. May Allah guide me.

To: Saira Alam
From: Khan, Ruhaba
Tues, Nov. 1, 3:13 p.m.

Dear Saira,
I am worried about Adil and his future. He is such a loving boy, your son. He and I have built an immense bond these past few weeks. He is a free thinker, a gentle soul, a feminist and a flutist! Please call me from your friend's phone soon,

so I can discuss with you a proposition about his further education.

This child has broken a spell. I always believed I could never tell a soul in our family, except you, about what happened to me that made me mistrust men, especially those from our world. But I hadn't known then that there was greater family to come. I hadn't known that one day a child named Adil would be my family. This child, with the same color of skin and hair and eye as my worst oppressors, would sleep soundly in a room in my home and I would feel safe. No whisper from the past could have willed in me the comfort—no, raging hope—that I feel when I hear Adil play his flute in his room.

Adil.

Does your name mean anything, people ask him and me. Yes, it means something. It means "the one who is just."

A boy whose name means "just" comes to live with an aunt who seeks justice, whose name means "open."

I hope you will forgive me, but he found me sobbing yesterday from the stress of a photograph of me that someone leaked on campus. I perhaps should not have done this, but I opened up to this teenager and told him about my past.

I told him. I told him about the men who didn't save me, the men who didn't stand up for me, the men who were charged with protecting me—but didn't—from the family men. I told Adil who they all were and how very unlike them he was now and how very unlike them he was forever to be.

Adil swore to never speak of it. He was shaken when I told him, that child the color of those men, so shaken that I was racked with self-doubt for a moment. But then, how else will we turn our boys into good men? How will we find in them the masculinity that melts into tears of compassion, of a right rage?

Adil had tears in his eyes. Adil cried tears for me. For the girl I was. For the girlhood I lost. I made a Pakistani boy cry for me.

I am invincible. He is brave. Your brave son. I am happy you found another way to escape our home, different from my way. I know you feel loved and cherished by the sweet family you made.

I will find a way to keep Adil here for as long as you want. I will come with him to Toulouse next summer and hug you and my brother-in-law and Naeema. I will have you all as my family and I will have Adil. He will keep his friends here. He will grow radical with me.

"Radical," I said, in a tenor just slightly above a whisper. I didn't look up. I sensed Ray Waters Jr. nodding. Sarah Kupersmith stood close and made notes.

For the love of Allah, we will be Muslims or we will be atheists. No matter who wins this fucking election, and no matter my many sins, I will wear my abaya in America the way you wear yours in Europe, and we will show Adil that no one dares rip it off our heads again. The white feminists will support me for their own reasons. They want me to be visibly the Other. The staunchest scholar of Said's Orientalism wants so badly to fight for Ruhaba Khan's right to bury her gorgeous mane under a rag; the loudest feminist wants to fight for Ruhaba Khan's right to wear it. And the haters want to be able to spot immediately, without all this nuance that's dulling as all, whom to hate. I'll make everyone happy. There, there.

I have found in my hijab a way to control the gaze, bend it to my will. In my hijab lies my defense against erasure.

But I am troubling you with all these thoughts. You should not have to worry about one more person. Don't worry. I will see you soon, my dear sister.

A film of moisture had crept over my eyes, and my heart was beating like a crazed lobster trying to pincer its way out of my chest. Something has been taken from me. Something tender has been taken from me.

And what was this girlhood incident she was speaking of? I could imagine, yes, but surely, she had written more?

I looked up at Ray Waters Jr. He was looking away, but Sarah Kupersmith seemed to be trying to burn a hole into my brain.

I looked back down, turned the page. There was no more. I will get no more of Ruhaba. There is only so much of the story I get to know. There is only so much of her story that I get to tell.

Sarah Kupersmith asked me what I thought the conversation between the boy and his aunt had been about that previous night. I have no idea, I said, looking at no one.

I need *you* to tell me, I wanted to say to them. Something has been taken from me. Something has also been kept from me. I have so much of them, the boy and Ruhaba, and I suffer now for the things I couldn't have.

Sarah Kupersmith drew in a breath to ask a question, but Ray Waters Jr. got there first—"During your relationship with her, did she ever allude to a matter she needed to hide?"

During your relationship with her . . .

"No. But I assume . . ."

"Did you know that women in Pakistan can be stoned to death for their own rape?" Ray Waters Jr. said.

"I think you mean Saudi Arabia," said Sarah Kupersmith, not looking at her associate.

If Ray Waters Jr. was slighted by this correction by the woman with him, he did not let on. Not that I was deep in any observation of them.

I was thinking of Ruhaba: Was she raped? What did they know?

"Did the boy seem disturbed?" Ray Waters Jr. said. "Especially in the last couple of days before November 1st?"

"I don't quite recall, but now that you mention it, perhaps yes," I said. I didn't tell them that I had been too preoccupied after that encounter with Meyer, too troubled about my own chances of finding my way into Ruhaba's arms.

Women who had been through rape were harder to seduce. Or way too easy. Given my experience with Ruhaba, she probably would never have been mine. *I could have rescued you, Ruhaba. You could have belonged.*

I don't have a good way to tell these federal agents that I suspect that the boy had walked in the door that evening when Meyer and I were talking, that he had overheard what we said about his aunt, what I said about my intentions. That's why he had followed her when she came to my office that day and he had lurked outside my door.

Ray Waters Jr. read me a primer on honor killings in the Muslim world. From the way Sarah Kupersmith slumped into a chair, I got the sense he was reading it as much to her as he was to me. He spoke of Muslim women being killed by their men—and boys—for what their world believed was wayward behavior. A chronicle took shape before us and burned bright as a flame that a female federal agent's sighs of indignance could not snuff out. Her notes are just notes, and the narratives of the men before her are in service of a more perfect story, a more perfect union.

CHAPTER TWENTY-ONE

The Laughter

When Chesterton was a child, his sister died. In all his years, nobody around him, not even his father, with whom he was close, talked to him about the dead girl. She was the only thing about which his father did not speak. Chesterton was left with little to go on. He did not remember his sister's death, but he remembered her once falling off a rocking horse. In his head, for years, the little memory grew and grew until it became something else and he came to imagine that his sister had been thrown from a real horse and killed. When he examined how he had come to conflate the rocking-horse incident with the separate and unrelated incident of his sister's death, Chesterton concluded that the real difficulty about remembering anything was that we may remember too much because we remember too often. The only true memory is the one that comes back sharply and suddenly, he believed. In that piercing instant, we remember things as they truly were.

I have avoided thinking about Ruhaba's visit to my office

on November 1st. I have neither remembered it too much nor remembered it too often. Now, I am sitting before my fire at home, Edgar at my feet, awaiting what I hope is the final visit from the federal agents before they make their address at their big press conference this afternoon. They want this all tied up. The presidential election is tomorrow, and there is much greater work to be done.

I must gather my thoughts. I think to that moment in which I went in search for Ruhaba the day after Meyer's visit to my home. I think of how I roamed, from her office to her classrooms to her home. I knocked on her front door and no one responded. I heard someone shuffle about inside, but her car was nowhere, so I imagined it was the boy, and he didn't, for some reason, want to open the door. I didn't give it much thought.

I returned to campus and went in search of Ruhaba at the library. I found her sitting there, curled up in a chair, reading in the light of a lamp in a quiet corner. If I had imagined that my feelings for her had coarsened, and indeed, I should have found it perfectly loathsome that she had stolen away for some blissful solitude after orchestrating such an upheaval in so many of our lives, I was once again floored by the very sight of her, diminutive, nodding off like a little girl. I steadied myself and swallowed hard.

It wasn't the best place in which to confront her, but perhaps I could keep my voice lowered. I forced myself to recall all that Meyer had told me the day before. For all the years I have known Meyer, I know he is a dirty little worm, but, like any worm, he has keen receptors for sensory information, whether or not he uses that information to evolve into a higher life form. I have never known that man to collect empty nuggets.

I would need to distance myself from this woman soon, I told myself. I told myself that she was a whore. She had been sleeping with a student, Meyer had told me. A student or *two*. Boys and girls! She wasn't inhibited by her culture or religion; she could have been sleeping with me, but she was sleeping with students.

And yet, there she had been, parading around as some sort of victim of our times, a victim with more power than anyone else right now in North America. A Muslim woman in a hijab. A woman from a religion on a rampage but a woman needing protection from those who fear her religion. What a perfect storm of identity politics this was, and look how it had whipped us all up into a fucked-up state of apologia.

Not me. She wouldn't have me. Oh, I would fuck her sooner or later, but it would be—how would she say it—on my own terms.

I should have turned around and left, but she had seen me, standing there, staring at her. She uncurled herself coolly, once again looking in total control. I walked to her.

"Hello, there," I said coldly, as coldly as I could in the lowered voice of the library.

"Hell-o!" she said.

Yes. Piercing, my recollection. Clear memory. Clear as day. Clear as a shout from hell. Hello.

"Looks like people are expecting to have a woman president," she said, waving me to sit in a chair near hers.

"Yes, it would appear so," I said, sliding into the chair.

"Did you know that a fair chunk of the Muslim community wants it to be Trump?" she said.

I didn't respond. I cared so little about this line of conversation. She could prattle on and she would get the message sooner or later.

"To be honest," she said, "I'd feel safer with him. At least we'd know what we have. It's like sitting in a well-lit room with a knife in your hand as a monster rushes at you. Versus sitting in a dark room hearing a voice that sounds like your mother's singing you a lullaby and then you feel your gut being ripped open."

I couldn't bear it anymore, the small talk. "You are sleeping with a student," I said.

I hadn't expected that. She hadn't expected that.

I thought she looked scared.

"How do you know?" she said, in a whisper. "Are you on the Inquiry Committee? Is *that* why you've been befriending . . . is that where that printout of that photograph came from?"

I was a bit surprised, but it pleased me that she could feel fearful of me now, not contemptuous, not betrayed, not entitled, but fearful.

"I am not on any Inquiry Committee," I said, matching her whisper. "And that picture is going nowhere. I just happen to know your secret."

She stood up. She started to walk away. Then, turning around, she said, "What do you intend to do about it?"

I sat there, silent, watching her. I wanted to look away from her fear. I had enjoyed it for a moment, and I no longer wanted to be the abyss into which she stared down in terror.

I did not want to be the monster or the mother.

"Nothing," I said. I stood up and walked up to her and stood close. "I slept with my students for years."

She was quiet. She stepped away. Then, walking away, she said, "*I* would have told on you."

"*What?*"

I had said that too loudly. A clutch of students bent over their laptops nearby looked up at us and then went back to their screens.

I walked a step behind Ruhaba as she strode past rows of towering bookshelves. She said, "If it had been the other way around, if I had discovered that you slept with your students, I would tell on you. I would see you as a predator. Perhaps because it's young girls and you're a man. A different power dynamic there."

I stared slack-jawed at the back of her head. No "thank you"? No "what do you want in return for your silence"? Instead, a challenge.

Was it a challenge? Or was it that same guilelessness that had kept me in her grip for months?

We were in a far corner of the library now. She was heading toward the elevator, but she paused, turned around to look me full in the face, and said, "Look, Ollie. I know you are attracted to me. I know you are probably angered that I sleep with students instead of sleeping with you. But you and I, we are two predators in our own way. Hyenas don't sleep with wolves. It would be disastrous. Ugly. Clumsy. Disappointing."

"How many?" I said.

"What?"

"Tell me it was only one time and I . . . I would forgive you."

She sneered at me. "*Forgive* me?"

"I mean . . . I could have the Inquiry Committee forgive you. They sometimes understand these . . ."

"They do? And what if it wasn't just one time? What if I am not forgivable? Why do you need me to be pure, Dr. Harding? Why does this university want me to be a pet and not a threat? Why do you people need me to be better than you?"

She turned away and stepped up to the elevator. I reached up to grab her by the back of her neck, to force her to stop, to reckon with what I had to say. But my hand stopped in midair as I saw a man shuffle out from behind a bookshelf. He stared at me, at my angry, grasping hand, at the woman walking away from me into an elevator.

It was a janitor. An old and shriveled man. He probably didn't even speak English. He stood there staring. I took a book out of a bookshelf and hurled it at him. He dodged it. I walked away.

If only Ruhaba had left it at that. If only she hadn't come back to me an hour later, to prod for deeper meaning, to poke the bear.

But, no. She came. I receded to my own space on a campus rapidly growing foreign. I sat in my office chair, my hand in my drawer, feeling the yarn of my neglected knitting, feeling something else beyond the yarn—cold metal, coiled in promise. It all calmed me. I was set to let it all be.

She walked right in through my office door. She pulled up a chair and sat in it as if she had all the claim on these halls. She spoke as if she had all the time in the world.

"I will not offer to sleep with you to keep you quiet," she said, calmly. "But I still have something to say to you. I will say it even though it will now sound like I didn't intend to say it and am only making it up to appease you."

She waited.

My memory tells me I took the bait.

"What did you come here to say?" I said.

"That, believe it or not, when you are being a better human, I feel safe with you."

I snorted.

"No, not the way I speak of feeling safe with Trump. Or perhaps in some way, it's the same. I am wary of America. I know of no place on earth where people are surer of the distinction between good and evil and see with such supposed clarity a chasm between the two. I don't know any other people who are more certain of their goodness than the white people here. I know no other culture in the world that can see every color but gray."

"What does that have to do with me?" I said, letting the impatience leap up in my voice like a ready whip.

"You see gray."

I stood up and turned away from her.

"I want to spend time with you because you step into the gray, Ollie."

I shook my head and waved my hand to dismiss her.

"Okay. You never have to speak to me again," she said. "But before I leave . . ."

My memory pierces me hard now. Clear as lightning. Gray as lightning.

"Before I leave, I want you to know that I am grateful that

you stepped up to Adil that night at the Provost's party when those kids walked away from him and his face fell. I saw it and I should have thanked you for it before but I . . . I waited. I don't know why. I decided in that moment that I wanted you as a friend."

"You should go now," I said.

I didn't want her to go. But I couldn't tell whether I was being played. I felt unsafe.

I turned around to fix her with a cold eye. As she stood up and nodded and began to turn to go, I snapped out of it. "No," I said. "Stay."

"I'd like to," she said. She reached out a hand and laid it on my arm. Something fell away from her face. She looked a little bit like the boy.

"I'd like to offer you my friendship," she said.

"An intimate friendship?" I said.

"What?"

"You . . . I want intimacy from you, Ruhaba." I pulled her toward me, to my side of the table.

"No! For goodness sake, wake up," she said.

"You . . . you *owe* me."

"I owe you nothing," she said, pushing me away. She started to walk toward the door.

"The university's inquiry . . ." I said, steadying my voice. "It's not just about you. Here, in America . . . that sort of thing could get in the way of your keeping Adil," I added. "I can make all that go away."

She froze. Her face turned into a mask of no lines, no maps, no strategy, no promise. With vanished eyes, she stared at me and said, "Why won't you let it go? Let them do what they will. What is it that bothers you all? Men like you. That I can get away with it and you no longer can?"

"Think of the boy. Think of someone other than you. *You*, with your savage degree of selfishness."

She smiled, slow, worse than a sneer this time. A snarl. "I *am* savage," she said, and then laughed the most hideous laughter I have ever heard, as if she relished my barbs.

She misunderstood me. She would *always* misunderstand me.

"And yes, I am selfish. So, shoot me."

And so, I did. In the shadow of a second, I slid open my drawer, picked up my gun, and, cold as the metal that touched my palm, I shot her square between the eyes and wiped the laughter from her face.

Grief has been described in so many ways. Some say it's a river, soothing one moment and readying to drown you the next. Others say it's the closest we can come to God. Chesterton called it superficial, said melancholy should be an innocent interlude. But the grief I felt in that moment just before the bullet left me to meet my beloved sits in me even now, as I write this. The grief holds me, slips and slides through me like a red silk demon, peering through my eyes one moment, whispering through my fingertips the next.

Everything else after that moment happened so quickly. The boy appeared in the next instant after Ruhaba fell. Now I realize that he had come to my office after he heard my urgent knocks on Ruhaba's front door. He had overcome his fear of the campus and he had found his way to my office to protect her. Because he'd heard everything I said to Meyer the evening before. He had come to my house to walk Edgar and he had heard everything. And now he'd heard everything I spoke about with Ruhaba. I watched his boyhood rush from his face at the sight of his aunt, headscarf and all, fallen to the floor, her blood already gushing like the Garonne, flooding her right eye.

"Khala Ruhaba!" he screamed, his voice breaking between boy and man.

I have to pause in my writing here. I have to breathe and let memory turn sharp, clean away every other instinct, every emotion, every resistance to the truth. Breathe against all will of the demon.

A silence I had known only when drowning in salt fell around us. Through its shroud, I saw a shadow inch toward my door. I reached into my drawer to put my gun away. My fingers brushed against my knitting.

The fibers of wool sent a message to my brain.

Kathryn. Sweet innocent child who may still want her father someday.

I threw the gun at the feet of the boy.

The shadow at my office door crouched forward. It was the administrative assistant. He peered in and his eyes almost fell out of his skull.

What did he see, that young administrative assistant? What did he know, from his training in the Run-Hide-Fight plan for an active shooter on campus?

He saw a boy, a boy he had made the mistake of sending into a faculty member's office without checking. He knew him to be a Muslim boy. Now he is a Muslim boy with a gun, shaking, leaning over one fatality.

Run-Hide-Fight had trained the administrative assistant to know that *an active shooter is an individual actively engaged in killing or attempting to kill people in a confined and populated area, typically through the use of firearms*. The past few days had put the administrative assistant on high alert, vigilant from the threat of a shooter.

What he saw was a white male professor standing with his hands raised and visible in the air, his face ashen. He saw a Muslim woman, no, a faculty member, on the floor, her eyes already dead in their stare, red blood gushing from her head and onto the office-gray of the carpeting in the Department of English.

The administrative assistant had been told: the event is unpredictable and evolves quickly.

What did he hear as the boy called out to his aunt, his voice rising, breaking, screaming? Did he hear a frightened and desperate lament to a dead aunt?

No, he heard something else. He heard a call to Allah. Allahu Akbar.

He had been trained, this administrative assistant, for just such a day, just such an incident, give or take. In the past week, he had listened for sounds and he had looked for signs. He was trained to *hide in an area out of the shooter's view*. He was told to *block entry to hiding places and lock the doors*.

He looked at me. I said: "I will talk to the boy. You go save the students."

The administrative assistant scurried out, kicked my office door shut from the outside, barricaded it with a filing cabinet from the hallway, ran down the hall, and put the Active Shooter Drill into motion.

Students and faculty would head in as calm a manner as possible—although I could already hear screams and thuds outside—to the escape routes that had been assigned to each building. They would leave their belongings behind. Public Safety police officers would be shouting instructions to the crowds, and visitors would follow the example of faculty, staff, and students. Everyone was to avoid sudden movements, especially toward the officers. They would provide the police with the location, room number, and description of the shooter: the Muslim boy with a limp. Dark-haired, olive-skinned, black-eyed. Fifteen years old. Speaks French and some English.

Loves Camille.

The campus would be locked down and the people would be evacuated. Classes in session would be told to lock and barricade their doors from the inside by moving heavy objects, such as desks or cabinets, in front of the doors. They would move away from all windows and carefully pull down any blinds or shades. They would silence all cellphones, radios, and televisions.

If anyone believed their life to be in imminent danger, they were to act as aggressively as they could toward the shooter. They were to be unafraid to fight, to overwhelm, and to take the shooter down.

The boy finally turned around to face me. His face was grotesque in the throes of fear and grief. He looked from his dead aunt to the live man before him.

I saw the will of all that is human drain out of the boy's face, his torso, his limbs. He picked up my gun from near his feet and began to raise it toward me. I held his gaze. I knew this boy from the gun range. *You will know his mind*. He wouldn't shoot me. The gun fell from his hand.

When the police arrived swiftly at my door, I was hiding securely under my desk, out of the way of any rain of bullets they planned for the active shooter. When they rescued me, I got one last look at the boy, through a huddle of men and metal, slumped from a single bullet the men had planted in his body. Dead? I couldn't tell.

They carried me to an ambulance and declared me to be in a state of shock.

In that state, I thought of Ruhaba. Gone. Lost. Never mine to gain, but always mine to lose.

I thought of the boy, of all the things he could say if he lived. I thought of the maps on the skin of his fingers and of the way they lay entangled and imprinted over mine on the one object he feared over all else. He had many stories to tell them, if he lived, and then they would come to me for mine.

CHAPTER TWENTY-TWO

Clean

To: Sugar High Bakery
From: Khan, Ruhaba
Oct. 28, 2016

Dear favorite baker,
That 6-inch vanilla-caramel cake with its black currant jam center is the most delicious thing I have eaten in all my life. I would like to order a regular-size, 12-inch cake of any flavor of your imagination to be delivered to my home on the night of the election. Something tells me my nephew and I are going to need some comfort.
With deep appreciation for your craft,
Ruhaba.

The boy is now conscious, the agents call to tell me. He is incoherent. He keeps saying that his aunt had extracted a promise from him. He kept murmuring, "I will not speak to the police outside your presence."

Your aunt is dead, they told him. You killed her.

He asked them if he was dreaming. Did he kill her in his dream? Did she drown?

The agents asked if I could come by the hospital tomorrow and speak with him. Perhaps I can help jiggle something in his memory, set it right? They will be by my side, they say, but I tell them I don't mind being alone with the boy for a bit. I will go see him after I cast my electoral vote.

I will go now for a walk with Edgar, breathe the fresh air of my free land. My hours and days of discernment have drawn to a close. Here on my desk in my study is the boy's letter. When I return, I will shred this letter with my hands. I will watch the pieces float into the flames of my fireplace that once again lies clean, uncluttered, sure of its purpose. Into the flames I will offer next every single page of this journal into which I have written my truths and paradoxes. I have committed it all to memory. I have no need for these pages, and neither does anyone else.

I am writing now in a small notebook as I sit on the same park bench on which the boy sat playing his flute some weeks ago. I must reclaim these spaces. I must continue my journaling, and then tend to the chapters in my book. In my email are two invitations to speak at conferences. My name has been in the news, and macabre though it may seem, an interest in my scholarship has been stirred.

The sun is out. The mountain is out, as we say hereabouts when the clouds clear and Mount Rainier becomes visible. In my backyard, a persimmon tree that Emily planted all those years ago has suddenly borne fruit after lying barren for an eternity. When I return home, I will pluck those little dollops of sunset yellow from the tree and enjoy that heavenly taste. A neighbor or two waved at me as I walked, as they do these days. Perhaps it is one of them who follows me around, in awe. I have been foolish to find in such admiration a foreboding. I thought I saw that figure again just minutes ago, dark, a bit too girlish to be Janet, vanishing behind a fence as I stepped out. I waved, but the shadow was gone, and I wondered whether I'd imagined her after all.

What good will come if the boy goes on living? If he dies, he will not have to face the heartbreak of going home only to lose his first love to another boy. For Camille will break his heart, of this I am sure. He ought to die with a heart in love. The one great love.

He should not have to answer to people about the shame of his aunt, about her dishonorable ways. He did not have to run in the streets and hide in a boat like that terrorist boy in Boston some years ago, only to be executed later by the state. He should go as a warrior. And, among some young men in his homeland . . . his homelands . . . he will be a hero.

I have been invaluable to their investigations, the FBI says. In the past few days since November 1st, after a brief statement explaining the bare bones of the case to the media and the American people, the FBI is moving to stall all tangential inquiries with this statement: The FBI is actively investigating Adil Alam's radicalization to include his history in Pakistan and France, his family, his associates, whereabouts, social media impressions, and potential motivations.

"This has been an active investigation that continues to unfold," I have heard Ray Waters Jr. say patiently into his phone several times. Today, his plan is to make some conclusive remarks at the press conference, about how the FBI had been investigating the boy for some time now, how they regret not taking him into custody before, how he had been seen skulking about the campus protests a few days ago, about how we were all fortunate that there had been only one casualty when several more could have been planned. The axis of inquiry lay somewhere between honor and terror.

Chesterton believed that fairy tales endure because the hero is a normal human boy startled by his adventures *because* he is normal. The fairy tale is about what a sane boy or man will do in a mad world.

They have been calling me a sane man, a hero. Do I have a choice? No. This story needs me to be a hero. The rapidity with which the American imagination has filled in the blanks in my story has left even me astonished. Look how neatly my narratives fall into a deeply etched template of immutable truths. They need me to tell it like they already know it happened. This story needs my voice to bring comfort. It needs your eye to seek an end with no wrinkle, but, perhaps, a frown.

From my voice, you pick up the pieces, you signal your grief and your virtue, your threads grow strong and thin, you find the larger stories to tell: The boy had a troubled past. Our boys are alienated. He may have been sent here to carry out an honor killing of his aunt, whose family believed her to have gone astray in the sexual liberties of the West. Those women there need our help. The boy may or may not have been a lone wolf. Yes, there was the matter of her own story, of joys and ecstasies, perhaps, and also of terrible past assaults. But not all stories are for our knowing. It's just better this way.

Who am I to whisper reason into these verses? Reason, not imagination, breeds insanity, Chesterton said.

Reason will tell you that the boy was just a boy, and that it was I who was the wolf. Poetry, however, will keep you afloat. Poetry tells me that they may come for me one day. Or I may go to them. Which one will buckle first, I wonder, my country or my conscience?

I now conclude my ritual of discernment. His letter to a sweet French girl tells a different story from the one in which we see ourselves clear as day. It will only serve to bring chaos to simpler, greater lives.

And the truth gets blurred like a wet letter
But since I gave up hope I feel a lot better

I am home now after a long and meandering walk, and I realize I had let myself be distracted on my way out. I left my front door unlocked. I threw it open and waited for Edgar to bark if he sensed an intruder. He ran happily to his water bowl. I walked through the rooms. Nothing seemed to be missing.

The agents just called and told me that "a person named Essence" has sent them a picture of a letter she has just procured from my study and is on her way to deliver to them a journal. She told them the boy had spoken to her about a love letter he gave to me and that she just had a feeling she must get her own hands on it.

She and some other students are demanding a different

inquiry. Why hadn't I handed the letter to them?, the federal agents ask. It reveals so much. It paints a different picture. They'd also like to talk to me about an account they heard from a university janitor that they had earlier ignored. And something from Ruhaba's department chair, about an email from Ruhaba regarding an altercation with me at the library on November 1st. Ruhaba had asked the woman for her advice about what to do. The woman chair had instructed Ruhaba to go talk to me immediately, make nice, maintain collegiality with senior faculty. She told the federal agents that she regretted sending Ruhaba to me.

Why hadn't I mentioned the altercation?, they ask me now.

There are too many threads to ignore now, too many questions that need answers from me, the federal agents say. I am not to leave my home until they get here, they instruct me. Agents have been assigned to read my journal, but my questioning will begin right away.

I have nowhere to go, I want to say to them. This is the only place to which I have any claim.

So much has been taken from me. And now, so much more. So, Ruhaba had come to my office that final time on instruction from her department chair. Not from some lingering desire for more of me, not even for closure. And yet, hadn't I seen a sincerity on her face when she had offered me something? An opening. A friendship. I wasn't sought to be replaced. I was invited to something, to a nearness and a vastness I still don't understand.

I push against the gravity of the gulf that wants to swallow me. I sit down at my desk, the one that just moments ago allowed itself to be burgled by a girl who ought to be thrown behind bars but instead has received an audience with federal agents. I pick up my phone to write a text to Meyer, to ask for his loyalty. My text doesn't go through. He has blocked me. When did he block me? It won't be long before they talk to him, too.

As I stare at the screen, I get a text from Kathryn. It has no message from her, no inquiry into my well-being, just a rude push of a link to a video shared on social media. Uploaded by one Saira Alam with the words, "Here's a video sent to me by my sister's student, taken on the morning of November 1st. You will see my son and my sister happy, on a walk, loving their lives. My sister is reciting a provocative Urdu poem by her favorite poetess, Fahmida Riaz. My son understands what she is saying. Does he look angry? No. He loved his aunt. He would never have killed her. He would never plan a school shooting. He was not a lone wolf, he is a lamb. Please find the man and the terrible force that took my sister's phenomenal life."

I watch Ruhaba smile into the camera from afar as she twirls slowly in a park. She kicks fall leaves high up into the air. The audio fills with laughter. It's when the leaves fall back down and settle onto her clothes and hair that I notice that Ruhaba does not have on her headscarf.

The boy is walking with her. He plays on his flute. Ruhaba speaks a verse. The camera turns dizzyingly onto the person shooting the video—Essence. She says, "I have no idea what Dr. Khan is saying, but yeah, I'll look it up later."

I was invited to go on this walk with them. I had declined because I wanted time alone with Ruhaba. I could have been in this picture, in this ordinary moment. Would that have changed the things that happened?

The video turns back around on Ruhaba and the boy. More verse. More leaves in the air. More dancing. More laughter. More flute.

I hear the flute this time.

I can't bear to hear the sound. The flute, the laughter. I halt the video.

I read the rest of the words Ruhaba's sister has written. They are lines from the poem Ruhaba is reciting and then a translation.

Apne lambe lambe baal udaati jaaye
Hava ki beti saath havaa ke gaati jaaye

There she goes, throwing her hair open to billow in the wind
There she goes, singing with the wind, the daughter of the wind

Epilogue

To: Khan, Ruhaba
From: Khan, Ruhaba

Dear You,
Come, bear witness to my silence. For, if you would have truly wanted it, I would speak, uninterrupted. I'd tell my own story, my truest story, for it's mine to be told and I don't lack language . . . but go on—have it your way.
Sincerely,
Ruhaba

ACKNOWLEDGMENTS

To be in the state of storytelling, over the hours and the years, the storyteller must find aid from magicians and muses beyond herself. Here are some of mine—

My agent, Soumeya Bendimerad Roberts, who *got* this book and then knew exactly what to do. My superb editor, Rakesh Satyal, and the team at HarperVia.

Readers who gave me feedback on different drafts—Ali Mian, Jane Anderson, David Neel, Ranjit Arab, Willie Fitzgerald, Kelli Connell, Anca Szilagyi, Jennifer Fricas, and Shahina Piyarali.

American and French students who provided editorial consultations—Haleema Bharoocha, Camille Canter, Laurel Mack-Wilson, Antonin Moncelet, Morgane Boistault, Ambrine Martin, and Ishaq Esnault.

Shiraz Sidhva provided connections in France, Ingrid Therwath-Chavier in Paris had good advice, Camille Sant and Bushra Mohammad generously shared stories in Toulouse. Ellie Kozlowski assisted me with research on the streets of Toulouse. Frances Dinger, Richard Chiem, Elizabeth Turnell, and Grace Turnell took care of my dog while I roamed for research and writing.

Places that gave me beds and desks and fellowships to work from—Hedgebrook (where I thrive), Residency L'Ancienne Auberge (thank you, Prajwal Parajuly), Playa Summer Lake (oh, those afternoon swims in the pond), Hugo House, and Seattle University.

My community of writers in Seattle—in particular, Claudia Castro Luna, Anastacia Renee, Ruchika Tulshyan, and Amber Flame were among those who looked me in the eye and said this strange book of mine was important. Françoise Besnard, conversations with whom lit up my imagination, again and again. My dear friend Theo Nestor, who rushed to check on my dog's injured paw and said no, I was not to cut my writing residency short and come home. Rick Simonson and Karen Maeda Allman at Elliott Bay Book Company, for cheering me on. My writing partners—Novera Alim King, Abigail Carter, Kim Fu, Waverly Fitzgerald, Lavanya Sankaran, Hye-Kyung Kang, Ellie Kozlowski, and Anca Szilagyi.

Natividad Gutierrez, for all the care and pastries and fresh flowers. My neighbors, for the love during the pandemic. My colleagues and students at Seattle University. My fiercely feminist friends in Seattle and all over the world—it is my deepest fortune that there are too many of you to list here.

And yes, my dog Tagore, because, let's face it, he is the only one who truly believes I have something to say.

As always and endlessly, I am grateful to my son, who was my first-draft reader and my final-draft sage. He reminded me why I should not change one thing about the woman in my book.

ABOUT THE AUTHOR

Sonora Jha is the author of the memoir *How to Raise a Feminist Son* (2021) and the novel *Foreign* (2013). After a career as a journalist covering crime, politics, and culture in India and Singapore, she moved to the United States to earn a PhD in media and public affairs. Sonora's op-eds, essays, and public appearances have been featured in the *New York Times*, on BBC, and elsewhere. She is a professor of journalism and lives in Seattle.

A NOTE FROM THE COVER DESIGNER

I devoured the manuscript for *The Laughter* over the course of a day, breathless and at times in shock. It's a stunning and challenging piece of literature, which makes designing its cover all the more difficult. I worked through quite a few ideas in the process of arriving at the final cover, but the one thing I was sure of was that I didn't want to depict any characters in a way that was too straightforward or photorealistic. I tend to think that doing so diminishes the reader's experience of the book—some things should be left to the imagination, especially for a story this complex and layered. Ultimately, I landed on a stunning artwork by the artist Vartika Sharma. The direct, unwavering gaze of the woman's eyes stand in sharp contrast with the distortion above them. The juxtaposition makes me think of Ruhaba's own sense of self, steadfast in the face of Oliver's twisted assumptions about her and her family.

Alicia Tatone

Here ends Sonora Jha's
The Laughter.

The first edition of the book was printed and
bound at LSC Communications
in Harrisonburg, Virginia, January 2023.

A NOTE ON THE TYPE

The text of this novel was set in Chaparral Pro, a typeface designed by Carol Twombly that combines the legibility of nineteenth-century slab serif designs with sixteenth-century roman book lettering. Its versatile, hybrid design allows accessibility and clarity in all text settings. Chaparral Pro remains true to its sixteenth-century print origins and has since become a popular standard for many print applications.

HARPERVIA

An imprint dedicated to publishing international voices,
offering readers a chance to encounter other lives and other
points of view via the language of the imagination.